Death Valley QTH

Printed in USA

Library of Congress Catalog Card Number:
85-073443

ISBN: 0-87259-503-X

First Edition

The Amateur Radio stations appearing in this book actually exist and are used by permission of the licensees and the Federal Communications Commission, whose cooperation is gratefully acknowledged by the author. Any resemblance of characters herein to actual persons, living or dead, is coincidental.

Death Valley QTH

A "Tommy Rockford" novel

By
Walker A. Tompkins
K6ATX

American Radio Relay League
Newington, CT USA 06111

Other Tommy Rockford adventures:

SOS at Midnight
CQ Ghost Ship!
DX Brings Danger

For
Edie N1CZC
wid TNX es 73

CONTENTS

CHAPTER ONE

CROSSBOW KILLER'S WARNING

Jouncing along the dusty graveled road in the Santa Bonita Radio Club's battered Volkswagen van, Tommy Rockford and his new friend Chub Downey were thrilling to the vast scenic panorama of California's Death Valley even as they enthusiastically argued the merits of their respective hobbies, ham radio vs. rockhounding.

Ominous slate-gray clouds were racking along the crest of the Panamint Mountains to the west, threatening a late June deluge to the region which National Park Service rangers considered to be the deepest, driest, hottest place in the entire western hemisphere.

Tommy, better known to amateur radio operators around the world by his call sign, K6ATX, was worried about what an electrical storm could do to ruin his upcoming Field Day operations. He switched on the van's AM-FM radio hoping to get a weather report from the nearest broadcast station, located in Las Vegas, Nevada.

By that act K6ATX changed the mood of the desert scene from peace and serenity to one which threatened danger and evil. He tuned in just as a radio newsman was airing a flash bulletin:

"...this is Barry Clark in the KVGS newsroom. We interrupt our regularly-scheduled programming to bring you the latest exclusive update concerning the two 'Crossbow Killers' who murdered a security guard at the Pharaoh's Palace casino on the Strip shortly before midnight, escaping with a reported $50,000 in gambling receipts. They shot down the guard, Hal Morehouse, as he was about to board his armored vehicle with a bag of cash. No shot was heard. The killers used a silent weapon—an arrow fired by a sophisticated crossbow, of the type used by hunters for shooting wild game.

"A valet parking attendant who witnessed the murder informed police that both robbers were wearing jackets bearing the insignia of the notorious Satan's Angels motorcycle gang of Southern California. The two made their getaway from Vegas on motorcycles and headed west on Interstate 15. This bulletin just in reports that at dawn today, a rancher in the Pahrump Valley saw the two cyclists driving over the open sagebrush terrain to cross the California border in the direction of Jubilee Pass, the southern gateway to Death Valley National Monument. Law enforcement officials fear that if the Crossbow Killers succeed in reaching Death Valley they will be practically impossible to locate and flush out of hiding. Stay tuned to this station for the latest developments as they occur. And now, back to John Lockhart and his award-winning Bandbox of Golden Oldies..."

Tommy Rockford snapped off the radio. In spite of the suffocating desert heat on this late June morning—the mercury was well over 125° —the nineteen-year-old radio ham felt a chill coast down his spine. Jubilee Pass, the killers' escape route, was visible through the shimmering heat waves to the south.

The knowledge that two desperate fugitives could be racing toward them at this very moment had shattered the tranquility of the desert scene, reminding Tommy that the haunting beauty of this sweltering pastel-shaded wilderness might also be concealing a hideout for men of violence.

Chub said facetiously, "I hope I don't meet up with those killers while I'm out rockhounding. I'd make too wide a target."

At age seventeen and a head shorter than Tommy's even six feet, Downey outweighed K6ATX by at least thirty pounds, which no doubt had contributed to his being nicknamed "Chubby" before he got out of elementary school in Los Angeles. A wag in Santa Bonita had commented "When Tommy and Chub walk down the street together they look like the figure 18!" Blond, blue-eyed Rockford was built like a quarterback without a surplus ounce of fat on his muscular frame.

Chub, possessed of an outgoing, happy-go-lucky personality to match his curly red hair and freckled face, always exhibited a monkey's insatiable curiosity about everything around him.

"What were we yakking about, Chub?" K6ATX asked.

Downey, who was a noted high school baseball pitcher back home in Los Angeles, took off his California Angels cap and fanned himself with it. "I was saying that desert country like this should be reserved for rock hounds like me. I've dreamed of getting to explore Death Valley ever since I became a pebble pup. But I can't understand why you radio hams would choose a bakeoven like Death Valley for your weekend gig. You can do radio hamming anywhere."

Tommy chuckled. "When the rest of my operating team get here this afternoon, they'll probably be telling me the same thing. No, Chub—we chose to come here because we have something to prove."

"But can't you prove it where the weather's more comfortable?"

"Once a year our ham radio organization, the American Radio Relay League, sponsors this radio operating event called Field Day. It is always in late June. We try to score points for the most contacts we work, all over the world. You may not believe this, but it's as much fun as the World Series—and don't forget, I'm a baseball fan too."

"But is there some law that says you have to do your hamming where the heat is popping thermometers? I don't see the point."

"The purpose of Field Day is to test operators and their equipment for the worst conceivable emergency. To prepare us for what we might have to face in times of disaster, like an earthquake or a flood or a forest fire. Anything that would destroy the power lines and roads. The government and public officials rely heavily on us hams to help out with communications during big disasters."

"So you're expecting a big disaster in Death Valley someday?"

Tommy said, "Actually, we amateur operators in Santa Barbara County's ham clubs probably don't have much of a chance of winning Field Day honors this year, but we want to test our skills and equipment and see how we stack up, according to ARRL rules. We're doing it to meet a challenge—to accomplish something unique that has never been done in history, sort of like climbing a mountain just because it's there."

"What's the challenge? The heat? The guy at the service station at Furnace Creek told me Death Valley was the hottest place in the United States last week, according to the Weather Bureau."

Tommy shifted the lumbering old van into a lower gear as they threaded through an oasis of mesquite shrubs and sand dunes which a rustic wooden landmark sign identified as the Bennett's Well. It was the campground where emigrants in a wagon train carrying the first Americans into Death Valley had been forced to butcher their oxen for food and proceed on foot in late December of 1849.

"Hot weather isn't the challenge I was referring to," K6ATX explained. "Electronics engineers have always claimed that radio communication is virtually impossible in daylight hours from the floor of Death Valley, which is below sea level, besides being hemmed in by high mountains. So the members of Santa Barbara County's four amateur radio clubs—at Santa Maria and Lompoc, Vandenberg Air Force Base and Santa Bonita—decided to prove that hams have the technical know-how and the high-tech equipment to make radio work here in the most hostile electronic environment in the world. We chose to do it the weekend of Field Day, because we know hams will be tuning the bands all over the globe."

Tommy had been peering through the dusty windshield at a pair of dust funnels on the south horizon. It actually came as a relief when the funnels proved to be dust-devils, not caused by two motorcyclists crossing the salt flats. The Crossbow Killers from Las Vegas had been weighing heavily on his subconscious all day.

"Some Field Day contestants even envy us being over here," he went on. "The League awards fat bonus points to anyone operating with power which doesn't come from the electric company or from petroleum-based fuels—natural sources like windmills, methane gas, tidal water, solar energy, or generators run by grain alcohol. One thing for sure, solar energy is never in short supply in Death Valley, California!"

Both teenagers lapsed into a lethargic silence, enduring the heat and discomfort as best they could. They had only known each other about three months. Tommy, who had just concluded his freshman year at the California Institute of Technology in Pasadena where he was studying for a future career as a NASA space scientist, had gone home to Santa Bonita, a hundred miles up the coast from Los Angeles, to spend Easter vacation with his folks, who operated a travel agency.

While there, Tommy had attended a teenage baseball game which matched the national champion Greater Los Angeles All-Stars and the champions of the Tricounty League, who happened to be from Tommy's alma mater, Santa Bonita High School.

The visitors had won a hard-fought three-to-zero shutout, thanks to the sensational pitching of their red-headed roly-poly mound ace, Chub Downey, who had more than lived up to his advance media hype as "the best control pitcher in his age bracket in the US." Sportswriters reported that scouts for the Los Angeles Dodgers and the California Angels were keeping a fascinated eye on young Downey as a future candidate for drafting into the major leagues.

Following the game, the visiting team's coach had sought out Tommy Rockford in the locker room.

"They tell me you and a Santa Barbara group are making a trip to Death Valley early this summer," the coach had said. "Would there be any possible chance that you could take my pitcher along? Chub Downey's an underprivileged lad from a broken home, ghetto background, lived in foster homes most of his life. The two things that have kept him from being trapped into the fast-lane lifestyle of drug abuse and street-gang warfare are his baseball and his hobby of rockhounding—amateur geology. Chub has confided that when he can earn enough money to take a trip, he wants to go to Death Valley and collect rock specimens out in a real desert. You see, I'm trying to encourage him to become a geologist some day."

Tommy had been struck by the coach's dedication. "Considering that baseball players make more than the President of the United States these days, I'm surprised you haven't encouraged him to go into pro ball, sir. From what I saw today, he could cut it."

The coach had shaken his head. "I've spent all my life in professional sports. I can tell you, an athlete's earning career is too short, even if he escapes injury. As his teacher and counselor, I want to see Chub cash in on his high IQ, not his ability to throw a screwball... Of course, if it isn't convenient to take him along, I apologize for even asking."

Tommy had not hesitated an instant in making his decision.

"It won't be a bit out of my way to pick Chub up in LA on my way to the valley. I'm driving a ham club van loaded with equipment and camping supplies, with an overnight stopover at Trona. You tell Chub I'll welcome his company. It's a lonesome four hundred miles."

Out of that locker room conversation had come what Tommy Rockford believed was the beginning of a worthwhile friendship. That was why, three months later, to kid Downey he had chosen to wear a Cal Tech baseball jersey with an orange block T and a blue and white Dodger cap to offset Downey's California Angels cap, with its logo of the Dodgers' cross-town rivals.

The Angels! That brought back in Tommy's mind an image of two desperate men from the Satan's Angels motorcycle gang, fleeing from a murder committed a hundred and twenty miles away in Las Vegas, who might very well meet them head-on around the next corner...

CHAPTER TWO

RADIO HAM VS. ROCK HOUND

Apparently Chub had something working on his mind that he deemed more important than worrying about the unlikely possibility of a face-to-face confrontation with a pair of escaping lawbreakers, for he turned suddenly to Tommy and asked, "How long did you say your Field Day contest lasts?"

"Twenty-seven hours. From 1100 hours Pacific Daylight Time tomorrow till 2 PM Sunday. Why?"

"And you said you get extra Brownie points for operating with solar power?"

"That's correct. The bonus helps to make up for having to operate in such a blast furnace as Death Valley."

"Aha! That means half of your operating will be at night. No sun, no power. That's an awful hunk of wasted time, seems to me."

Tommy was impressed. Chub's coach had stressed the fact that Chub was blessed with a higher than average IQ, and these intelligent questions, about a totally new subject, proved it.

"I've got to hand it to you, Chub, you're a sharp cookie. But operating on solar-generated power at night is no problem. You see, the photo cells collect the sun's energy all day and use it to charge a number of 12-volt storage batteries which give us a leeway of more than forty hours operating time during periods of darkness or heavy fog or overcast when the sun isn't shining. As a matter of fact, we expect to log more stations after dark than we will in daytime—especially our high-bonus QSOs with satellites. Night-time radio reception is always better in the desert."

They rode on in sweaty silence for several minutes. Then Chub spoke up again: "You radio hams seem to talk a different language than the rest of us wimps. What's a QSO?"

Rockford explained patiently, "It's a form of radio shorthand, just like the Ten-Code that you unlicensed Citizens' Banders use on the air—ten-four for okay, ten twenty-three for stand by, and so on. Except that we licensed radio amateurs, especially those of us who prefer Morse code CW to voice transmissions, use what is known as the International Q-Code."

"Never heard of it."

"Well, I'll admit that Q-signals might be becoming obsolete, Chub, because most hams nowadays prefer a microphone to a radio key. But the big advantage of the Q-Code is that no matter what language you speak, they mean the same. QSO means a two-way conversation, QRX means stand by, QRM means interference, QRZ means who is calling? and so on. Very simple to learn and saves a lot of time. Although sometimes the Q-sigs get ridiculous. Like when you want to stop, why not say so, instead of saying you are 'going QRT?' The same silliness applies to you Citizens' Banders and your Ten-Code."

Chub said, "Driving over from LA yesterday, I remember you said you were being sent to Death Valley a day early so as to find a QTH for your Field Day operations. Tell me what a QTH is and I'll help you look for it."

K6ATX ducked down to peer through the grimy windshield at Telescope Peak, coming up alongside on their right. He believed their destination was somewhere near the base of that mountain.

"QTH means your location. The Radio Club wanted me to find a place below sea-level for our operations. I had planned to set up for business at Badwater, over on the east side of the valley about ten miles east of here, because it is 282 feet below sea level, the lowest spot in North or South America. Unfortunately, the Space Shuttlers ham radio club from Vandenberg Air Force Base beat me to it by coming over here yesterday."

"So what QTH are we hunting for?"

"I'm trying to find an abandoned miner's shack that my Dad and I spent a night in back when I was about nine years old, on my first visit to Death Valley. All I can remember is that the shack was at the foot of Telescope Peak. Of course, after ten years it may not even exist anymore. I sure hope it's still standing, because we need a sheltered place to work in, out of the sun. Ground temperatures can hit two hundred degrees in Death Valley this time of year."

Both teenagers lapsed into another lethargic silence. Finally Tommy roused from his torpor as Chub started chattering again: "You know, I have had fun yakking around my neighborhood on CB radio. But I know what I'm missing, not having an FCC license and being able to talk to people anywhere in the world, like you hams do. It was the Morse code that scared me off. Why can't they grant a ham ticket without having to learn code? It's as old-fashioned as smoke signals or beating out messages on a jungle drum, seems to me."

"Spoken like a true CBer," K6ATX chuckled, sensing that he had a prime candidate to recruit for the incomparable hobby of Amateur Radio. "But learning the Morse dots and dashes—we call 'em *dits* and *dahs*—is a lot easier than learning all the rock-hound language you laid on me yesterday—words like Pliocene, Paleozoic, travertine, rhyolite, gneiss, schist—that's a high-powered vocabulary you rock hounds use. As for learning Morse code—before we drive another mile I can teach you how to say 'HI' just like our OSCAR up in space. We can use the auto horn for a key."

"I didn't know they gave Oscars to radio hams!"

"In this case, OSCAR is an acronym, Chub. It means Orbiting Satellite Carrying Amateur Radio. The first OSCAR we hams put in space, riding piggyback on a NASA rocket, carried a transmitter that broadcast only one message—Hi! When you tuned in OSCAR's frequency and heard that friendly Hi! coming at you from outer space—it was more thrilling than hitting a grand-slam home run. Want me to teach you how to say HI in one easy lesson?"

"Lay it on me heavy, man! The only code I know is SOS, and that's kind of hard to work into an ordinary conversation."

"Okay, le's go. The letter H is four dits. I'll play it for you on the VW horn—*bee-bee-bee-beep*! Now the letter I is two dits, like this: *Bee-beep*! Put 'em together and what have you got? You've got HI. . . *Bee-bee-bee-beep*. . . pause one beat. . . *bee-beep*! Try it."

Chub Downey, dark eyes glowing with the thrill of learning, put his thumb on the horn button and tapped out four beeps like an expert brasspounder, following it with a hesitant *beep*!—pause—*beep*! knowing instantly he had flunked his first code lesson.

"What you tapped out spelled HEE, not HI," Tommy explained.

"In Morse, the letter E is a single dit. Put a space between them, and two dits become two letter Es instead of the single letter I. Okay, have another go at it. It's all a matter of rhythm."

For the next five minutes, anyone who might have been within earshot of the jouncing old van would have wondered why its horn kept emitting a series of short bursts which, after a dozen tries, flowed into a smooth pattern which spelled "HI" and, to Chub's boyish delight, merited an A grade from his instructor.

K6ATX said, "That's it for now. We're coming up on ten o'clock. Turn on the Las Vegas station again and maybe we can catch a weather report. I don't like the looks of that storm gathering up on the peak. An electrical disturbance this weekend could knock out our Field Day reception, to say nothing of the danger of lightning hitting our skyhooks and forcing us to close down."

Chub Downey leaned over to switch on the dashboard receiver, flooding the cab with Golden Oldie music. As he was reducing the audio so they could tell when the news break came on, Chub let out a squeal of excitement and pointed off through the dust-powdered windshield, crying: "Hey, there's an old shack, Tommy! Might be the QTH we've been hunting for, think so?"

K6ATX crouched low over the steering wheel for a look in the direction Chub was pointing. Through the shimmering heat waves he recognized the mouth of a canyon he recalled as having the name "Avalanche Gulch" on his father's Auto Club road map of Death Valley. On the north rim he saw a small sway-backed cabin of weathered boards, with a lacy green tamarisk tree partially overhanging the roof, a tree grown to twice the size he remembered from his long-ago camp out with his Dad.

"You've got sharp eyes, kiddo!" Tommy said exultantly. "That's the QTH we wanted, all right. Buckle your seat belt—I'm about to turn this bucket of bolts into a ORV—an off-road vehicle!"

Tommy yanked the wheel to send the Radio Club van sloughing off the graded road onto the sand and gravel slope of the alluvial fan which spilled from the throat of Avalanche Gulch. Shifting into low gear, he angled off to the right. The sturdy old Volkswagen bounced up the slope like a mountain goat and swung to a dusty halt in front of their destination hut.

He knew the shack was more than a hundred years old, dating back to the Panamint silver boom of the 1870s. The roof's ridgepole swagged like the seat of a saddle, its warped shingles patched with rusty tin from kerosene cans pounded flat. The board-and-batten walls had been seared a reddish tobacco-brown by long decades of exposure to sun and wind, the grains of the wood etched into stark relief by abrasive particles of wind-driven sand.

As the two boys alighted stiffly from the van, the first thing that caught Chub Downey's notice were three oblong earthen mounds alongside the cabin which looked suspiciously like graves. Above them a sign hung askew from a broken-out window that had been curtained with a gunnysack. It carried a threatening admonition: BEWAR!! TRESSPASSERS WILL BE SHOT!! SAML SUTKLIFFE OWNER.

"I remember seeing those graves and that sign as a nervous nine-year old," Tommy laughed, "and my Dad telling me that while he didn't condone trespassing on private property, he doubted if anyone had lived in this cabin for over fifty years."

Chub found an old gunnysack on the ground and used it to brush the dust off the side panels of the white van, so as to reveal the red signs painted there, lending authenticity to the scientific expedition which he was proud to be accompanying:

EMERGENCY MOBILE STATION
RADIO K 6 T Z
SANTA BONITA AMATEUR RADIO CLUB
SANTA BONITA CA 93101

K6ATX was peering up at the crest of Telescope Peak directly above them, at 11,049 feet the highest point on the skyline. Up there at this very moment, his Uncle JC Ellison, W7OE from Seattle, was preparing to camp out during Field Day, along with his adopted son Noisy Noyce, KA7XNN, and several other newer hams. They would assist JC in manning a two-meter intercom station to provide communication among the four Radio Club lash-ups from Santa Barbara County—Santa Maria at the Death Valley Sand Dunes to the north, Lompoc atop Dante's View on the east, the Vandenberg AFB group at Badwater, and the Santa Bonita operation here at Sam Sutkliffe's cabin at sea level.

"I can't wait to head up that canyon yonder," Chub exclaimed, reaching behind the passenger seat to haul out his proudest possession, a Little Jim Dandy Mineral Detector.

"Gosh, what if I discover uranium? Or gold? Can I go now, Tommy, or is there anything you need me to help with, like unloading the van? I don't aim to be a freeloader on this trip, you know."

Tommy said, "Thanks, Chub. There's one little chore I need your help on. I want to string an eighty-meter dipole between the shack and that dead juniper up on the ridge. You'll tie one end to the tree while I'm up on the roof. Then you're free to take off rockhounding—as long as you check in with me every thirty minutes on your CB rig. And make sure you're back before sundown. It's easy to get lost in Avalanche Gulch, especially after dark."

From the rear of the van Tommy took a 133-foot coil of Number 12 copperclad iron-core wire, fitted with heavy ceramic insulators and guy ropes at each end. He passed one end to Chub Downey, who trotted off toward the juniper snag Tommy had indicated. K6ATX, unreeling the coil of wire between them, climbed the rough stone fireplace chimney on the east end of the cabin, his Nike jogging shoes ideal for the task.

Firmly astraddle the cabin roof, Tommy fastened his end of the antenna to the fieldstone chimney.

Chub Downey, displaying remarkable agility for such a heavy-set teenager, scaled the juniper like a monkey and, pulling the antenna wire taut, secured his guy rope around a projecting limb. Then, climbing down from the dead tree, he jumped to the ground and started down the slope, intending to pick up his backpack before starting for Avalanche Gulch and the first real rockhounding adventure of his restricted city-bred life.

Chub had not taken three steps before a gasp of horror escaped his lips and he froze in his tracks, staring off toward the south, unable to believe the sight that met his eyes.

Coming toward him from the direction of Avalanche Gulch was a bewhiskered old man wearing a sweat-stained sombrero, frayed blue shirt, bibless overalls and patched boots. He was trailed by a flop-eared, heavily-loaded pack mule. The man was aiming a .30-30 rifle straight at Chub Downey's head.

"Just stand hitched," the old desert rat growled. "You two claim-jumpers ain't going' nowhars. Fust I'll knock the big feller offn the roof, then I'll drop you like a hydrophoby skunk."

Tommy had his back to them, unaware of danger. Before Chub could break his paralysis to scream a warning, the old man swung his

Winchester barrel toward the cabin below, drew careful bead at the unsuspecting radio ham straddling the roof, and pulled trigger.

Flame spat from the rifle muzzle. Chub squeezed his eyes shut, the deafening concussion of the shot smiting his eardrums like a thunder clap rebounding in angry echo off the mountain wall. He steeled himself for the grisly sound of Tommy's corpse crashing to the ground alongside the shack.

CHAPTER THREE

THE DEMENTED PROSPECTOR

A microsecond ahead of the crack of the gunshot a bullet chipped rock dust off the chimney less than an inch from Tommy's head, stinging his cheek with mortar fragments as it ricocheted into space with the diminishing whine of a plucked guitar string. K6ATX twisted around in time to see the wisp of smoke unraveling from the muzzle of a deer rifle held by a long-bearded stranger a dozen feet away from where Chub stood alongside the dead juniper.

"Hey, mister!" Tommy managed to shout. "Hold it, okay? What call do you have to shoot at *me*?"

The desert rat levered another shell into the breech of the smoking rifle and shouted back, "You're both claim-jumpers, ain't you? An' if you don't git offn my roof pronto I'll leave you both for the buzzards to peck the meat off yore bones. I could just as easy have clipped a notch out of your ear as hit that chimbly."

Tommy Rockford did not doubt the old man's marksmanship skills for a minute. A brassy taste of fear corroded his tongue as he carefully unstraddled himself from the ridgepole and began skidding down the steep-pitched roof, hurtling over the eaves with a ripping sound as a protruding nail snagged the seat of his jeans. He flexed his knees like a skydiver landing to cushion the shock of his eight-foot drop to the ground.

The old man turned his attention to Chub, whose normally caramel-ruddy cheeks had turned the color of banana meat. "Tubby, if you don't want me to render you down for lard to grease my flapjack skillet, you'll hustle back down there and stand beside the big feller. We'll see what far-fetched excuse you'll give for jumpin' my old Daddy's mining claim, and if either one of you try to lie, I'll lead-pizen you like I would a foamy-mouth coyote."

The noise Chub made scrambling down the slope to the level ground in front of the cabin was drowned by the incongruous sound of country and western music coming from the van's radio, which Tommy had left tuned to the Las Vegas station in hopes of getting an updated weather prediction for the weekend.

The old man, rifle stock hugged against his rib cage as he led his jenny mule down to the cabin, halted in front of the two boys, who were careful to keep their arms raised.

"We're not claim-jumping, sir," Tommy Rockford protested. "We were just trying to find overnight shelter from that storm that's brewing up on Telescope. We'll leave right now if you say so."

The old man squirted a stream of tobacco juice at a darting lizard and drawled, "You two ain't goin' *nowhar.* Man an' boy, I been prospectin' Death Valley for over seventy year. My old man built this cabin fer Ma after Borrowed Time got knocked out by the big rock slide, aimin' for me to be borned under this roof, only she decided to go back to the Gunsight Lode Hotel for the birthin'. You young rascals ain't learned to read? Cain't you see that no trespassin' sign on the winder yonder?"

Tommy was surprised to note that Chub Downey had stopped shaking with fear and was now eyeing the old prospector with more curiosity than anxiety. The red-head said eagerly, "Haven't I seen you someplace before, Mister? You a movie actor, maybe?"

The old man grunted, but it was obvious that Chub's question pleased his ego. "I been on the TV onct. Sierry Club fellers filmin' a Death Valley pitcher. They tried to worm the secret of Borrowed Time out of me, but I'll take that to the grave, like I promised my old Dad I would. The newspaper fellers, they call me Seldom Seen Sam, because I'm always out prospectin' an' only show up onct or twict a year to buy beans an' chawin' tobaccy."

"Seldom Seen Sam, the last Death Valley pioneer!" Chub exclaimed, turning to Tommy. "You remember that show, on PBS—"

Chub was interrupted by a sudden break in the loud music coming from the van's radio. Then an announcer's excited voice rang out:

"This is Barry Clark in the KVGS newsroom with the latest bulletin concerning the two Crossbow Killers wanted for last night's murder of a local casino employee. They have been identified by a parking lot attendant who knew them both, as Rusty Hilton and 'Goldielocks' Lesher, who were once arrested in Reno for possession and sale of narcotics, and are wanted in Los Angeles for the shooting of a police officer two years ago. According to this witness, Rusty Hilton is red-headed and rides a red 'Harley hog' chopper-style motorcycle, while Goldie Lesher rides a bright yellow Yamaha, the machines they were reportedly seen riding toward Death Valley earlier today. Stay tuned for further developments. And now, back to the music of Bob Senn and the Haybarn Five—"

It was Seldom Seen Sam who lurched over to reach into the VW and switch off the blaring music. His face, purple with rage when he had confronted the two "claim-jumpers" a moment before, had bleached bone-white while listening to the radio news bulletin.

As if talking to another human being, the old prospector called over to his jenny mule, "You hear that, Hernia? Two long-haired hippies on motorsickles, one red, one yella. The same pair that shot pore ol' Hector with a bow an' arrer last winter. Now it looks like them two polecats are headin' back to Borrowed Time. Well, this time we'll be ready fer the skunks, won't we, Hernia?"

The shaggy old mule nodded vigorously, as if she understood every word her master had said. The two boys remained in a frozen posture, arms over their heads, knowing they were at the mercy of a demented old desert dweller who, judging from the way he conversed with his mule, was well advanced into a state of senility, if not actual insanity.

Tommy, hoping to stall for time by keeping the old man's thoughts diverted from his absurd accusation of claim-jumping, spoke up sympathetically: "Did I understand you to say a friend of yours was killed by a crossbow, sir?"

Seldom Seen Sam appeared to snap back to the present. He kept his rifle trained on his young prisoners as he jerked his head to indicate the mule. "Two long-haired hoodlums on motorsickles came bustin' into Avalanche Gulch last winter. I'm perty shore they had been hangin' out in Borrowed Time the past six months. I was up on the rim of the Gulch chippin' an ore sample offn' a ledge, when I seen them motorsicklers spot the two mules I had grazin' down in the gulch, Hector an' Hernia. One of the rascals, the yella-haired one, takes out a crossbow like the one William Tell used to shoot the apple off his son's head in a storybook I used to look at as a kid. He shot pore ol' Hector in the gut, just for the fun of seein' the critter fall an' kick. An' me caught without my rifle. The two of 'em seen me up on the rim, though, so they didn't shoot pore ol' Hernia here. They hopped on their sickles an' lit out o' there, headin' south out of the Gulch, an' I ain't seed 'em since."

The shock of the cruel scene old Sam had described made both boys forget their own peril. It was against federal law to shoot feral burros, mules or bighorn sheep inside Death Valley National Monument, but the law was ignored by so-called weekend hunters, mostly from the Hollywood area, who commonly used crossbows instead of firearms because of the silence factor.

"That's the most terrible thing I ever heard of, shooting a harmless animal just for sport!" cried Chub Downey, a very sincere catch in his voice. "Poor old Hernia, she must be lonesome—"

The prospector turned his attention back to his captives.

"Now, what are you city dudes doin' on my Dad's silver claim? And don't tell me you're sightseers! Not this time of year. They don't show up in Death Valley until October or so, when it cools down to a hundred-ten in the shade. Anybody comes in summer, they are up to mischief. What's yore mischief? Runnin' from the law, like them motorsicklers with the crossbow?"

Tommy felt nausea stab his stomach, knowing that a whit more pressure of the old lunatic's finger on the trigger could blast them into eternity. He knew he could never get old Seldom Seen Sam to understand what a ham radio Field Day was all about.

Before Tommy could come up with an answer, the addle-headed old man gestured to the row of three earthen mounds next to the cabin. When Tommy had first visited this cabin as a nine-year-old the mounds had grave markers on them. Somebody's idea of a prank, his father had said, not wanting Tommy to have bad dreams that night.

"See those graves?" Seldom Seen Sam asked. "That's where I buried the last three claim-jumpers. You two wallopers are next!"

Chub made a frightened choking sound deep in his throat. Tommy Rockford stood in stony-faced silence, like a prisoner who had just heard a judge pronounce his own death sentence. In this case, the judge was a mental case festering with hatred and paranoia.

Seldom Seen Sam continued, "I see you're carryin' a shovel

behind the driver's seat o' yore truck. I got another one strapped onto Hernia's pack. Two claim jumpers, two shovels. Grab them tools. You're diggin' a double grave alongside those other three."

Chub felt his knees go rubbery. He had never been placed in a life-threatening situation before, and it seemed as if his blood was changing to ice water. At his side, Tommy Rockford whispered, "Do as he says for now. Keep him talking. Once I get hold of a shovel I'll try to bash that rifle out of his hands."

Chub Downey, responding to the confidence in Tommy's bearing, walked over to the Volkswagen and removed an army surplus entrenching tool which the Radio Club carried for emergencies. He saw their captor swing his rifle to follow Tommy as he walked over to the jenny mule and untied a miner's shovel from the diamond-hitched pack, a shovel with a well-worn blade due to decades of trenching for ore samples in the desert. Now, if Chub could just keep on distracting the old man...

The pudgy redhead called over to Tommy, who was still standing alongside the mule, biding his chance to jump old Sam: "Tommy, you remember last winter when Channel 28 ran that Sierra Club documentary about keeping strip mining out of Death Valley? And they interviewed an old-timer who talked about a long-lost ghost town and the announcer challenged him to prove the town ever existed at all? Well, that man was Seldom Seen Sam here!"

Tommy, picking up Chub's cue, began strolling toward the prospector. He responded excitedly, "By golly, you're right! Mr. Sam, I knew your name and face were familiar, but I never dreamed I would get to meet a celebrity like you in person!"

The taut fixture of the old man's mouth corners was replaced by what could only be called a shy blush. Both boys got the impression that behind his formidable thicket of whiskers old Sam was actually grinning. Most important reaction of all, his calloused thumb eased his gun hammer off full-cock position.

Seizing his opening, Chub prattled on, "I'll never forget how the Channel 28 people were trying to get you to admit you knew where some lost ghost town was, the one with the funny name that mysteriously vanished off the maps more'n a hundred years ago—"

Seldom Seen Sam cleared his throat and grinned modestly.

"Aye-yup. Fer over fifty year people have done their dangest to pry my secret out of me, but you notice I didn't talk, eh? I promised my Daddy on his deathbed I would never reveal the secret of his lost Gunsight Lode, long as I have a breath left in me. An' that applies to you two, even though you won't be alive long enough to double-cross me."

The old man's rheumy eyes misted over with memories as he seated himself with an arthritic grunt on the front bumper of the VW van, cuffed the sweat-stained Stetson off his brow, and grounded the butt plate of the Winchester between his boot heels.

"A fine man, my Daddy was," the old man reminisced. "Name was Rudy, short for Rudolph Sutkliffe. From Ioway. Raised corn an' hawgs before he come West in the Gold Rush of '49. Stayed in Californy an' wound up buildin' a hotel at Borrowed Time, when that camp was boomin' in '74. Married my mother on a trip to Sacrymento, God rest her soul. Brung her as a bride to help run the Gunsight Lode Hotel that them TV galoots claimed was just a tall tale I had made up, a legend. Hah! Ifn' I hadn't promised my old Daddy as he lay dyin', I could of taken them city dudes to Borrowed Time an' *showed* 'em the hotel, an' my parents' graves! Fer as I know, the only outsiders who ever stumbled onto my secret are them two Crossbow Killers from 'Vegas. They ever come back, Hernia an' me will be waitin' for 'em, an' I'll bushwhack the two of 'em without showin' 'em any more mercy than they showed when they crossbow-kilt pore ol' Hector... Okay, I'm in a hurry to get movin' before that storm breaks. So let's get on with our grave-diggin', shall we?"

CHAPTER FOUR

THE PURPLE CRYSTAL BALL

Chub Downey acted as if he had not heard the order. Oblivious to the menace of the rifle, he walked over to the old derelict.

"Mister Seldom," the redhead said with all the adoration of a hero-worshipper, "I've wanted to talk to you ever since I took up rockhounding. The Mystery Man of Death Valley, the magazines call you. Disappear for months at a time, then show up at some trading post to get supplies, then disappear again. But what was important to me, was how the papers call you the last old-time Western prospector left alive, which makes you the world's champion rock hound! And here I am talking to you! I can't believe it!"

A rumble of thunder high on the shoulder of Telescope Peak made the jenny mule twitch her furry ears apprehensively. Tommy was reminded that he had not yet made radio contact with Uncle JC up there on the mountain where the storm was gathering.

Seldom Seen Sam, a man whose brain was subject to wild swings of mood, appeared to have been genuinely flattered by Chub Downey's obviously sincere demonstration of respect. As if he had totally forgotten the subject of grave-digging, Sam reached up to give his shaggy tobacco-stained mustaches a twist around a forefinger which Tommy could only interpret as a preening gesture.

"I seed myself on the TV," the old man chuckled. "They had one set up at a bar over in Beatty, Nevady. Looked like a movie I seen onct that the park rangers put on at the Furnace Crick museum, all in perty color, with talking to boot. Ya-up, they call me the last o' the Forty-Niners, which I really ain't, of course, it was my Dad who was the real Gold Rush Forty-Niner. But I'm eighty-seven, and all of them years spent around Death Valley."

It suddenly dawned on Tommy Rockford that Chub was no longer trying to divert the old man from the grave-digging project by playing on his obvious vanity. The worship showing in Chub's big brown eyes was the real thing. Collecting rocks and minerals was a hobby he had been introduced to as a Cub Scout—a hobby, as his coach had told Tommy back in Santa Bonita, which had rescued Chub from the drug addiction and street-gang violence of his peers while growing up in the Los Angeles barrio, and had given him a possible goal to strive for, a future career as a geologist. Now he was face to face with the ultimate rock hound—a fossil from another era, one generation removed from the 'Forty-Niners, last survivor of a breed which was almost an extinct species today. But until Sam's rifle was in Tommy's hands, their danger remained very real. The old man's next change of mood could be to one of homicide.

"Tell me," Chub asked, leaning on his shovel, "when you're out prospecting, do you use modern gadgets like Geiger counters? Do you have a Mohs Scale kit to test the hardness of a rock when you find one you can't identify?"

Seldom Seen Sam resumed his seat on the VW bumper. He extracted a plug of tobacco from his overalls, worried off a cud, tucked it between tongue and cheek, and turned back to his fan.

"Ain't no rock ever invented ol' Seldom Seen Sam cain't identify, son! Moe's Scale? Don't recollect I know any Moe."

Chub squatted at Sam's feet, the tyro worshipping the master, his face shining with excitement—an excitement Tommy did not share, because as long as the old man sat on the van bumper there was no way to get behind him and seize the Winchester .30-30.

"A Mohs Scale kit—it's for raw beginners like me to test minerals for hardness," Chub explained. "Wait. I've got one in my backpack. I'll show it to you. I was just getting ready to go out hunting rocks when you and Hernia showed up. I'm glad I didn't miss you—the chance of a lifetime to meet the champion rock hound!"

The old man flicked a wary glance toward Tommy Rockford as if to warn the older boy to keep his distance, while Chub went back to the van and brought out his canvas backpack. He unzipped a side pocket and produced a wallet-sized pigskin case. Opening it for Sam's benefit, he revealed six pencil-like brass rods, each tipped with a point made from a different mineral.

"What in tarnation would I carry a set o' pencils around fer?" the old man scoffed. "I kin barely read or write and don't mind admittin' it. Only eddication I got was from my old Daddy, seein' as how Ma died bringin' me into the world."

Chub said eagerly, "You know how to grade rocks when you find 'em, Mr. Seldom, but us rookies, we have to depend on a Mohs Kit. We know that talc is the softest rock there is, and the second hardest is gypsum, the third is calcite, and so on. This kit is graded from Number Five to Number Ten on the hardness scale, each tip one grade harder than the last one—apatite, quartz, topaz, sapphire, and diamond. This weekend in Death Valley is my first chance to test rocks with my Mohs Kit on a real geology trip."

Seldom Seen Sam examined one pencil-shaped Mohs testing rod with the primitive curiosity of a monkey fingering a strange new object. Then he handed it back to Chub.

"I be dawged," he said, "I never even *heard* o' most of these here minerals. O' course, I'm only interested in gold or silver, not borax or onyx or stuff like that. What I got loaded on old Hernia now is what I figger will assay out as high-grade silver ore with some gold. In this business it's either bonanza or borasco."

Tommy, relaxing for the first time since a .30-30 bullet had missed him by a hair, said laughingly, "I can see why you named your packmule Hernia. That load she's carrying will give her one."

Seldom Seen Sam bristled. "A park ranger's wife named her that," he said archly, "because she said it has a nice feminine ring to it."

Chub hurried over to the van and returned with his mineral locater, an instrument resembling a vacuum cleaner with a pair of headphones attached to the long handle. It was a lightweight version of the mine detectors that soldiers had used in Korea and Vietnam to locate booby traps and land mines in wartime.

"This is my Little Jim Dandy mineral detector," Chub said proudly. "Had to save up for two years to buy it. You know how it works, don't you? This one's got a Geiger counter in it for detecting radioactive rocks like radium and uranium—"

To Tommy's surprise, old Sam nodded. "Now *that's* one newfangled gadget I *do* recognize," he boasted. "Every summer a swarm of city dudes start combin' the hills with these gadgets, like a bunch of idjits sweepin' gravel with a broom. Owned one onct myself. Don't like 'em. Got no use for fancy fooferaw. What was good enough for my Daddy is good enough for old Sam, I always say. A pick, a pan, a jackass to tote your grub—that's all you need."

Chub said, "I heard you tell the TV man you had located some uranium deposits. Have you really?"

"Young feller, I got me a whole shoebox full o' uranium ore in my room at the Gunsight Lode Hotel. Ore that would make your machine buzz like a rattlesnake. Not a mile from where we're standin'," he added mysteriously. "You know, young feller, I've taken a shine to you. I'm goin' to show you a rock that will make yore eyes bug out like a tromped-on toad-frawg's. Wait here."

The old man got to his feet—and Tommy Rockford pounced like a cougar on a jackrabbit. A brief struggle, and the Winchester rifle had been wrested out of Sam's grasp without having to risk inflicting injury on the old man. K6ATX jumped back, rifle poised, blue eyes sparkling with the triumph of his surprise coup.

"Don't shoot him, Tommy!" Chub cried anxiously. "He wants to show me something!"

K6ATX ejected a live shell from the .30-30. He did not lever a new one into the breech. "Mr. Seldom is going to have to ride with us over to Furnace Creek Ranch and the Park Police station," he said grimly. "Whether I file charges against him depends on the advice I get from the rangers. This man is a menace to society."

Seldom Seen Sam seemed not in the least dismayed to find himself a captive rather than the captor. "Pshaw, you got no cause to be aggravated with me," the prospector chuckled. "I was just bluffin' about the grave diggin', to throw a skeer into you so's you wouldn't trespass again. Now, sonny, what I had to show you—"

Totally ignoring the rifle in Tommy's hands, the oldster strode over to his patiently waiting mule, rummaged in a gunnysack, and came back with an object which caught the sunlight and refracted it with dazzling purple brilliance. It was a baseball-sized globe which Chub Downey at first mistook for natural crystal, until he saw a threaded hole which identified it as having been a glass doorknob. Its purple color was what geologists called amethystine—a pure color which reflected light like a diamond. Had it been a real amethyst it would have been worth a fortune.

"Ever seen the like o' this here?" Sam asked. "I taken it offn a saloon door over in Ballarat, the old freighters' camp on 'tother side of the Panamints. You know what that ball is made of?"

Chub turned the purple crystal sphere over in his hands, caressing it as if it had been a sacred object.

"Sure I know what it is. Amethystine glass. Finest specimen I ever saw. Back in the old days," Chub explained condescendingly for Tommy's benefit, "they made glass with manganese in it. Leave it out in the hot desert sun for fifty-odd years, it turns purple. Today's glass won't turn purple, because they don't use manganese."

Seldom Seen Sam smiled pityingly. "*Glass*? Son, that purple ball is a *diamond*! Very rare. Park geologist told me so. Money couldn't buy it. And all the years it was a doorknob on that saloon in Ballarat, none o' them galoots guessed it was valuable!"

Chub glanced at Tommy, who shook his head ever so slightly. Any visitor to the deserts of the Southwest knew about purple glass, created by years of exposure to the violet rays in sunlight. Specimens of purple glass were getting hard to find outside of souvenir shops, so they were now collector's items, usually in the form of bottles or random shards. As Chub had said, modern glass did not acquire amethystine coloration when exposed to the desert sun. But why disillusion the old man about his "diamond"? Even as purple glass, this doorknob had a high commercial value.

"Chub," Tommy said gently, "get some rope from the van. We've got to secure his wrists for the trip over to the Furnace Creek ranger station."

Chub's eyes were filled with anguish as he handed the purple crystal ball back to the old man.

"Thanks... for letting me hold it," he said huskily. "It's the—prettiest and biggest—diamond I ever saw."

A snag-toothed grin appeared behind Sam's whiskers.

"Like I said, son, I taken a liking to you. That diamond is yourn! To keep. To remind you that you once met Seldom Seen Sam. Not many people do. And I won't be around much longer."

The old man returned the purple doorknob to Chub's keeping. Then he said, "How long are you kids going to be stayin'?"

Chub, too flabbergasted to answer, heard Tommy's reply: "This is Friday. We have to leave Sunday afternoon. You mean it's okay if we use your father's cabin for the weekend?"

"O' course, why not? Now that I know you're not like them motorsickle hippies who come here last winter and kilt ol' Hector."

He peered up at the sky, where the storm clouds showed occasional flickers of lightning. "We got to be leavin', Hernia an' me."

He turned to Tommy Rockford, who had a foolish look on his face as he stood there gripping the old man's hunting rifle. K6ATX said awkwardly, "Okay, you can go, Mr. Sam, but I'm afraid I'll have to keep your rifle. You can pick it up at the ranger station."

The old man shrugged. "Big feller, I got no need for the Winchester the next few days. When you kids leave, you stow the gun in the cabin there, understand? I'll pick it up on my way back to Borrowed Time where I always spend the summer months. In case those motorsickle fellers show up like the radio thinks they might, I would need that rifle. You savvy."

Tears of gratitude trickled down Chub Downey's cheeks as he stroked the purple glass globe with his palms. The giver of this gift believed he was bestowing the world's rarest diamond. It was a souvenir Chub knew he would cherish as long as he lived.

"I—I wish you didn't have to go, Mr. Seldom—but thanks for letting us stay here. We won't litter up the place with trash."

Sam walked over to pick up Hernia's halter. "Sorry you can't stay longer. I'm headin' for Furnace Crick to ship my ore samples to an assay office, and pick up supplies. But I won't get back here for mebbe a week, ten days."

Disappointment put its stamp on Chub's features. "Sure wish I could have seen your uranium samples," he said wistfully. "I've never seen a chunk of real uranium ore except in the museum at Exposition Park in LA, and that don't count... You say you keep yours in a hotel room only a mile from here? I thought the nearest hotel was the Furnace Creek Inn Tommy and me passed coming in—"

Sam answered, "The Gunsight Lode Hotel was the one my folks ran in Borrowed Time back in the '70s—the 1870s, that is. I'm the only person alive who knows where it is. Except maybe them motorsickle crooks, an' I ain't sure about them, except I found a couple of sleepin' bags on the jailhouse bunks I couldn't account fer."

"But you said on TV the ghost town vanished almost a hundred years ago—"

Chub broke off his questioning when he caught a hand signal from Tommy. It was obvious that Seldom Seen Sam was playing the game of life with a lot of cards missing from his deck.

An angry drumroll of thunder volleyed across Death Valley. To the north and east the sky was enamel-blue over the California-Nevada border, and in the smog-free atmosphere they could see every vivid detail of the multi-colored Grapevine and Funeral and Black Mountains forming the east wall of Death Valley, from Jubilee Pass on the south to the area of Scotty's Castle on the north.

"Hernia an' me got to be shakin' a laig," the old man repeated. "Looks like she's fetchin' up to sprinkle, an' I wouldn't want to be caught in a flash flood out on the alluvial fans—most turrible thing that kin happen to a body in Death Valley is bein' hit by a flash flood. Land as dry as a bootsole one minute, an' up to yore armpits in a millrace the next."

Without so much as a handshake or wave of farewell, the remarkable old desert man set off at a reaching stride down the slope, following the tracks of the Radio Club van. He had a good ten miles to cover across the salt flats to reach Furnace Creek Ranch, slowed by the pace of his overloaded mule. Both boys reflected sadly that they would probably never see his like again. Both felt equally sure that their lives had been enriched by their brief encounter with the picturesque old eccentric.

Chub, polishing the purple doorknob on his T-shirt, asked wistfully, "You believe what he said about a ghost town, Tommy?"

K6ATX said gravely, "The history books tell us that Borrowed Time was once a famous old mining camp like Ballarat or Rhyolite or Bodie, but we also know it disappeared from the face of the earth a long time ago. Old Sam's brain has retreated into a time warp. He's sort of reliving his father's time."

"You'll think his craziness rubbed off on me, Tommy, but I—I believe his ghost town story."

Tommy said, "Maybe Sam is crazy like a fox, putting the world on by hinting that Borrowed Time still exists somewhere around Death Valley. Maybe it's a publicity stunt. Tourists probably buy Sam a lot of free drinks, just to hear him spin his wild yarns."

They stood beside the van, watching the old man and his mule thread their way through the mesquite scrub and creosote brush to disappear into a wash in the fan-shaped alluvial sprawl from Avalanche Gulch which formed one of the skirts of Telescope Peak.

"All kidding aside, we had a very narrow escape just now," Tommy said. "Sam could very easily have forced us to dig our own graves, shot us and forgotten all about it by tomorrow. I'm terribly sorry for him, but I think we're lucky to have gotten out of that mess alive."

Tommy carried the prospector's rifle over to the van and stowed it under a pile of tarps. It was a museum piece, the classic Winchester '73, the lever-action .30-30 which had won the West.

He heard Chub Downey saying, "The poor old geezer told us he had come from over the mountain. I know he came out of Avalanche Gulch yonder. That means he must have been out of sight in the Gulch for several miles coming down this side of Telescope Peak."

"What are you getting at, kiddo?"

"I can't get it out of my mind how he said he spent the hot summer season in the Gunsight Lode Hotel, in a ghost town not one mile from here. Well, that means Borrowed Time must be somewhere up Avalanche Gulch, doesn't it? He was so determined not to give away his Dad's secret, but he talked *too* much. I think I know his secret! While I'm rockhounding, *I'm going to find that town*!"

Tommy shook his head, sorry that he had to break the bubble of Chub's fertile imagination.

"No way, amigo. Hikers, hunters, geologists, government surveyors in helicopters—every square inch of this desert has been explored and mapped, long ago. I tell you, Borrowed Time is a myth, a tall tale, like all the other fictitious legends of lost gold mines you hear all the time. Borrowed Time doesn't exist, Chub, so stop daydreaming."

Chub's shoulders lifted and fell. "Just the same, like I was telling you when you were up on the roof fixin' that antenna to the chimney, I'm going to do some heavy rock hunting up that Gulch while you're setting up your radio equipment in the cabin. And who knows? I might just accidentally stumble over Sam's vanished ghost town! Stranger things have happened."

"Yes," Tommy thought, "especially in Death Valley..."

CHAPTER FIVE

ROCK HOUND'S DISCOVERY

Tommy Rockford realized that Chub Downey was impatient to be on his way into Avalanche Gulch on his rockhounding jaunt—after all, that was why he had come along on this ham radio expedition to Death Valley in the first place.

"Okay, pal. On your way. There's nothing you can do to help me set up the station. Have fun."

Chub snatched up the faded khaki canvas bag with a shoulder strap which he used to carry rock samples in the field, a bag he had picked up for two bucks at a military surplus store, its original purpose having been to carry a soldier's gas mask in combat.

Slinging the bag over his shoulder, Chub dug his geologist's pick-ax from the back of the van along with a pair of binoculars Tommy had loaned him for the trip. Shouldering his Little Jim Dandy Mineral Detector, Chub jogged toward a nearby ravine which led down into rock-ribbed Avalanche Gulch.

"Whoa, boy—QRX a second!" Tommy shouted after him. "Cool it! Aren't you forgetting something?"

Chub halted a few yards away from the cabin and began checking out his prospecting gear. "Nope. Got all the stuff I need. It'll be an uphill climb in that canyon, I figure, so I'm travelin' light. See you later, pardner."

Tommy shook his head. "Hold it a minute, kiddo. Your CB rig? Remember I told you never to leave this base camp without a radio? I want you to check in on Channel Fourteen every half hour while you're out of my sight. I'll be monitoring that freq. Unless you give me your solemn promise to do that, I can't let you go at all, Chub.

Sorry, but that's how it has to be."

Chub grinned triumphantly as he fished inside his knapsack and drew out his five-watt CB transceiver, a TRC-211 walkie-talkie with a "rubber ducky" stub antenna and crystals for six basic channels. It had a twenty-mile transmitting range under line-of-sight conditions.

"Ten-four," he said, lapsing into Citizens' Band jargon meaning "Okay, message received." "While we're at it, Tommy, let's synchronize our chronometers, shall we? Mine says 11:12."

Tommy consulted the solar-powered quartz wristwatch his parents had given him for high school graduation a year ago. It registered three minutes faster than 11:12. Since he would be using his watch for keeping official Field Day logs tomorrow, he had carefully synchronized it to the government's WWV time signals. But knowing how proud Chub was of the cheap digital watch he had won as a prize for pitching a no-hitter in the All-City League, he replied "Right on the nose. Okay, your first check-in will be at 11:30, then noon, and so on, every half hour. If your rig can't punch any RF through those canyon walls—in other words, if I don't come back to you—don't get so carried away with your rockhounding that you forget to check in. If you do, I'll jump in the van and come up Avalanche Gulch looking for you. Okay?"

"Okay, boss. Hey, why didn't you tell me to bring a raincoat on this trip? I might get drenched before I get back, from the looks of those clouds."

Tommy paused in the act of dragging his sleeping bag out of the van. "Oh, yes—one other thing. I'll expect you back here by five o'clock, Chub, no later. The other operators will be here by then and we might need a hand setting up solar panels. But I promise, you'll be free all day tomorrow for your rock hunting."

"Gotcha. See you at five. Loaded with gold nuggets and uranium dust, who knows? Hi-ho, hi-ho, it's off to work I go—"

Impatient to get free of the leash, Chub set off down the brush-choked ravine toward the floor of Avalanche Gulch, which was hemmed in by sheer hundred-foot lava cliffs. Over the centuries the Gulch had spilled out deposits which had spread skirts of sand and gravel and boulders toward the flats on the valley floor, known to tourists as the Devil's Golf Course. In prehistoric times Death Valley had been a fresh-water lake; when earthquakes shut all its inlet and outlet of water, the lake had eventually evaporated, leaving a glistening white dry bed of salt deposits more than a thousand feet thick.

K6ATX toted his sleeping bag into the old shack and tossed it in a corner. On his next trip to the van he got the hand-held Radio Shack Citizens' Band tranceiver the club used as a short-range intercom, in this case his communications link with Chub Downey.

Knowing that Seldom Seen Sam's father had built this rickety old cabin before the turn of the century—Tommy wondered where the lumber had come from, so long ago and so far from civilization—he eyed the cobwebby rafters and the newspaper-covered walls with new interest. Except for recent graffiti, nothing had changed in the ten years since he and his father had camped here overnight.

The dirt floor was about twelve by fourteen feet, with a rock-and-mud fireplace at the eastern end—a fireplace from which Tommy's antenna lead-in wire emerged, since there would be no fires needed in that ancient hearth on Field Day. Not in Death Valley in late June, when air temperatures soared to 120 degrees and higher. Humidity was so low, of course, that you couldn't breathe on your sun glasses to fog them for cleaning—the fog wouldn't form. The ham gang would be doing their cooking on Coleman camp stoves.

The cabin had two windows, and only one door, on the north side. Vandals had long since carted away the table and stove and bunks which had once been here, but the ham operators would be using folding chairs and bridge tables for their gear. As befitted his role as advance scout for the Santa Bonita team, Tommy spent the next half hour lugging in folding tables and chairs along with cardboard cartons containing all manner of Amateur Radio gear—transmitters, receivers, power supplies, testing equipment. The solar panels and storage batteries were still in the van.

Tommy snapped on the club's battery-powered AM-FM solid state BC receiver which he placed on a wall shelf, tuning it to the Las Vegas station in hopes of getting an updated weather report. In case of floods occurring this morning over in Panamint Valley, which paralleled Death Valley on the west, roads might have become temporarily blocked by mudslides. If they were too serious, Field Day would be cancelled for this year, a gamble they had to take if their QTH was to be in such an exotic place as Death Valley. Well, after all, the whole idea of Field Day was to operate under extreme emergency conditions, wasn't it?

He turned down the audio to keep the country and western programming at KVGS from blocking out Chub's first half-hourly check-in on the CB rig, and began busying himself hooking up the club's equipment which they would be entering in the contest on 160, 80, 40, 20 and 10 meters. Other operators, one for each band, including his long-time buddies Roy MacCormack, W6AMD, Doc Baldwin, K6CRJ and Spud Kleveland, WA6IBR, all of Santa Bonita, were due at four o'clock. They would not know the location of this sea-level QTH until Tommy contacted them on a prearranged sked as they were entering Death Valley in the vicinity of Stovepipe Wells, their ETA being around three o'clock this afternoon. By then, Tommy hoped to have everything in readiness to begin operations tomorrow morning. It gave him a feeling of community, knowing that all over the world fellow radio amateurs were busy with similar preparations.

Firing up the portable generator for his personal hundred-watt single-sideband rig, Tommy was relieved to find that it loaded up well on the eighty-meter dipole he and Chub had been stringing up outside the cabin prior to Seldom Seen Sam's interruption. That was only one short hour ago, but it seemed like something in a half-remembered dream.

Tommy took time out to park the Volkswagen van in the shelter of the lean-to which had once served as a stable for mules. Back inside, K6ATX was deep in his concentration with knobs and dials, tuning his transmitter to peak efficiency on the emergency antenna, when he was startled by Chub's raucous voice issuing from the CB rig he was wearing in a belt holster.

"KBR8243, Tommy Rockford, sea-level in Death Valley, California, this is Humpty Dumpty, operating in Avalanche Gulch. Do you read me, Tommy? Am I getting out?"

"Humpty Dumpty" was the Citizens' Band "handle" which Chub Downey had adopted for identifying himself on the air, an appropriate nickname considering his rotund build. Lifting the walkie-talkie to his lips, Tommy thumbed the transmit button and replied, "Ten-two, receiving you okay. You sigs's on the weak side, but perfectly readable. Over."

Tommy was sorry they weren't on FM, as static generated by the nearby electrical disturbance wouldn't have bothered them.

"Wanted to let you know you can't drive the van into Avalanche Gulch, Tommy. Big boulders everywhere. I see some old tire tracks, but they look like some guy with an off-road bike has been up here.

You couldn't drive up this Gulch even with a four-wheel-drive jeep. Over and possibly clear."

"Roger-dodger," Tommy answered, lapsing into ham talk. "I'll be monitoring at noon sharp. Don't forget. Over and out."

"Seventy-three," Chub Downey responded, conversant enough with ham jargon to know that 73 meant "best regards." "I'll BCNU at high noon. Gosh, this is an exciting place to explore! Over and out, and I wish I had brought along a sandwich."

It gave Tommy a sense of relief to know that Chub's CB rig could punch a signal out of the canyon, since the redhead's safety was Tommy's responsibility. Now he had a clear mind to focus on other duties, the first of which was contacting their Field Day central control station up on Telescope Peak, where his Uncle JC would be monitoring two meters, waiting for the various ham clubs comprising the Santa Barbara County contingent to check in as each group reached Death Valley and took up their assigned stations.

Because a high altitude seven-mile hike along a snow-crusted trail from Mahogany Flats was required to reach the summit of Telescope Peak, Uncle JC and his son Noisy Noyce were limiting themselves to a two-meter transceiver for local communications.

Confident that his own ICOM two-meter hand-held model could reach Uncle JC's QTH on the peak, Tommy switched to transmit mode and began his calling sequence, thankful that FM would eliminate the atmospheric hash on the band caused by those angry storm clouds which had probably reduced Uncle JC's visibility.

"W7OE Slant Six, William Seven Over-Eater Slant Six, this is K6ATX, King Six Always Take X-lax in Death Valley, calling and standing by." Tommy repeated the calls three times before releasing the push-to-talk button and listening.

Almost instantly, to Tommy's vast relief, he heard his Uncle's familiar voice: "K6ATX, this is W7OE/6 returning... Wow, you can have California, Tommy, I'll take Puget Sound! Seattle was never like this! Cold as the devil's ice-box, windy like you wouldn't believe, and socked in solid. In June! So far the thunder and lightning is north of us but the storm front's heading our way. It may get too bad for you to read me before long. Where's your QTH, Tommy, so I can notify the others? This is W7OE/6 standing by."

Tommy came back, "Mighty relieved to know you and Noisy got there okay, Unk. Everything is fine business down here. Chub

Downey's out rockhounding at the moment. Have you heard from 'AMD or the other ops yet? I'm expecting them to show up around four."

Uncle JC's signal was almost lost in a thunderclap: "I raised them down in the Panamint Valley about an hour ago, heading for Towne's Pass. They were afraid to take Wild Rose Canyon into the Valley, because of the storm threat, which was wise of them. Give me your QTH, Tommy, so I can let 'em know where you are in case they can't work you."

"Roger. I found an abandoned shack for shade—" At that instant the CB at Tommy's belt interrupted with Chub's excited shout: "Tommy, Tommy! Do you read me? Urgent! Urgent! This is Humpty-Dumpty calling and standing by, come in—"

Such was the urgency in Chub's voice that Tommy called into his own microphone, "QRX one, Unk—I've got to find out what's bugging Chub. Be back in a sec."

"Roger," W7OE answered from Telescope Peak. "The way the kid was yelling, I could have heard him up here. Sounded scared. Hope a bighorn sheep hasn't butted him off a cliff or something, hi."

Tommy set aside his mike and picked up his CB rig. He pushed the talk button and, forcing himself to sound calm, said "What's the scoop, Humpty-Dumpty? You all right? I'm reading you solid."

Subconsciously he noted that the time was 1220 hours—twenty minutes later than Chub had promised to check in. Tommy had the distinct impression, almost a premonition, that something had gone wrong up in Avalanche Gulch.

"Ten-four, Tommy," Chub's transmission came loud and clear. "Tommy, listen to this. You won't believe it, man! I found this pile of loose rock leaning up against the south cliff, see? It looked like old mine tailings to me, not natural stones, so I climbed up to take a look. At the top of this triangle of loose rock was a thicket of green bushes. I poked through this jungle and guess what I found? You'll never believe it! You still reading me, Tommy? This will knock your Dodger cap off."

"For gosh sakes, Chub, drop the other shoe! What did you find behind your bleeping bushes?"

"Tommy, I found a horizontal hole in the cliff—a man-made tunnel, because it had wooden braces, shoring timbers. And at the other end of that tunnel I can see—now this is the impossible part—

you still there, Tommy?"

K6ATX found himself shouting in frustration, "*Chub, under no circumstances go into that tunnel! It's probably an old prospect hole and they can be extremely dangerous for spelunkers—*"

But Chub had apparently started transmitting before Tommy had signed off, for K6ATX cut back to catch Chub in mid-sentence:

" . . .can see daylight at the end of this tunnel! Outside are old wooden buildings, like you see in western movies! Sign painted on the door—I'm reading it now: GUNSIGHT LODE HOTEL, in old-fashioned capital letters. . . Seldom Seen Sam's hotel! He wasn't feeding us a line of bull after all! I'm going into the tunnel now, Tommy—I'll keep transmitting, but if my signals fade, don't worry—I'll check out this hotel and then get back to you—"

Chub's radio signal faded slowly, then cut off as if he had pulled the big switch to end his transmission. Panic stirred in Tommy Rockford, realizing he had failed to warn Chub about the danger of poking around abandoned mine tunnels and shafts. If the ceiling collapsed, as it might well do if Chub stumbled against a decayed shoring timber, nobody would ever find his bones.

Guilt lay heavy on K6ATX from another angle: Chub's chances of running into the Las Vegas murderers. Old Sam had said the Crossbow Killers may have discovered his ghost town. Chub had reported seeing old motorcycle tracks. Why had he allowed Chub to enter Avalanche Gulch? Tommy had failed in his responsibility to the kid.

There was only one alternative. As long as Chub was inside the tunnel, there would be no radio communication between them. He would have to go into Avalanche Gulch after Chub Downey—and fast.

Completely forgetting that he had left Uncle JC standing by on two meters, Tommy stuffed the CB rig back in its belt case and ran out of the shack, intending to take the van. Then he recalled what Chub had told him about the Gulch being impassable even to a four-wheel-drive vehicle. He was willing to trust Chub's judgement on that.

He raced on past the stable now serving as a garage and headed down the narrow ravine leading into Avalanche Gulch, following the tracks of Chub's jogging shoes down the sandy slope. He was sprinting so fast when he reached the bottom of the ravine and plunged out onto the floor of Avalanche Gulch that he could hardly keep from sprawling headlong.

Below and to his left the Gulch opened out into the vast white expanse of Death Valley's salt flats. To his right, the narrowing cliffs framed the upper Gulch where Chub's footprints led.

Even as he skidded to a halt and regained his balance, Tommy Rockford heard the ear-shattering roar of two motorcycles bearing down on him from the direction of the Gulch mouth and Death Valley. He jerked his head around and received in the space of an eye-blink a series of kaleidoscopic impressions:

Two big motorcycles, one a blood-red Harley "hog" chopper, the other a big yellow Yamaha V-Max, were racing toward him at high speed, spewing rooster-tails of sand behind churning wheels... Shaggy-bearded riders with long hair bannering under their helmets like monsters in a science-fiction movie... Chrome handlebars jutting from either side like the horns of stampeding bulls...

There was no time to shout a warning, no time for him to dodge or the cyclists to veer aside. Tommy was caught between the two thundering machines. The Yamaha's handlebar clipped him behind the left ear. He felt himself cartwheeling through space in a shower of stars, then crashing into something cushiony that broke his tumble.

The two motorcyclists braked hard, motor exhausts filling the rocky canyon with their alien roar as they tilted into a skid and spun around, heading back to where Tommy Rockford was sprawled dazed and bleeding against a clump of silver-leafed desert holly.

Through slitted lids, Rockford saw a red-bearded rider—Rusty Hilton, the radio had called him—lean his red Harley hog on its kick-bar and dismount, striding over to stare down at the fallen youth, his muscular torso stretching his black leather jacket to capacity. He was joined by his companion, a heavy-set man with hair like golden fleece which streamed out from under his skull bucket like stuffing from a ruptured mattress. Goldie Lesher...

"Just a kid," Lesher muttered... "Too young to be a narc cop."

The redhead squatted down for a closer look at his victim. Some primitive instinct made Tommy feign unconsciousness.

"You smashed his head, whoever he is. Came barrelin' out of that crack in the cliff like he was trying to cut us off or something. You veered to hit him on purpose, didn't you, Goldie?"

The blond rider prodded Tommy's inert body with a boot toe as he might the carcass of a run-over animal. "Well, like they say, Rusty, dead men tell no tales... Maybe we, like, ought to see if he's got a wallet? Watch? Ring? He won't be needin' 'em."

An obscene oath of disgust came from Rusty as he stalked back to mount his red Harley.

"Has the angel dust completely rotted what passed for your brain, Goldie? What if this kid ain't travelin' alone? Want some snoop to find him and think he was killed and robbed intentionally? This way it looks like he fell off the cliff accidental."

The yellow-haired man shrugged and went back to mount his Yamaha. Tommy Rockford's senses had faded into oblivion, so he was unaware of hearing the two motorcyclists as they roared off up Avalanche Gulch and around a bend, to vanish ahead of a sifting pall of dust which floated back in clouds to settle slowly over the unconscious youth's body.

High overhead, a black speck against the threatening, slate-colored sky, an alert buzzard began wheeling down in ever-lowering spirals, as if it had sighted carrion. Buzzards, scavengers of the badlands, only eat dead flesh...

CHAPTER SIX

IN AVALANCHE GULCH

Tommy's return to his senses duplicated the slow, nightmarish progression of sensations he had once experienced while scuba-diving for abalone along the Santa Barbara Channel's offshore Santa Cruz Island. That time he had become entangled two fathoms deep in a kelp bed, with the air in his tanks nearly exhausted.

His first conscious sensation was of watching a fireworks show exploding against the night-black curtain of his eyelids. Then confused, weird sounds penetrated his head: the grinding of sand particles between his molars, where his mouth had been slammed against the ground hard enough to make his lips bleed.

Taste was next: the saltiness of blood on his tongue, followed by touch: the sticky wetness in his hair as he groped trembling fingers up to explore the throbbing pain where the fireworks seemed to originate. Mingled with those sensations was the lingering stink of motorcycle fumes trapped between the basaltic walls of the canyon, a stifling alien scent in his nostrils.

Only then, having marshaled his dazed senses one by one, did Tommy Rockford find the will and the strength to open his eyes.

At first he could not recognize where he was. Gray daylight was streaming into the rocky throat of Avalanche Gulch, which curved off to the left, blocking the long view up-canyon behind an intervening outthrust of cliff.

He was lying on his right side, his legs partially under a tangled thicket of silvery desert holly—the cushion which had absorbed his fall and undoubtedly saved him from fractured bones. The sun, past high noon, was a coppery blur behind a deck of storm clouds massing on the zenith, allowing no pattern of light and shadow, no accents down here at the foot of the Panamints.

Tommy painfully pushed himself to a sitting position. His brain spun like a gyroscope, threatening another blackout. He closed his eyes and sucked oxygen into his lungs. When he opened his eyes again they came into focus on a double set of tire marks which snaked out of sight around the nearest bend in Avalanche Gulch. Motorcycle tracks. That brought comprehension flooding back to fill the vacuum in his mind.

"Those two guys on the cycles... had to be those Crossbow Killers we heard about on the radio this morning... latest bulletin warned they were believed... heading toward Death Valley..."

Confused recollections swirled through Tommy's head as he forced himself to stand up, leaning on the lava wall for support until the world stopped whirling around him and his knees stopped wobbling. How long had he been knocked out? A minute? An hour?

He lifted his wrist to bring his watch close enough to focus on, recalling that it had been 12:20 when he had last talked to Chub on CB Channel 14...

"Chub! Oh my gosh—*that's* what I was doing when I ran down here and got clobbered by those motorcycles. Trying to keep Chub from exploring some old mine tunnel and getting himself killed—"

He was astonished to see that it was now 1:15. That meant he had lain unconscious for thirty-five or forty minutes, although the time lapse seemed like an eye-blink.

He gingerly examined the throbbing welt on his scalp where the rubber grip of the handlebar had struck him, hard enough to flip him to one side like a tiddlywink. His fingers came away with the tips stained bright crimson.

He tried to sort out a few facts while he waited for enough equilibrium to return so he could start walking up the canyon without falling on his face every few steps.

One fact he had to accept was that the two motorcyclists who had left him for dead were armed and dangerous—fugitives from a Nevada manhunt, the murderers of a security guard at a Las Vegas casino last night.

Something in his favor: the waffle-iron prints of the jogging shoes which identified Chub Downey's passage up the Gulch were easy to track in the loose sand, although obliterated at times by the tire marks left by the Crossbow Killers' motorcycles.

Relief washed over Tommy Rockford as logic told him that the two fugitives had probably not overtaken Chub, who according to his own radio report had left the canyon floor to climb what he thought was a pile of mine tailings spilling from a prospect hole, the opening of which was hidden behind a thicket of brush higher up the face of the cliff. Such holes were common throughout the Mojave and Amargosa desert country of California and Nevada.

If Chub had seen the motorcyclists, he would have mentioned them. There was every reason to hope that by the time the outlaws had passed along the canyon floor, Chub was safely out of sight in his mysterious tunnel.

One grim reality Tommy Rockford had to accept—as long as he and Chub were inside this canyon along with two leather-jacketed cyclists who had murdered a man, they were in great danger. Tommy put no credence at all upon Chub's fanciful tale about having seen Seldom Seen Sam's lost ghost town hotel, the Gunsight Lode, visible at the far end of the tunnel. That smacked of a childish association of ideas, a fantasy taking root in the fertile, receptive soil of an adolescent imagination.

"I've got to get... up canyon... and find that heap of mine tailings piled against the cliff," Tommy panted hoarsely. "Locate Chub's tunnel, if any, and get both of us out of here before those Crossbow Killer hoodlums catch us... "

He caught sight of the CB walkie-talkie he had been carrying at the moment disaster overtook him. It had been knocked out of its belt holster and was lying a dozen feet away, the telescoping chrome antenna impaled in the sand like a javelin.

Tommy stumbled and fell twice in those dozen feet, nausea stabbing him repeatedly. He felt the warm wetness of fresh blood leaking down his ear and under the collar of his baseball jersey. Common sense told him that his first responsibility was to himself, to get that head wound bandaged before the hemorrhaging weakened him further. Otherwise he was subject to a blackout at any moment, with possible serious results if he fell.

Extricating the Citizen's Band transceiver from the dirt, he saw that it was damaged beyond repair. A motorcycle wheel had passed over it, crushing it flat. This meant he couldn't give Chub a call, or hear Chub in case the youth had come back out of the tunnel and tried to contact him.

Or was there a tunnel in the first place? On the trip over from the coast yesterday, Chub's incessant chattering had often verged on pure fantasy. Had Chub made up the whole story about climbing a pile of loose mine tailings to discover a tunnel mouth concealed behind a clump of brush, somewhere on the face of the south wall of Avalanche Gulch?

Tommy Rockford turned and headed back up the ravine to return to the Field Day site. His watch showed 1:30 when he finally came out into the open again.

Everything was as he had left it—the VW parked in the stable shed, the strand of copper wire dipole leading from the dead juniper on the ridge down to the shack's chimney. He had left this scene only an hour and ten minutes ago, but already it seemed like something remembered dimly out of his boyhood. The blow to his head had put his time machine out of sync.

Death Valley's white-streaked salt and borax flats were not as blinding-bright under the subdued sunlight as they had been earlier. The high-altitude storm clouds, scudding in from the north, were now spilling over the stony summits of the Panamint Range to fill the great sink with blue shadow.

If California Highway Patrolmen were looking for motorcycle tracks anywhere off the paved highway in the valley proper, a gully-washer rain would wipe out the fugitives' spoor forever.

From a metal box in the van, Tommy got out his emergency first aid kit. He found his shaving supplies and dug his mirror out of the depths of the water-resistant nylon bag.

Then K6ATX headed for the cabin door a dozen feet away. Twice in that distance his knees caved under his weight and waves of weakness flooded his senses, as they had on his short climb up the ravine from Avalanche Gulch. He was thankful he had had training in first aid, first as a Boy Scout and later as a summer lifeguard at Santa Bonita's public beaches. Cleansing and bandaging his own head wound would be hard to manage, though. It would be at least a couple of hours before he could expect Doc and Spud and Ray to show up to assist him. Another problem to be contended with was keeping the news of his injury from Uncle JC, who would be torn with worry for his nephew and his obligations as Field Day coordinator.

"I hope I'm able to do my share of hamming tomorrow," he muttered, pushing open the shack's flimsy door on its bullhide hinges.

He dragged his feet across the hard-packed dirt floor and laid his first aid kit and shaving mirror on one of the card tables he had set up for the club's radio equipment.

When he had swabbed away the dried blood and dirt from his hair he revealed a four-inch scalp laceration, which he sterilized with rubbing alcohol—it felt like he was cauterizing the wound with a red-hot iron—and applied a dressing of antibiotic ointment from his emergency kit, binding it securely into place with strips of sterile gauze like the sweat bands worn by athletes.

Stomach pangs and general weakness reminded Tommy that he hadn't eaten since he and Chub had breakfasted early that morning at Trona, the chemical-refinery town southwest of Death Valley. Although he had no appetite, he rummaged in a grub box and forced himself to drink a can of orange juice and choke down some cheese, raisins and bread. Almost immediately he could feel the energy surging back into his body.

A growl of thunder, loud enough to make the old house rattle, reminded Tommy Rockford that he had left his Uncle JC holding the phone up there on Telescope Peak, just prior to his mad dash down into Avalanche Gulch, almost two hours ago.

He unpacked the Radio Club's 45-watt TR-7950 Kenwood two-meter rig from its cardboard container, set the digital dial to the club's operating frequency, and switched it on. As if on cue he heard his friend Roy, W6AMD, in the act of resuming a QSO with Uncle JC up at the net control station:

". . . W6AMD—A Million-Dollar station!—operating mobile at Stovepipe Wells resort, Death Valley. Roger, W7OE. Reason I'm giving you this shout is because we haven't been able to raise K6ATX yet to find out where he located our Field Day QTH. We don't dare drive south down the valley toward Furnace Creek for fear he may have headed north toward Ubehebe Crater, or maybe as far as Scotty's Castle. Has Tommy contacted you with any information? This is W6AMD mobile standing by in a royal tizzy."

Before Tommy could press the transmit button to break in, he heard Uncle JC's anxious voice returning without call-sign preamble: "Yes and no, Roy. I worked Tommy on two meters, just long enough to hear him say he had found an 'abandoned cabin'. Where, he didn't say—and Death Valley is a hundred miles long and over ten miles wide, you know. Before he could give me his QTH, Tommy got interrupted by some sort of emergency call on a CB channel from his friend Chubby somebody. Said he'd be back immediately. That was two hours ago—and I haven't had a dot or a dash from Tommy since. W7OE/6, back to W6AMD, but keep it short, Roy, I may have to QRT any moment if lightning starts striking around here."

Tommy's thumb hit the push-to-talk button a microsecond after Uncle JC's squelch tail went off the air, hoping against hope he had beaten W6AMD. He almost shouted into the mike, "W7OE/6, this is K6ATX coming back to you. Do you copy, Unk?"

Frustration touched Tommy as he heard W6AMD come back to JC atop Telescope Peak:

"Roger on your having to QRT any second, JC. Guess all we can do here is stand by at Stovepipe Wells until K6ATX keeps his sked with us. It'll sure put a crimp in our Field Day score if Spud and Doc and I can't man the station at wherever Tommy's mystery shack is, though. We have all those solar panels to set up for our power supply et cetera. W6AMD mobile in Death Valley, off and clear."

K6ATX immediately gave W6AMD a call—but apparently the fates had decreed that the two, like Kipling's East and West, would never meet. W6AMD had returned to the air, but to acknowledge a call from Fred, KB6JIP, one of three Technician Class hams who were with Uncle JC up at the control station on Telescope Peak.

With a sigh of resignation, Tommy switched to the alternate intercom frequency, planning to hook up with Uncle JC, only to find W7OE/6 engaged in "talking in" a station wagon containing the members of the Santa Maria Amateur Radio Club, presently on Highway 195 at Lone Pine in the Owens River Valley.

Giving road directions and weather reports to a group still a hundred miles away would be a time-consuming matter, especially when Santa Maria's driver was letting JC, from seven-land, know that Mt. Whitney, the highest mountain peak in the 48 contiguous States, and Badwater in Death Valley, the lowest spot in the hemisphere, were both inside Inyo County, one of America's largest counties.

Tommy turned off the rig, having no time for ragchewing. His first priority was finding Chub, hoping the kid hadn't stumbled into the two Crossbow Killers in the Gulch. That couldn't wait.

His own CB transceiver had been flattened into a battered piece of junk, so he would have no way of contacting Chub by radio. However, Tommy still had his own two-meter FM hand-held job, and decided to take it with him into Avalanche Gulch and bide his time to break in with a report to Uncle JC concerning his QTH.

There was a ghostly green half-light over Death Valley as K6ATX emerged from Seldom Seen Sam's cabin and headed back down the ravine for the second time. He had a splitting headache but was almost unaware of the pain in the urgency of locating his redheaded companion.

Under the head bandage Tommy's brain throbbed as if someone was pounding him with a hammer every time his heart beat. But he was no longer bleeding, and the food in his stomach had relieved the original light-headedness that had plagued him on his way back up to the cabin earlier.

CHAPTER SEVEN

FLASH FLOOD WARNING

Back again on the gravelly floor of Avalanche Gulch, Tommy started off up the canyon following Chub's easy-to-read trail. He knew the basalt walls rising sheer to the rimrocks fifty feet on either side would serve as amplifiers to funnel any sound of motorcycle engines to his ears long before the two Satan's Angels came in sight. That would give him time to hide in the brush and rocks which littered the canyon floor.

K6ATX followed the winding tracks made by the two motorcycles around the first long curve of the canyon, the floor of which was rising at a ten-degree angle. From time to time he could pick up the familiar prints left by Chub's jogging shoes. They reminded him of photographs which NASA had published years ago, of bootprints the Apollo astronauts had left in the moon dust back in '69. It was that achievement during his childhood that had inspired Tommy Rockford to strive for a future career as a space engineer. It was not outside the realm of possibility that some day he might travel to the moon himself, make a pilgrimage to the historic spot where the *Eagle* had landed, and view those very bootprints in the shadow of the Stars and Stripes!

Working his way around another S-bend in Avalanche Gulch, Rockford scanned the shadow-filled canyon ahead for any trace of movement. A few yards ahead were the first of the jagged boulders which blocked off the Gulch to any other than two-wheeled traffic. They were rocks which apparently had tumbled down from the south rim—and in comparatively recent geological times, Tommy judged, since they had not yet taken on the blue-black sheen known as "desert varnish," which rocks acquired after thousands of years of exposure to the sun's heat, which sweated oxides from the rock.

"Just what am I supposed to be looking for, other than a red and a yellow motorcycle?" Tommy asked himself out loud.

The answer, of course, was a sprawl of mine tailings chipped out of a concealed tunnel opening somewhere up the sheer stone cliffs which formed the left-hand side of Avalanche Gulch. The heap of tailings would be identified by a clump of brush that had taken root at the apex of the triangle of loose stone. However, another bend in the Gulch limited Tommy's vision to less than fifty yards.

He picked up Chub's clear trail again and followed it until the kid's shoe tracks entered another jumble of rocks which almost blocked the canyon floor. He saw where the two motorcyclists had gone into single file, as if aware of narrower spots up ahead—confirmation of Tommy's conviction that the Crossbow Killers' long-sought secret hideout was indeed located somewhere up the miles-long length of Avalanche Gulch.

Because he was close to physical exhaustion from the trauma of his head injury, Tommy was forced to sit down and rest. While regaining his wind, he switched on the two-meter hand-held rig.

Down in this rock-ribbed slot at the base of Telescope Peak he hardly expected to hear anything. But from the speaker issued a signal so potent that Tommy had to reduce the volume to prevent the sound from possibly reaching hostile ears farther up the canyon.

"WA6IBR at Stovepipe Wells, this is WB6FZV with the Vandenberg Air Force Base ham station at Badwater, Death Valley, returning. Hi, Spud! The guys here are busy setting up our solar-cell array to generate electricity... Don't you think my preamble to a QSO will thrill Field Day hams when they pick it up tomorrow? 'The West Coast space shuttle gang, operating from the deepest hole in the western hemisphere!' That's a blockbuster combination!"

Tommy knew why the signal was pounding in so loud. Badwater was less than ten miles away, line-of-sight across the open floor of Death Valley. He knew the man at the mike, Steve Bauer, one of several blind operators in the Santa Bonita Ham Club, who had been invited to share the Field Day experience with fellow ham hobbyists who wear the proud uniform of the United States Air Force.

Tommy had a crucial decision confronting him. Should he contact Uncle JC up on Telescope Peak now and break the news that the Crossbow Killers had been sighted going up Avalanche Gulch?

He decided that could wait. To bring a swarm of law enforcement officers to the area might very well hand Chub Downey a death warrant, in case the kid was being held hostage by the two felons somewhere up the canyon.

In a sense the outlaws were trapped; Tommy doubted if there was any other exit higher up the canyon that a motorcycle could negotiate. In case he did see the pair coming back, heading out toward Death Valley, there would be plenty of time then to contact Uncle JC with the news, and let him attend to relaying the message to the law. The Crossbow Killers could never get out of the valley.

K6ATX could not rest any longer. It was time to resume his climb along the trail which snaked up the Gulch, although the very thought of exerting himself in such heat was frightening.

Wild burros, descended from the pack animals of the pioneer prospectors back in the legendary twenty-mule-team borax era of Death Valley history, had left their hoofprints and droppings along the Avalanche Gulch trail, on their way to feeding grounds higher up the slope of the Panamints.

The National Park Service rangers who administered Death Valley urgently desired that all feral burros be exterminated, but public opinion would not permit. Burros were not indigenous to the region and their habits of denuding the landscape of plant life by devouring foliage to the root line and fouling water holes were driving such native animals as bighorn sheep to the edge of extinction—a tragedy which the tender-hearted animal lovers of America did not seem to understand.

Tommy had a strong hunch that the next bend of the canyon might reveal Chub Downey's triangular-shaped sprawl of mine tailings piled against the south cliffs, with a thicket of brush masking the tunnel entrance at its apex. He doubted if his overweight friend had the energy to have hiked much higher up the Gulch than this.

Tommy left his two-meter rig on, keeping the speaker barely audible, attached to his clothes by a metal belt clip to leave both hands free for rock-scrambling. As he was working his way around the long crescent curve of the canyon, hoping at any instant to come in view of Chub's mine tailings, he noticed that the static discharges were gaining in volume. Flashes of far-off, unseen lightning were flickering over the fifty-foot-high walls of Avalanche Gulch, followed moments later by ear-jarring thunder. The desert storm was about to break over the desolate land.

It was at that moment, with a suddenness that caught K6ATX entirely by surprise, that he heard his Uncle's frantic voice burst from the tiny speaker on his two-meter transceiver:

"Emergency! May Day! Emergency! CQ all stations—Emergency!

Of all the code words used in radio communication, May Day was the one calculated to put a chill down the spine, to freeze the heart in mid-beat. The English pronunciation of a French call for help, May Day was the internationally-recognized distress signal, the phone equivalent of the SOS distress symbol used in wireless telegraphy's Morse code. Had JC been operating *CW*—continuous wave rather than a frequency- or an amplitude-modulated *voice* signal—he would have tapped out three dots, three dashes and three dots with his key to form the letters SOS.

Uncle JC was in some kind of trouble up there on Telescope, or he wouldn't be shouting "May Day" or "emergency" into his mike. Had a lightning bolt struck nearby? Or had young Noisy fallen off a cliff?

"If anyone can hear me," JC's voice sounded behind the steady roar of thunder and falling rain, "this is a life-and-death emergency warning to everyone on the west side of Death Valley for a distance of five miles north or south of Telescope Peak. I have just witnessed the most violent cloudburst a human being could conceive. Heavy rain clouds ripped open their bellies on the Panamint peaks and millions upon millions of gallons of water are now plunging down the eastern slope toward Death Valley like a tidal wave. It is beyond human comprehension. The run-off will be heaviest in the canyons, so if anyone hearing this emergency message is in a canyon or low spot of any kind, get out while you can! The water will hit the valley within minutes. Move to higher ground! May Day! Flash flood warning..."

The horror-charged voice faded out under a jam of static. It took K6ATX no longer than ten seconds to realize that he, himself, could be in mortal danger. Avalanche Gulch thrust its gash up the mountainside almost to the summit where Uncle JC's catastrophe of nature was taking place, forming a natural channel for a surge of water which would wipe out everything in its path.

Even as the terrifying thought entered his mind, the sky seemed to open and swollen raindrops spattered the rocky terrain around him, a few at first, then coming in torrents.

Tommy Rockford had been hearing of flash floods in the desert area of California all his life. He knew their incredible destructive potential, the way they could change a region's topography forever in a matter of minutes. He remembered how Seldom Seen Sam had hurried on his way this morning because he didn't want to run the risk of encountering a flash flood which could turn a bone-dry gully into a raging millrace without warning.

The rain was coming down in buckets now, stinging his skin, bouncing off the nearby boulders. And then to Tommy Rockford's ears came a strange rumble, similar to the indescribable subterranean roar one hears during an earthquake. An organ swell of sound that boomed louder with each passing second, deep, malignant, and incredibly frightening.

The earth under Tommy's feet began to vibrate. Powder-dry cascades of dust spilled from ledges in the cliff above, as some elemental force, thunderous as an approaching freight train, caused the rock walls of Avalanche Gulch to tremble.

The cloudburst which had dumped its untold millions of gallons of rainwater on the Panamint peaks was using this very canyon as one of its obvious sluiceways en route to the sprawling alluvial fans at the foot of the gulch—fans five miles across at their bottoms, formed by the build-up of similar flash floods that had been creating the beauty of Death Valley over the millions of years that the vast sink had been evolving from an inland sea.

Tommy refused to yield to terror. He started climbing the piles of wet boulders which had spilled over the south rim in some monumental avalanche in the past—perhaps the rock slide that had given the gulch its picturesque name. If a flash flood was plunging toward him, as he was now sure it was, his only hope to save himself was to get above the high-water mark in time.

It was too late. In that terrible instant Tommy's eyes beheld a scene out of a horror movie: a twenty-foot wall of coffee-brown water and debris rounding the canyon ahead of him to explode in sheets of dirty yellow spray against the north wall, caroming back to crash with equal force against the south wall, then foaming in a debris-choked cascade to burst like a bomb against the very rockpile Tommy was climbing like a bug.

He felt the raging floodwaters snatch at his legs, felt his fingers being torn loose from their death-grip on the rocks he was climbing.

Then he was snatched like a leaf out into the awful surge, and undercurrents sucked him below the brown millrace of angry water. The one corner of consciousness left to him was enough to tell him that no power on earth could save him now, that he was being swept downcanyon to his death and an unmarked grave under sprawling tons of mud and detritus dating from the dawn of time.

CHAPTER EIGHT

AFTERMATH OF TRAGEDY

He came to the surface in a smother of foam, riding the curling crest-wave of the flash flood. Pure instinct, born of a thousand surf rides inside the rolling tube of an ocean breaker, served the young radio ham in good stead now.

He had never done any skydiving—a sport he had always wanted to try, but had promised his nervous mother he wouldn't—but he knew that body attitude can be controlled in space by using arms and legs as a pilot would use the control surfaces of his aircraft's wings, rudder and elevators. Would the same idea work in water?

He was able to stop his barrel-rolling motion by hugging his elbows tight to his ribs and letting the savage thrust of the racing water strike his palms and fingers as if they were ailerons on an airplane wing, instinctively banking his body as the vanguard of the wave swept him toward the north cliff and around the curve in the canyon, thus saving himself from being dashed to death against the rock wall and using the water itself as a shock absorber.

Once around the lowest bend of Avalance Gulch, Tommy felt the violent turbulence of the flood tapering off as it was no longer churning over enormous piles of boulders. Because the canyon widened out from rim to rim as it approached its mouth, the water had more room to spread, and consequently became shallower.

Tommy saw the familiar holly thicket zooming toward him, the one marking the entrance to the ravine which led up to the Field Day cabin. It blurred past him, like leaning from the window of a car and seeing a tree coming closer and then zipping past.

The roar of the floodwaters was less deafening now as he was swept out through the yawning gateway of Avalanche Gulch, onto the alluvial fan which sloped all the way to the soda flats and stretched across the valley to the Badwater depression.

Wrapped in a tangle of foliage and other debris which the plunging wall of water had scoured off the floor of the Gulch on its miles-long rush at almost waterfall speed, Tommy Rockford lost control of his body-surfing position as the water depth lessened.

He felt his knees and elbows bump solid earth for the first time. Looking back on it later, Tommy realized how easily he could have been disembowled by his long skidding slide down the canyon, escaping being ripped open by protruding rocks and thorny bushes through sheer luck.

At the end Tommy rolled and skidded up onto a wind-heaped hump of sand. The water gushing out of the canyon mouth behind him was dissolving the big dune, but for Tommy it was like tumbling into a deep snowbank after a ski run, or riding his surfboard safely to a stop on a smooth and shelving beach.

Sprawling to a halt on the crest of the melting sand knoll, he dug his fingers into the earth and tucked up his legs as he felt the ebbing waters of the flash flood clutching at his body, as if reluctant to give up a victim.

The waters divided on either side of the sand dune upon which he had come to rest. He was perhaps a hundred yards outside the rocky portals of Avalanche Gulch, and a hundred feet lower in elevation. What was left of the spent flood still spewed from the canyon mouth, tumbling huge boulders like marbles out onto the alluvial fan. The foaming surge split into two forks, and in a matter of seconds carved waist-deep gullies in the sand and gravel detritus.

Then it was over, spent. The flash flood subsided as suddenly as it had been created ten thousand feet up the canyon. The rain was gone. Sunshine glinted blindingly on the last traceries of water flowing down the mountainside. And then, between two eye-blinks, the flood vanished, drunk up by the thirsty sands. Here and there pools of trapped water glistened briefly under the desert sun like shattered fragments of mirrors, and then disappeared.

"Thank you, God," Tommy Rockford whispered prayerfully. He had never been one to shout his religious beliefs from the house tops, but his faith in his Creator and the teachings of the *Holy Bible* had been deeply implanted in his psyche by devout Christian parents, a strength which served him in good stead in times of stress and danger such as today. Lying here on the sand hill like so much jetsam cast up on a beach, Tommy knew he had been in God's hands during that terrifying toboggan slide down Avalanche Gulch.

Tommy came shakily to his feet, clawing tangled brush from his waist and shoulders. Suddenly he was struck by the fact that tendrils of steam were lifting like smoke from the sands around him. The entire weather picture had changed within minutes; the punishing June heat had returned.

His gaze lifted to scan the tumbled slopes of Telescope Peak, where the cloudburst had left the naked rock glistening in the sun. Already its rays had raised the temperature to the 120-degree mark; his soggy baseball jersey and jeans were already almost dry. Where an ugly, bloated rain cloud had been ruptured on the sawtoothed Panamint peaks was now the pure electric blue of the Death Valley sky, clean-washed and without a trace of smog or haze. Given a pair of binoculars, Tommy believed he could have picked out the camp of his Uncle JC and cousin Noisy up there on the skyline—assuming they had survived the cloudburst.

It had been Uncle JC's awareness of the resulting flash flood in the lower canyons, and his being able to transmit a warning on two meters, that had saved Tommy's life. If he had been caught higher up in the canyon when the water struck he would have been smashed to pulp against the jumbled rocks. As it was, through sheer instinct he had combined the techniques of a scuba diver and a surfboard rider—both of which he was, back home—to go with the tide and survive his wild ride down the canyon.

Tommy ran spread fingers through his shock of blond hair, and winced, straining the muddy water from it. All about him the earth was bubbling and gurgling, little air vents popping open in the sand from the waters which were percolating down into the soil. He wondered how many rodents and tarantulas and rattlesnakes had drowned in their flooded burrows, lost without chance of escape.

In the wake of the storm, visibility had expanded to reach the farthest horizons. Eastward, Tommy Rockford could see the sheer chocolate-colored walls of ancient rock which spanned more than a vertical mile from Badwater, at 282 feet below sea level, to Dante's View, the popular tourists' vista point on the skyline.

Steve Bauer and his Air Force buddies were setting up their Field

Day ham station at the foot of that cliff. K6ATX wondered if they had enjoyed their view of the flash floods tumbling down the western wall of the valley, or if they had even been aware of the drama transpiring a scant ten miles away.

Closer at hand, to the north and east, were the adobe ruins of the historic Eagle Borax Works where twenty-mule team wagons had loaded in pioneer days. Still nearer lay the clump of green mesquites marking the oasis of Bennetts' Well, which he and Chub had driven through this morning. The covered wagon party which had been stranded there in late December of 1849, the first Americans to see Death Valley, had crossed the Panamints on foot, possibly by way of Avalanche Canyon, in search of civilization.

Legend had it that when the emigrants finally reached the summit of the mountain wall to escape the bake-oven valley, the matriarch of the Bennett family had looked down for the last time on the sink that prehistoric Indian dwellers had named Tomesha, or Ground Afire, and had cried "Farewell, Death Valley!—thereby bestowing upon one of America's most scenic and mysterious places a totally inappropriate name. US geodetic surveyors, drafting topo maps for the government, had bestowed other dire-sounding labels on Death Valley landmarks—Funeral Mountains, Hell's Gate, Dante's View, Desolation Canyon, Devil's Cornfield, Dry Bones Canyon.

Shielding his eyes with trembling hands, Tommy Rockford scanned the long sweep of Death Valley to the northward, toward Stove Pipe Wells and Scotty's Castle. Sunlight glinted off the chrome bumper of a vehicle crawling along the paved road from the date-palm oasis of Furnace Creek Ranch. He wondered if that might be Roy MacCormack and his other ham friends, hunting him.

Lost in the spell of the desolate beauty of the scene, Tommy Rockford finally returned to reality, and the emergency which had sent him down into Avalanche Gulch in the first place. Chub Downey! Tommy could not help but feel that the redhead had been safely above the high-water mark of the flash flood, if he had indeed been exploring a mine tunnel leading to a lost ghost town, as he had claimed in his radio check-in.

"At least there's a chance he's still alive," Tommy said in a croaking voice. "I won't give up until I find his body to prove otherwise..."

He started slogging his way back up the slope. It was heavy going, for what had been flinty hard earth furred with creosote brush when he had driven his VW van across it earlier today to reach Seldom Seen Sam's cabin was now a naked, treacherous shelf of quicksand, a cake-frosting of fresh silt into which his feet sank to the ankles, making each step a physical effort.

As he was entering the rocky portals of the Gulch his eye was attracted to a bone-white, skull-like object which the flood had cast upon the fast-drying mud a few yards off to his left. The thought crossed Tommy's mind that the flood had exhumed a prospector's or Indian's grave, but as he walked closer to the object he recognized it as a fiberglass motorcycle helmet.

Tommy's heart hammered his ribs as he found a stick and pried the molded fiberglass helmet out of the mud. The temples bore a painted insignia of a scarlet-faced, black-bearded, double-horned devil riding a thunderbolt, and gold letters which spelled out SATAN'S ANGELS—the motorcycle gang which had defied the police of California and Nevada as long as Tommy could remember.

Closer examination of the webbed sweatband inside the crash helmet revealed a number of cinnamon-red hairs, hinting that this helmet could have belonged to Rusty Hilton, one of the Crossbow Killers who had staged the $50,000 hold-up at the Las Vegas casino last night.

Tommy flung the helmet aside as if it were something unclean, wiping his hands on his Levis. He wondered, was Hilton wearing that skull bucket when the flood hit him? The back of the helmet had been caved in, a dent which would most certainly have resulted in a crushed skull.

He continued on up the steep slope, where wisps of vapor were being drawn by the heat from bubble-marks pocking the surface of the fast-drying mud. He worked his way outside the wet path of the flood onto hard dry ground. Now the urgency of getting up Avalanche Gulch to see what had happened to Chub Downey made him overlook the pounding throb under his head bandage.

Out of the open sun, in the shadow cast by the south cliff, Tommy was forced by sheer exhaustion to sit down on a slab of polished gneiss to rest. Once again a glitter of sunlight on something bright and metallic drew his eye to an object caught in the thicket of white holly scrub across the canyon at the exit of the ravine trail.

Curiosity brought Tommy to his feet and sent him slogging across the mud to investigate. Drawing nearer, he recognized the curving metal shape as one handlebar of a half-buried motorcycle. It was the yellow-enameled Yamaha that the other Crossbow Killer, Goldie Lesher, had been riding.

Only the one handlebar, a smashed headlight and part of the fork assembly were visible above the mud. He told himself that later, when this nightmare was behind him, he would bring his entrenching tool and attempt to dig Lesher's cycle out of the mud. The pair of leather saddlebags he remembered seeing lashed to the sissy bar at the rear might contain the $50,000 loot which had cost a man his life during the Pharaoh's Palace robbery.

But right now Tommy had no time to dwell on buried-treasure fantasies or wonder what fate had overtaken the two motorcycle fugitives. He had no doubt but that the flash flood had drowned both of them, and good riddance. He might even stumble across their waterlogged corpses farther up-canyon, although he hoped to be spared such a grisly discovery.

He wondered what had become of the two-meter handie-talkie he had been carrying when the flood's crest snatched him off the rocks. If he still had it, right now he would be attempting to contact Uncle JC up on the peak to make sure he was okay after the storm, and to tell him where Roy and Doc and Spud could find him—although the events of the past hour had made his ham radio Field Day plans seem secondary.

He had plodded another hundred yards up the Gulch, noting that the flood had completely stripped away all vestiges of plant life, when he made his next exciting discovery. It was nothing as gruesome as the drowned bodies of Rusty Hilton and Goldie Lesher. It was a twist of two-inch wide canvas webbing, a strap attached to something buried under the silt.

A sickish sensation went through K6ATX as he tugged at one end of the strap to expose a canvas carrying case for a World War Two vintage gas mask. It was the bag that Chub Downey used to collect rock specimens.

CHAPTER NINE

CODE TEN THIRTY-FOUR

Overcoming an intense feeling of revulsion, Tommy Rockford cupped his hands and began clawing away at the moist sand under Chub's knapsack, as a dog might dig for a bone.

Relief flowed through him as he excavated the loop of carrying strap and found that it had only been snagged on a buried root. He got to his feet, peering up-canyon as he repeated aloud his conviction that his portly buddy was alive and safe, in spite of the flash flood which had scoured all living things from Avalanche Gulch:

"Chub said he had climbed a tailing heap to reach the mouth of a mine tunnel. Okay, that flood wasn't more than twenty feet high. His mine tunnel could have been higher up the cliff than that..."

He resumed his trek up the canyon, this time with no helping footprints to read. The ground still gurgled and made sucking sounds as bursting air bubbles came up through the silt with little popping noises, to leave craterlike pits in the muck.

By the time K6ATX had rounded the first bend in the Gulch and reached the point where he had been when the floodwaters roared down upon him, he was able to hop from boulder to boulder, which was easier than slogging his way through ankle-deep mud.

The changes which the raging waters had wrought seemed incredible to Tommy. He carried a camera-clear memory of the jumble of avalanche rock which had cluttered the trail ahead on his first visit. That pattern had been altered beyond all recognition. Boulders the size of grand pianos had been rolled a hundred yards beyond their original locations and were draped with brush and weeds on their upper sides, brush which had been uprooted farther up the mountain.

With increasing difficulty, K6ATX made his way around, over and across the jumbled rocks until he reached the next twisting elbow of the canyon. Here the rock walls faced each other across a gap less than a hundred feet wide, narrowed to only a third of the width at the canyon mouth. From this vantage point, Tommy could see an unbroken vista of over half a mile of Avalanche Gulch's crease in the Panamint mountain wall. He judged that at the upper end the Gulch rimrocks were less than fifty feet apart before coming together near the summit of Telescope Peak.

"Chub couldn't have climbed much farther along than where I am now when he called in his noon check," Tommy panted aloud. "So his heap of mine tailings should be visible from this spot."

His gaze carefully traced the south, or left-hand wall of the gulch, the lava shimmering like tombstones in the sunlight reflected off the north cliffs. But he saw nothing that resembled the pile of mine tailings Chub had described as leaning against the south cliff. Nothing but sheer, time-scarred rock, mottled in places with the blue-black crust of desert varnish.

Was his memory at fault—had Chub Downey described his discovery of the mine tunnel as being on the *north* cliff?

Again Tommy came up against a dead end in his search. Nothing resembling a pile of loose mine tailings spilled from a mine tunnel could be seen along the opposite wall of Avalanche Gulch.

Then Tommy deduced why. The incredible power of that flash flood could have undermined the tailing dump from the bottom, causing the upper end of the loose rock to slide downward into the water to be swept down onto the alluvial fan at the foot of the Panamints. That water action would also have carried away the thicket of brush which Chub described as growing at the top of the heap of mine tailings to conceal the entrance to the mine tunnel he had discovered. If this reasoning was correct, it meant that the mine tunnel opening should now be plainly visible to anyone working his way up the floor of the Gulch!

A renewed excitement thrilled through Tommy Rockford as he again began studying the face of the cliffs forming the south wall of the Gulch. The highwater mark still showed on the rock, attesting to the fact that the flood had crested at less than twenty feet in height where it was compressed here in the narrows.

Above the wet line was another expanse of sheer or overhanging basalt ending in the rock-littered layer of whitish capstone which rimmed the entire length of the Gulch. Tommy found it difficult to judge heights from this low angle, but he guessed that the rimrocks were at least fifty feet above the canyon floor at most points.

He started stumbling his way through the boulders again, eyes searching the tricky shadows on the cliff face, which fast became less distinct as the sunlight reflecting off the opposite cliffs was beginning to diminish.

Tommy was so absorbed with his hunt for the black maw of a mine tunnel showing itself like a window in the scarred rock face above that he tripped and fell headlong over an obstacle underfoot. When he saw what it was he reacted as if he had fallen on a coiled rattlesnake.

He had stumbled over what was left of a battered and flattened Harley-Davidson "hog" motorcycle, its grotesquely elongated front shock absorbers leading to the bent and twisted front wheel of what riders called a "chopper." The ruined machine had literally folded itself around a boulder. The ruptured fuel tank was enameled a bright blood-red.

"Rusty Hilton's cycle," Tommy muttered. "It got hung up on this rock while his partner's machine washed all the way to the mouth of the gulch—" At any rate, both outlaws' fates had now been accounted for, leaving only Chub Downey to track down.

Tommy glanced around apprehensively, bracing himself for the shock of seeing the red-bearded outlaw's corpse sprawled somewhere near his wrecked wheels. In a subsconscious effort to avoid making such a grisly discovery, Tommy lifted his eyes to study the sheer face of the cliff once more. And then, almost by accident, he saw what he had been searching for.

Thirty-odd feet directly over the spot where Hilton's wrecked motorcycle lay in mute testimony to the terrible destructive force of the flood, the smooth face of the cliff was broken by the black entrance to a tunnel of some kind. As Chub had said, it was not a natural cavity. Plainly visible from below were weatherbeaten shoring timbers supporting the ceiling of the tunnel.

Below the tunnel entrance, and spreading like a fan down the cliff, was an area of lighter-colored rock, as if the sun-glazed desert varnish had been erased in a triangle shape, its apex pointing to the threshold of the tunnel.

The variation in coloring of the cliff face was easy to explain.

This was where Chub's pyramid of loose mine tailings had rested against the cliff until the flash flood had undermined it and swept it away, like a broom brushing away cobwebs.

A feeling of guilt coursed through Tommy Rockford, recalling the skepticism with which he had greeted Chub Downey's report of finding a pile of mine tailings leading up to a mysterious tunnel in the cliff. So far, facts bore out Chub's story. But how about what he said he had seen at the far end of that tunnel—weathered false-fronted wooden buildings with the legend GUNSIGHT LODE HOTEL painted on a door, readable only to someone peering down the tunnel? That part of Chub's story was too absurd for belief, of course. Either Chub had been kidding him along, because he had said he was going to hunt for lost ghost towns as a sideline to his rockhounding today, or else Chub's over-productive imagination had carried him beyond the limits of plausibility.

But K6ATX was faced with facts he could not dismiss as adolescent fantasy. The ghost town might not exist, but the mouth of a tunnel half way up a cliff was certainly real enough. And, Tommy now realized, that tunnel mouth was as inaccessible as if it had been on the moon. Without the stairway of mine tailings which Chub had used to reach the tunnel, it would now require a forty-foot extension ladder to reach that aperture in the cliff. But why, he wondered, had any miner dug a hole so difficult to reach?

Tommy put his forefingers between his teeth and gave vent to an ear-splitting whistle. If Chub Downey was anywhere inside that mine tunnel up there he had to hear that whistle! Tommy hadn't been the loud-whistle champion of his Cub Scout pack for nothing.

When the echoes of the whistle had died away in the distance, Tommy strained his ears for an answer. He heard only the sluicing of hidden waters trickling down through the rocks, and the cry of a startled wild bird somewhere afar off.

"Chub! Chu-u-u-u-u-b! Are you still up in that tunnel?"

Tommy's shout, megaphoned through cupped hands, set up the same annoying echoes as the QRM that had followed his whistle.

And then—was it his imagination playing him tricks? He thought he heard the faintest of voices, distorted as if by an electronic echo box at a radio station... or was it like a whisper issuing from the depths of an opened grave in some half-remembered TV horror thriller he had seen as a kid?

No—there it came again!

"Tom-meeee! Ten..thirty... fo-o-u-ur!..."

The ghostly whisper died away, putting a tingle on the hairs of Tommy's neck nape. He had no way of orienting the source, but from the hollow timbre of the voice, he knew it must have come megaphoning out of the mine tunnel up there.

He called Chub's name again and again, but got no answer.

Tommy picked up small stones and tried to throw them up into the maw of the tunnel to attract Chub's attention, but his aim was faulty and he could not seem to summon the strength to throw that high at a near-vertical angle.

Tommy sat down on a ledge near the wreckage of Hilton's red motorcycle and tried to plot his next move. Scanning the cliff's surface, he knew it would be impossible to scale from below, even though he was a skilled rock climber. The climb, short though it was, would require special equipment such as drills, pitons, coils of nylon rope and crampons.

Rope! The ham club's VW van carried a thirty-foot coil of rope for towing purposes. Peering up at the mine tunnel, Tommy calculated that the opening in the rock wall was less than thirty feet down from the caprock above it.

With that fact established, planning came easily. All he would have to do would be to get a coil of rope, then hike up the south rim of Avalanche Gulch until he came to the spot directly above Chub's mine tunnel. There he could secure his rope to a handy boulder, then let himself over the rim and rappel down the face of the cliff until he reached the level of the tunnel mouth. It would be as simple as that!

Now that he had figured out a plan of attack, Tommy wasted no more time in contemplation. He walked over to the base of the opposite cliff and began studying the precise shape and appearance of the broken rocks immediately above the opening of the mine tunnel, so as to identify the exact spot when he reached it later.

He noticed a distinctive boulder of an odd yellowish color, as if it contained sulfur, and next to it a leaning slab of conglomerate rock like a shoring timber supporting a boat hull in a shipyard. There was also an ocotillo cactus plant growing at the edge of the caprock, its spiny green stalks tipped with red.

He might be confused by other rocks or clumps of brush on the south rim, but with three unique check points to work with—the odd yellow boulder, the leaning slab like a shoring timber, and the ocotillo—he would be able to recognize the exact spot where he could lower a rope and, sliding down it, find himself alongside the mouth of Chub's tunnel.

With frantic haste, oblivious to his physical fatigue, Tommy Rockford began racing back down the canyon. Not until then did his mind backtrack enough for him to inquire about Chub's cryptic numbers "ten thirty-four."

Did it refer to something that had happened at 10:34 this morning? No, that didn't make sense. Ten thirty-four... More likely it was part of the "ten code" which Citizens' Band radio hobbyists had adopted for a second language. But there were scores of Ten Code combinations, which K6ATX, his attitude typical of radio hams who felt somewhat superior to their unlicensed CB colleagues, had never bothered to memorize since he would not be using them on the ham bands. "Ten four," for example, meant "Okay, message received," a commonly-used bit of CB jargon which even Amateur Radio operators occasionally employed in their QSOs. "Ten two" stood for "Receiving well," and so on. But ten thirty-four? Tommy hadn't memorized the Ten Code that far.

Tommy was gasping for breath when he finally arrived back at Seldom Seen Sam's abandoned shack. He found everything as he had left it, but he hadn't expected to find it otherwise.

A shattering disappointment awaited him in the club van: the expected coil of rope was not there. It had been replaced by a heavy ten-foot tow cable with an iron hook at either end. And he would need a minimum of thirty feet of rope in order to lower himself from the cliff rim to the level of the tunnel opening.

The sun, blazing now in a storm-washed sky, was just touching the Panamint skyline far above, promising an early twilight for Death Valley. Its blinding glint on a strand of copper drew Tommy's attention to the radio antenna he and Chub had erected this morning for Field Day; strong copper-jacketed, iron-cored No. 12 wire, at least 133 feet of it, since it had been cut for eighty-meter use. Ham radio had supplied the answer to reaching the otherwise inaccessible mine tunnel! Wire would be a lightweight substitute for rope.

Tommy was dumping the gear from his knapsack, planning to take along a few items of food in case he and Chub got caught overnight in the mine tunnel, when his eye fell on a small booklet which

Chub had brought along. It was entitled OFFICIAL NATIONAL CITIZENS' BAND RADIO TEN-CODE.

Chub had shouted—or at least Tommy imagined he had shouted—the numerals "ten thirty-four." The answer to that mysterious symbol might be in this book!

Tommy ran a fingertip down the long list of Ten-Code signals which ran from Ten-one, "Receiving poorly," to "Ten-two hundred," which stood for "Police needed," a call frequently used by CBers arriving on the scene of a traffic accident.

Ten-thirty-four... When Tommy's finger came to rest on that symbol he knew he had verified Chub Downey's message. This proved that Chub was alive, although not necessarily safe. For according to the code book, Ten thirty-four meant "*Trouble at this location, help urgently needed!*"

CHAPTER TEN

THE MYSTERIOUS TUNNEL

What kind of "trouble" did Chub Downey mean?

Tommy Rockford's over-wrought imagination conjured up any number of possibilities: Trapped by a cave-in, legs crushed, dying, somewhere in this mysterious tunnel or its offshoots. Maybe he had stooped to examine a pebble and a sidewinder had bitten him! Rattlers were not common in Death Valley—in fact, Tommy had never seen a rattlesnake in any of his numerous past visits—but they did exist. Nor did they always use their rattles to sound a warning. Their venom could be fatal, especially in hot weather. Then there were poisonous scorpions, black widow spiders, tarantulas...

Tommy forced himself to stop thinking so negatively. He had to find out for himself what "ten thirty-four" meant in Chub's case.

He climbed up the ridge overlooking the cabin and untied the west end of the radio antenna where Chub had fastened it to a limb of the dead juniper, letting the weight of the insulators pull the antenna to the ground. Then he hurried back down to Seldom Seen Sam's shack, climbed to the roof by means of the rock-and-mud fireplace chimney, and unfastened the other end of the center-fed wire dipole.

Back on the ground, K6ATX coiled the wire into a convenient roll he could sling over his shoulder while scrambling over the boulders and loose debris which carpeted the mountainside on the south rim of Avalanche Gulch.

As he worked, Tommy peered off into the distance toward the dark green blur which marked the date palm grove, motel complex and public campgrounds at Furnace Creek Ranch. In the glass-clear air of the desert, Tommy could see the paved highway which led up

Furnace Creek Wash between the Grapevine and the Funeral mountains, leading past the multi-colored hills of Zabriskie Point on its way toward Death Valley Junction, Las Vegas and the outside world. A mile from the Ranch, opposite the deluxe Furnace Creek Inn perched incongruously on the hillside, was the road leading southwards toward Badwater, the Ashford borax mill and Jubilee Pass, the southern exit which linked Death Valley to the vast Mojave Desert.

He was surprised to see virtually no traffic on those important roads; if the California Highway Patrol and the Inyo County Sheriff had any manhunters out combing the area for the Crossbow Killers, Hilton and Lesher, they were invisible.

Tommy regretted loaning his binoculars to Chub, for with them he could have scanned the gravel road which intersected the main paved highway near the exit of Artist's Drive, crossing to the west side of the valley via the Devil's Golf Course and flanking the foot of the Panamints. That was the route he and Chub had taken this morning on their way to Seldom Seen Sam's shack.

Right now, Tommy imagined, the old prospector and his jenny mule, Hernia, were probably plodding along that graveled road toward their destination at Furnace Creek Ranch. If by any chance Tommy's three friends from Santa Bonita, Roy, Spud and Doc, happened to be on that road hunting for K6ATX, the old desert rat would be able to tell them where he was. But that was unlikely. W6AMD and the gang were probably still waiting up at Stovepipe Wells Resort, seething as much from frustration as the day's heat.

Tommy buckled a quart-sized canteen of water to his belt. He packed some canned tomatoes, pork and beans and applesauce into a backpack, and selected one of the ham club's IC-2AT two-meter hand-helds in case he could link up later with JC and the other hams. He tucked a pair of buckskin gloves under his belt. Then, slinging the coil of antenna wire over his shoulder, Tommy set off through the stifling heat toward the ravine which would take him down into Avalanche Gulch.

Back again on the canyon floor, Tommy headed downgrade out of the gulch mouth. Once on the open alluvial fan he began the slow and arduous ascent of the south rim, pausing frequently to rest, drink, and swallow a salt tablet. He estimated that the ground temperature had passed 150 degrees and was mounting—a heat factor to be reckoned with as much as the air temperature. This, he fervently hoped, would be the last ham radio expedition ever to visit Death Valley—unless it was during the tourist season, October through April, when the valley temperatures were mild.

On one of his rest stops along the south rim, he switched on the two-meter rig and had a listen on the Field Day intercom frequency. Even without the telescoping Vocom antenna being extended to five-eighths of a wavelength, reception was perfect. It was comforting, knowing he had a radio link to the outside.

Tommy resumed his way up the rocky slope, following the south rim of Avalanche Gulch. To his left lay an immense field of loose lava rock, the result of some prehistoric volcanic action. It gave Tommy the shudders, noting how loose those rocks were as he clambered over them, knowing how easily he could set off an avalanche of stone, far more hazardous than snow slides he had experienced on High Sierra skiing trips.

The twisting chasm of Avalanche Gulch carved a line of blue shadow across that frozen rock slide. It was not difficult for Tommy to understand how government surveyors had chosen to name the canyon "Avalanche Gulch." That slide rock, suspended in place for perhaps ten thousand years, was a massive disaster just waiting to happen. He hoped it would wait until he was safely off the slope. But it was inevitable that some time in the future—maybe in the next minute, maybe not for a thousand years—that poised sprawl of loose lava would be jarred by an earth movement, or set in motion by gravity pulling on its own incalculable weight—perhaps triggered by a sonic boom from some passing jet aircraft—and Avalanche Gulch would be obliterated forever under millions of tons of broken stone.

Tommy's heart was slugging his ribs from overexertion in the blazing heat but he kept going, knowing he was nearing his three identifying markers—the yellow boulder, the ocotillo cactus in bloom, and the leaning stone like a ship's shoring timber—which would tell him when he had come abreast of the tunnel entrance.

He found himself gasping like a landed trout when he finally reached the yellow boulder. From the perspective of the shack across the Gulch, these hundreds of acres of poised avalanche rock had looked marble-sized; close up, the rocks averaged better than three feet in diameter.

The yellow boulder—a geological freak amid the black lava debris around it—was shaped like a rhino's horn and must have weighed tons.

It would make a solid anchor post around which to loop the antenna wire he would be using to slide down over the edge of the cliff.

Knowing he would need to be thoroughly rested for the physical ordeal facing him, Tommy forced himself to relax, thankful that the sun was behind Telescope Peak. He doubted if he could have made it if the rocky slope had been under the direct blaze of sunlight.

He turned on his 2-meter rig again. Scanning through the band, he heard radio hams making idle chit-chat, worse than a bunch of rag-chewing truck drivers on CB. The club's local frequency, with Uncle JC acting as net control, remained active on legitimate communications as Field Day preparations continued on several fronts.

Tommy rested as long as he dared. It was now 4:33 PM by his sun-powered wristwatch which, fortunately, being shockproof and waterproof, had survived his watery ordeal earlier that afternoon. This period of the year the light held longer than at any other time, and twilight lingered here in the desert country anyway.

With any kind of luck, he and Chub would be safely back at the cabin, or perhaps headed for Furnace Creek Ranch for a cafeteria meal, before it got dark. Then, tomorrow, he could devote his full mental energies to Field Day activity, turning Chub loose to pursue his rockhounding activities. Or would he? Tommy tried not to think that he might find his plump friend seriously injured, or even dead. He had difficulty trusting his own ears, that he had ever really heard Chub's faint cry issuing from the hole in the cliff. Heat and physical exertion can do strange things to the mind, making it subject to hallucinations. On the other hand, his mind couldn't have invented the ten thirty-four signal.

He uncoiled the roll of copper antenna wire and found its halfway point, which he looped around the horn-shaped yellow rock. This gave him two wires to work with as he dropped both ends over the brink of the rimrock, checking to make sure the wire would not jam in a crack or crevice anywhere when he started pulling it down later. It would be impossible to climb from the tunnel mouth back up to the rimrock; the No. 12 wires would cut into his flesh, even with gloves. But if he could retrieve the wire, he would be able to anchor it to a timber or projecting rock inside the tunnel and use the twin strands to slide back down to the floor of the Gulch when they were ready to leave.

He stuffed the two-meter hand-held into his backpack along with the canned food, slung it into position, and donned his buckskin gloves. Taking a good grip on the two wires leading back from the yellow boulder, he knelt down backwards on the brink of the cliff, slid his legs over the edge until he could brace his entire weight on his elbows, and then lowered his full weight.

His very life was committed now. Under the soles of his Nikes was fifty feet of empty space. Instant death would result if he lost his grip on the wires, or if the wire snapped, or if the yellow boulder toppled over and released the loop of wire. But Tommy was confident none of these dire things would happen; the odds were in his favor that his descent of the cliff face would be without incident.

He took a bight of the dangling parallel wires around his right leg to serve as a brake and began sliding hand-over-hand, inch by inch down the sheer brow of the cliff. Even with the sturdy gauntlets to protect his palms and fingers, the wire seemed to cut into his flesh like knife blades.

Foot by cautious foot he rappeled himself down from the rim overhead, letting his rubber-padded toes bounce off the fluted basalt face of the cliff. The pounding of blood in his ears told Tommy Rockford he was overtaxing himself.

The wires were not long enough to reach the canyon floor. He knew it would be impossible to climb back up. His very life now depended on how accurately he had placed the dangling wires in relationship to the six-foot-wide hole in the cliff—a tiny target to shoot for, going at it blind.

He could tell he was nearing the lower ends of the wires by the clatter of the porcelain insulators against the cliff below him. If he had misjudged... he thrust that disconcerting possibility from his mind. And at that moment he felt his shoes slide from abrasive rock onto splintery wood, and then swing into an empty cavity. He had come abreast of Chub's mine tunnel!

Three more jerky, sliding descents, and Tommy swung his feet inward to plant them solidly on the floor of the tunnel. He let go the supporting wires with his right hand and used it to snatch out and get a secure grip on one of the weathered ceiling timbers he had spotted from the canyon floor thirty feet below.

A current of fetid air fanned Tommy Rockford's neck as, again clinging to both wires, he toppled forward into the mine tunnel and lay panting on a floor of solid stone. Air was flowing *inward* through the tunnel, a fact which started Tommy's adreneline pumping furiously. It meant that Chub's mine tunnel had an outlet through which air was circulating from Avalanche Gulch!

He disengaged his hands from the wires, tugged off his gloves, and lay panting for long moments, finding it difficult not to surrender to the temptation to roll over on his back and go to sleep. Then, raising himself to his knees, Tommy Rockford took his first real look into the jet-black gut of the mine tunnel ahead.

Perhaps a couple of hundred feet ahead, a square of gray daylight revealed the other end of the tunnel. Like a telescope mounted on a tripod, the tunnel framed a view, exactly as Chub had said, of a weather-grayed wooden building. Tommy saw porch pillars, murky windows, and a badly-warped door. On a transom above the door was a time-faded, painted sign: GUNSIGHT LODE HOTEL.

CHAPTER ELEVEN

THE CROSSBOW'S ARROW

Tommy Rockford's common sense told him that he was being tricked by an optical illusion, a mirage. Or more likely, hallucinations brought on by too much exposure to sun and heat.

What was it that Seldom Seen Sam had said this morning about being born in the Gunsight Lode Hotel, "the best hotel in the whole camp"? If a relic from the 1870s actually lay outside the end of this tunnel, then would he find the rest of the long-lost ghost town of Borrowed Time also? A town he had always assumed was legendary?

Tommy took a deep swig from his canteen, shook his head to clear it, and rubbed his eyes before taking another look down the long dark tunnel.

The weatherbeaten door and the transom with the sign were still there, shimmering in the heat waves.

Trembling, K6ATX came to his feet, resisting an impulse to beat a retreat from this tunnel instead of exploring it further.

Cupping his hands around his mouth, he shouted at the top of his lungs, "*Chub! Can you hear me, Chub?*"

Confused echoes, amplified like shouting down an open well, made a din in Tommy's ears, then slowly died away into silence.

He waited. The silence seemed to press in about him.

There was no answering shout from Chub Downey.

After another long pause, Tommy rummaged in his knapsack for his flashlight, hoping to find the familiar prints of Chub's tennis shoes leading along on the floor of the tunnel, to confirm that this was indeed the cavern from which he thought he had heard Chub's faint voice warning him of trouble at his QTH and that he urgently needed help.

But countless years of desert winds and winter's snow-water drainage had scoured the rough rock floor clean of any sand or dirt which could have preserved a footprint.

He no longer had any pretext to delay checking out what lay outside the other end of the tunnel. Stowing the flashlight back in his knapsack, Tommy Rockford groped forward in a stooped position, since the shoring timbers spaced along the tunnel did not give clearance for a man of his height to stand upright.

He kept his eyes on the door of the ghost town hotel, as if hoping that between eye-blinks it would go away. But as he drew nearer he made out new details of the door, sagging on rusted hinges, and a narrow porch floored with warped boards, on which sat a couple of rickety straight-back rocking chairs.

The south portal of the tunnel proved to measure roughly a hundred feet from its entrance to the exit overlooking Avalanche Gulch. Pausing to look behind him, Tommy could see only a rectangular view of the cliff face forming the north wall of Avalanche Gulch.

"Well, here goes." Sucking in a deep breath, K6ATX stepped out of the tunnel to find himself facing the most unreal scene his eyes had ever beheld in his nineteen years, even surpassing the sunken Spanish treasure galleon he had explored on the ocean bottom off San Miguel Island the year before.*

Fifty yards to his left was the dead end of a narrow gorge, a steep face of slide rock which towered a hundred feet before it was shut out of view by a bulging wall of rock which formed the overhanging south wall of the inner gorge.

Behind him, another cliff sloped skyward at a forty-five degree angle, paralleling the overhang of the southern cliff, and shutting off Tommy's view of any strip of open blue sky which he knew was the source of the vivid daylight that filled this defile at the foot of Telescope Peak.

That took care of three directions—north, south, and east. But to Tommy's right, or west, the defile extended for perhaps the length of a football field before ending in another broken jumble of spilled avalanche rock.

The two rockpiles sealed off the defile from both ends like a pair of bookends, leaving the mine tunnel as apparently the only way in

---

*See DX BRINGS DANGER, Published 1985 by ARRL

or out of this lost cavity in the base of Telescope Peak.

Against the south cliff, facing north, a row of unpainted wooden buildings stood cheek by jowl, tucked out of sight under the overhanging loom of the rock ceiling in much the same manner that the ancient Anasazi cliff dwellers of the Southwest had constructed their pueblos under sheltering stone archways to protect them from the elements and to defend against enemy attack.

The comparison was apt, except that these were not Anasazi cliff dwellings. These buildings were made of milled lumber that had somehow been transported across Southern California's deserts to build this string of houses a century or more ago when America was in its brawling period of conquering the Western frontier.

This had to be Seldom Seen Sam's birthplace, the ghost town of Borrowed Time. It was infinitely more exciting than a Zuni pueblo or a Hopi cliff dwelling. Here was a forgotten fragment of Western American history, a mausoleum of Americana, preserved like some Egyptian temple for the ages.

"Borrowed Time... you existed after all... And the news media thought Seldom Seen Sam Sutkliffe was loco and ridiculed him—"

Tommy uttered the words with prayerful awe and respect. He had stumbled across the secret the old desert rat had guarded so tenaciously through the decades—the existence, and the location, of a mining camp which had mysteriously "vanished" in some natural disaster before the turn of the century.

Tommy recalled vividly how the old prospector had phrased it in the television interview: "Borrowed Time vanished, but that didn't mean it was no longer in existence."

It was obvious to Tommy why the pioneers who had built this mining camp in the 1870s had named it "Borrowed Time." If the avalanche rock ever slid into the center of this defile, as it had already done to seal off the upper and lower ends, the town would be crushed, the ruins buried forever without hope of being exposed to daylight again.

Tommy tried to reconstruct the history of Borrowed Time. An avalanche had closed off the road leading out of the open end of the defile in the direction of Death Valley. The upper end of the defile was already closed off by a rockslide. Whoever remained alive in the camp when the disaster happened were forced to dig their way out to the nearest daylight or perish of starvation. That escape hatch would be the tunnel Tommy had just traversed, bringing him in from Avalanche Gulch. The same tunnel that Chub Downey had accidentally discovered this morning while on his rockhounding expedition. The same tunnel, undoubtedly, which Seldom Seen Sam had used to enter or leave Borrowed Time over the years.

Again Tommy shouted Chub's name. Again he was answered only by taunting, ghostly echoes. The weird acoustics of the rocky cavity in the mountain put duck bumps on Tommy's skin. It was almost as if the ghosts of those who had perished in the rockslide which had buried a portion of Borrowed Time were greeting him from the void of eternity.

The fact that Chub did not answer could mean many things. Maybe he was exploring some other mine tunnel—the mountains around Death Valley were honeycombed with prospect holes. Or he could be frantically trying to find his way out of Borrowed Time at this very moment. Tommy could visualize the terror Chub must have felt when he retraced his steps to the front of the tunnel only to find a flash flood had destroyed his rocky stairway back to safety. Then, hearing Tommy's voice, he had managed to scream a message: "Ten thirty-four... Trouble at this location, help urgently needed."

Tommy headed across the strip of open ground which formed Borrowed Time's narrow street until he reached the sagging porch steps of the Gunsight Lode Hotel. He dropped the burden of his knapsack and canteen onto one of the dust-covered chairs on the porch and decided to do some exploring himself.

A time-bleached sign had been tacked onto a porch post:

IF DOOR IS LOCKED, RING BELL FOR NIGHT CLERK.

The door hung ajar, seemingly held in place by spider webs. The night clerk who had posted that sign had probably been in his grave for more than a century.

Tommy stepped over the threshold into what had been the hotel lobby. To the left of the doorway, a flight of stairs led down into the pitch blackness of some kind of cellar. On the clerk's reception counter facing the door, under a rack of dusty pigeonholes where patrons had kept their mail and their room keys in the long-gone era when this mining town was booming, Tommy saw what he took to be a stack of fresh-looking newspapers which should have been yellowed with age.

The floor boards creaked eerily under his weight as Tommy

crossed the frayed carpeting of the lobby and picked up one of the newspapers. It was the Los Angeles *Times*—dated only two weeks ago! With it was a copy of the Las Vegas *Sun* only eight days old!

Cold perspiration popped out of Tommy's pores, although the interior of this ghost-town hotel was stifling from stored heat that had radiated off the lost canyon's stone walls.

But the mystery of the newspapers, in a ghost camp which had disappeared from the face of the earth three generations earlier, was easily explained. Seldom Seen Sam had said he made his home at this hotel between prospecting trips. He had spent the last several months prospecting along the western side of the Panamints, he had said, so these were probably newspapers discarded by tourist litterbugs driving along the highway, which Sam had scavenged.

A flight of dusty stairs led to the balcony above the lobby. Tommy put off a strong curiosity to explore the rooms up there, and made his way back outdoors instead. Finding Chub was still his major priority, and daylight would be failing soon.

Now that his eyes had grown accustomed to the dim light, he could see where the building next door on the east had been half-crushed by the wall of broken stone spilling into the defile from the direction of Death Valley. This meant that every building along Borrowed Time's single street east of this point was buried under the rockslide which had sealed off the camp from the outside world. His explorations would therefore have to be in a westerly direction only.

The bedrock floor of the canyon held no dust or dirt which could tell him where Chub Downey might have gone. Tommy noticed that the rusty tracks of a narrow-gauge mining railroad had been laid along the street. The rails disappeared under the rockslides at either end of the camp. Originally the rails had probably been used by small iron cars in transporting raw ore to a stamp mill, both mine and mill having been victims of the avalanche.

Walking between the rails, Tommy headed westward, flanking the row of ghost town buildings. All were unpainted and ramshackle. Some had been stripped of siding, cannibalized perhaps by Seldom Seen Sam to repair other buildings, or for use as winter firewood—Death Valley's surrounding highlands were under snow in wintertime, probably turning Borrowed Time into a refrigerator.

Alongside the west end of the Gunsight Lode Hotel was a circular stone coaming with a windlass and suspended bucket—a fresh-water well, the one essential without which Borrowed Time's residents could not have survived.

The one-storied structure next door to the community well, the glass long since knocked out of its two front windows, bore a faded sign across its false front identifying it as **Honest Jas. Garrett's Assay Office & Miners' Tool & Supply Depot.**

A tarpaper-roofed shack abutting the assay office still had its single window intact. Stenciled thereon were the words **John Dell's Tonsorial Parlor. Beard Trim 2 bits.** What appeared to be a hitching post in front of this building had once been a traditional barber pole with red and white stripes, now faded out.

The presence of warped hitch rails, and a hollowed-out log which served as a watering trough for animals, was evidence that livestock had once been able to reach Borrowed Time from Death Valley, before the access road had been destroyed by a rockslide.

The sagging-roofed shoebox of a building next door to Dell's barber shop still had a legible sign on a board above the doorless entryway: WELLS-FARGO & CO. EXPRESS AGENT.

Over everything hung a century's odor of heat and decay.

Walking along in gape-jawed wonderment like a kid visiting Knott's Berry Farm's reconstructed ghost town—yet wholly aware that this was the real thing, not a counterfeit built for the pleasure of tourists—Tommy came to the last structure in the row of buildings, and the only one built permanently of mortared stone quarried and cut on the site. It had narrow loophole windows heavily barred with what had once been discarded miner's drilling bits, and the door was of rust-red iron panels. The massive lintel over the rivet-studded door reminded Tommy of a tombstone epitaph because of the whimsical legend some miner had chiseled on it:

BORROWED TIME JAILHOUSE
Easier to Enter than Exit!
Erected A.D. 1879

Beyond the stone-walled jail was an area enclosed by a stone fence—obviously a stock corral for mules and saddle horses, back when Borrowed Time was a thriving camp. It was now littered with the rusting wreckage of mining machinery, broken wagons, heaps of whiskey bottles which undoubtedly could be mined like treasure trove by any of several purple-glass collectors Tommy knew back home, and the assorted accumulation of mining-camp junk which proved that litterbugging was not a Twentieth Century innovation.

So far, there were two staple features of the stereotypical western ghost town of the movies which Borrowed Time seemed to lack—a saloon and gambling hall, plus a graveyard for the interment of citizens who had died with their boots on.

Even as Tommy Rockford rounded the corner of the stone corral, he caught sight of the straggly row of wooden crosses on a weed-grown slope at the base of the overhanging southern cliff.

That was the town's boothill, apparently, and since the saloon would have been the most popular place in camp, it had probably been located farther west, long since buried under the sprawl of avalanche rock which sealed off the canyon's upper end.

A hundred feet of empty ground lay between the corral and the rows of grave markers, the wood burned a silvery brown by the elements. Impelled by a curiosity too great to resist, Tommy momentarily forgot that the purpose of his search was not the fun of exploring a ghost town, but to find some trace of his missing buddy Chub Downey. He found himself jogging toward the cemetery.

He counted nearly forty grave mounds, some of them unmarked, some with warped pine headboards dated in the 1870s and 1890s. Two more recent graves, overgrown with weeds, placed side by side in an obscure corner of the cemetery, drew Tommy's special interest.

One marked the last resting place of "*ROXANNA SUTKLIFFE. Born San Francisco 1856 died in Borrowed Time 1898. R.I.P.*"

The adjoining headboard, baked tobacco-brown by time and weather, read "*RUDOLPH SUTKLIFFE. Born Ft. Atkinson Iowa 1824. Discovered Gunsight Lode 1870. Came back after the Big Slide. Died 10 July 1916. Grave marked by his son Saml. R.I.P.*"

It took Tommy Rockford a moment to catch the significance of the two epitaphs. Then he recalled how Seldom Seen Sam had mentioned digging his father's grave in Borrowed Time's cemetery. These warped boards perpetuated the memory of Sam's parents.

The weed-grown graveyard marked the end of Tommy's explorations. He had seen no sign of other mine tunnels along the street or behind the buildings where Chub might have gone, exploring for rocks or hunting for a way out.

A battered and rusty iron ore car sat on the rails which led under the rock slide that had forever sealed off the canyon's upper end. This indicated to Tommy that the rich silver lode which gave the camp its original reason for being—rumored to have been the legendary Lost Gunsight Lode of song and story—was probably located somewhere far back under that pile of rock, buried forever deep in the core of Telescope Peak.

That lost mine was Seldom Seen Sam's secret...

Tommy lifted his eyes upward and saw the ribbon of blue which was the only place in the canyon where the rimrocks were wide enough apart to afford a view of Telescope Peak. Dusk would soon set in. He could see the pink, sunset-tinted contrail of a high-flying jet, a chalk mark crawling across the indigo sky.

"All I can do now is check each house, room by room," Tommy decided. "But if I don't find some trace of Chub, what—"

K6ATX didn't get a chance to finish his thought.

Something zipped past his ear with a whining sound like a wasp would make—or a bullet—followed by a thud as the object struck a heavy wooden cross marking one of the older boothill graves.

Tommy whirled to look at the cross. Vibrating there on one arm of the crosspiece was a steel-tipped arrow which had completely impaled the thick wood. Only one weapon could have delivered a shaft with that much penetrating power. A modern steel crossbow.

Tommy Rockford knew he had been the bowman's target. He stood there frozen, rooted to his tracks, eyes shuttling left and right in a frantic search for some place where he could dive for shelter before a second arrow could be loosed by the concealed attacker.

The nearest shelter was the rusty boiler of an overturned donkey engine which had probably supplied power for the ore cars, but it was a good twenty feet away. But before he could take his first stride toward that boilerplated refuge, a harsh voice shouted an order from somewhere in the direction of the jailhouse:

"Just cool it, big feller! Both arms reaching, okay?"

A blur of motion drew Tommy's eye to the tall figure of a red-bearded man who stepped out from the concealment of the jail.

Tommy Rockford recognized the bearded man instantly; they had met before, as his bruised head testified. *Rusty Hilton*! One of the Crossbow Killers fleeing from Las Vegas...

CHAPTER TWELVE

PERIL IN BORROWED TIME

Hilton had stripped off his black horsehide jacket with its Satan's Angels design. His naked chest with its powerful pectoral muscles was thatched with thick curly hair, and the beginnings of a paunch sagged over the belt of his faded Levis. Without his motorcycle helmet, Hilton revealed an onion-bald head with fuzzy red sideburns blending into his unkempt beard.

At the moment, the outlaw was cranking the ratchet on his custom-made crossbow, the mechanism which enabled him to pull back the bowstring into readiness for a new arrow. A walnut stock similar to that of a shotgun was fitted to the grooved hardwood trough which supported the arrow and was bolted to the steel bow. The tension on such a bow, as magnified with mechanical help, was sufficient to give an arrow the velocity of a bullet. Tommy knew that these bows, some of which cost many hundreds of dollars, had long been a fad with so-called "sportsmen" in Hollywood.

With his silent weapon now cocked for a follow-up shot, Rusty Hilton removed a slender, steel-tipped arrow from a tubular plastic quiver strapped between his shoulder blades and fitted it carefully into its groove, the bowstring seated in the V-shaped notch at the feathered end of the arrow. Hugging the gunstock grip securely between forearm and ribs, the hairy fugitive beckoned for Tommy to come toward him, arms raised.

"Okay," Tommy said with an attempt at bravado. "Now what?"

Pound for pound, K6ATX believed he could out-match Hilton in man-to-man combat; his speed would compensate for Hilton's weight. But it would be foolhardy to attempt to wrest the crossbow away from the burly criminal. If Hilton's finger pulled the weapon's trigger the arrow could skewer his body like a needle through a beetle. This was probably the same weapon which Seldom Seen Sam had witnessed killing Hector the mule at long range.

Not since his encounter a couple of years back with a smuggler from the notorious Purple Shirt Gang* had Tommy looked into a pair of human eyes filled with such menace and malevolence.

In Hilton's case, as Tommy discovered when he had walked near enough to see into the shadows under Hilton's shaggy-browed eyes, the pupils were contracted to pinpoint size—a sure sign that he was high on drugs. That being the case, Tommy knew he was not only the captive of a known slayer, but one whose brain was made irrational by chemical poisons.

Tommy halted six feet from the jail door, obeying a gesture from Hilton. He said, "All right—what have you done with Chub Downey? I know he's around here somewhere."

Hilton's brows drew together.

"Who?" he demanded.

"Chub Downey. The fat kid with hair the color of yours. I came here looking for him. As I'm sure you must know."

Hilton was silent for a long moment, obviously thinking over his answer. Finally he said, "The only reason you aren't lying out there with this arrow punched through your gizzard is because I got to know how you managed to get up into our tunnel. That flood this morning swept away our rock pile, so you would have to be a human fly to climb up that rock wall. How'd you do it?"

Tommy swallowed hard, playing for time.

"Before I tell you my secret," he countered, "you tell me where Chub is. He's just a poor kid from a foster home in LA who was out hunting for rock specimens. He had no idea you and Goldie Lesher were using Borrowed Time for a hideout. Chub discovered your tunnel by pure accident—and he would have been long gone by now if that flash flood hadn't cut off his way to get out."

Tommy saw Hilton's flushed face go bone-white and he belatedly regretted having blurted out so much information. By mentioning Goldie Lesher's name, he had tipped his hand about knowing the identity of the fugitive Crossbow Killers and their reason for hiding out here in Borrowed Time.

---

*See SOS AT MIDNIGHT, Published 1985 by ARRL

"You seem to know quite a bit about Lesh and me," Hilton sneered. "Your friend was a spunky little tub of lard, I'll grant you that. He wouldn't even admit he was with you, claimed he was alone. Even after we told him we had run you down with our choppers down at the mouth of the gulch and had left you for dead with a bashed-in skull. Your head must be made of solid bone, kid."

Tommy's eyes misted over, learning of Chub Downey's loyalty in trying to keep the two killers from knowing he was not alone.

"What have you done with him?" Tommy asked huskily. "Whatever it is, let him go. He can't harm you in any way."

Hilton shrugged. "And who are you, big feller? I suppose you're from the same outfit as the fat kid?"

Tommy saw no harm in identifying himself. "I'm Tommy Rockford. I go to college in Pasadena. Chub and I were—having a Death Valley vacation. Like I said, he stumbled on your tunnel by pure accident while he was out prospecting for rock specimens. When he didn't come back for lunch, I went looking for him."

At that moment Goldie Lesher came lurching out of the jail door and shuffled toward them. Hanging from his lower lip was a brown "sherm" or Sherman cigarette which had been dipped in liquid PCP, one of the most potent narcotics on the junkie market.

Spitting out a profanity, Lesher snarled at his partner, "Why ain't you told him we killed his buddy, Rusty? Then put that arrow through his guts. You know why he trailed us here. He's a spy for the fuzz, if he ain't a narc agent himself. So why not waste him and play it safe? What are you stallin' around for?"

As he spoke, Lesher reached in his tight-fitting jeans and pulled out a staghorn-handled knife. There was a clicking sound like a gunhammer being cocked as the yellow-haired ruffian pressed a release button with his thumb. Like magic, a razor-edged switchblade jutted from Lesher's fist.

"If you won't butcher this cocky punk, then I will!" Lesher bellowed hoarsely, and sprang at Tommy Rockford with the knife coming up in a stroke which could have disembowled its victim had not Rusty Hilton reached out a leg to trip his partner. As the golden-haired outlaw sprawled heavily to the ground, Tommy kicked the switchblade knife out of Lesher's grasp. The man reared to his knees, red-shot eyes blazing furiously as he howled at Hilton:

"Why are you wasting time rapping with this dude? If he knows how to get into our hideout, then the cops will be following him! Are you losin' your nerve, Rusty?"

Although he had no reason to sympathize with the blond-bearded ruffian who had been about to stab him to death, Tommy could not help wincing when he saw Hilton kick Lesher brutally in the mouth as the blond-haired man struggled to regain his feet.

"That's exactly why I *am* rapping with him, you dim-witted moron!" Hilton shouted. "We got to know how he got through that tunnel after the rock pile was washed out. Did it ever occur to your burned-out brain, Goldie, that maybe this kid knows *another* way in and out of this camp? So get back into the slammer and lie down and sleep it off while I handle the big guy in my own way!"

Blood leaking from a smashed underlip, Lesher retrieved his switchblade, snapped it shut and pocketed it. Mumbling obscenities, but plainly yielding to the superior authority of his bald-headed partner, Goldie Lesher staggered back inside the ghost town calaboose and slammed the iron door shut, muttering curses.

Hilton jerked his head in Goldie's direction and said in a conspiratorial tone, "He's blitzed out on PCP. If it turns out to be another bad trip I'll be having to chain him down to his bunk again tonight. The dust turns him into a maniac."

"And who chains you down, Hilton?"

"Me? I do cocaine. I don't touch angel dust. It rots the brain. Goldie used to make his own, until the US made the chemicals illegal. Then he bought it from veterinarians who used it to tranquilize injured animals. Now he buys Sherms and soaks 'em in PCP he buys from street pushers. It turns him into a killer."

Tears were swimming in Rockford's eyes as he said huskily, "So he killed Chub. What did it get him? Chub was a harmless kid."

Hilton raised the crossbow to warn Tommy not to come too close.

"Your tubby friend didn't suffer, trust me. Never knew what hit him... Now, getting back to you. You say you and the kid were on a vacation? To a blistering hell-hole like Death Valley? Why should you lie to me like that? I'm betting my last blue chip you're a rookie on the narc squad in 'Vegas, sent to track us down—"

"I'm from Santa Bonita. On a week-end trip to the desert."

Hilton said, "Goldie an' me found this place two years ago and made it our home base ever since. We never saw the likes of that flood that hit the Gulch out there. We heard a roar, went to the mouth of the tunnel and looked out, and Avalanche Gulch looked more like the rapids of the Grand Canyon when the Colorado's in flood stage. When Goldie an' me saw our rock pile ladder wash out, we both figured we were bottled up in this old minin' camp for keeps. But you found another way to get in and out, didn't you?"

Tommy evaded answering that direct question. As long as Hilton believed he knew of another escape hatch from Borrowed Time, it was unlikely he would have murder on his mind.

"Even if you *could* get back into Avalanche Gulch, you'd find yourself stranded in dangerous country, Hilton. You wouldn't have a chance at escape. You know why? Both of your cycles got smashed up in that flash flood. I saw the wreckage myself, half-buried in the mud. Your red Harley-Davidson, Goldie's Yamaha V-Max. Twisted like pretzels and smashed flat, both of them."

Hilton nodded bleakly. "Whenever Goldie an' me were holed up here we couldn't very well get 'em up to the tunnel, so we stashed our wheels back in the rocks, out of sight of random hikers or hunters who might drift up the canyon, which ain't happened yet. I didn't expect our cycles to survive that gully-washer... If we ever thought about it, which we didn't, we would know it took water to carve that gulch in the first place, but who would expect a flood to come along in summertime?"

"If you knew this country you'd know this is flash flood season, Hilton. You may be street-smart, but you're obviously not a desert man. Now you see the price you paid for your ignorance."

Hilton fell silent, brooding over what Tommy had said. Finally he asked, "Tell me, kid—how do you know so much about Goldie and me? How would you even know our names if you weren't a narc?"

"Simple. Radio and TV newscasts have been full of nothing else all day, ever since you killed that man in Las Vegas last night. A rancher saw the two of you cutting across the Pahrump Valley heading toward Jubilee Pass this morning, and put it on the air. Right this minute you've got police from two states closing in on you by air and land. They've already got Death Valley cut off."

Tommy saw that his words had visibly shaken Hilton. "And we thought we had found the perfect place to hide out in," the outlaw mused, rubbing the heel of his palm along the polished stock of the crossbow. "We first got wise to this old mining camp being here when we saw an old prospector with two mules seem to disappear into thin air after he went into Avalanche Gulch. Picketed his mules in the Gulch, then disappeared. Goldie an' me couldn't figure it out, so we spied on him. Saw him climbing up and down that rock pile. After he left with his mules, we located his tunnel, and followed it into this crack in the mountain—and laid eyes for the first time on this old mining camp. We'd found the ideal hideout!"

"I'm surprised you didn't murder old Seldom Seen Sam—"

"No. He never knew we were here! He was away eleven months out of the year. Harmless old coot, looney as a tick. We used to see him bring in supplies on his packmules. I doubt if he even wondered what happened to the stuff Goldie and I helped ourselves to. I don't think he remembered buyin' the supplies and bringing 'em here. But one thing the old duffer couldn't pack in for us—cocaine, horse, acid, not even marijuana. Or most important of all, cash. The old fool apparently lived without using money."

"And you needed lots of cash to support your drug habits."

"Sure. Why do you think we robbed that casino in Vegas?"

Tommy said, "One thing old Sam *hasn't* forgotten. We met him this morning. He told us how you and your junkie friend shot his pet mule last winter. It takes a real sportsman to gut-shoot a poor old jackass, especially one that packed in supplies for you to steal! Guess you're pretty proud of that big game hunt, huh?"

Hilton had the good grace to blush. "That boner was Goldie's idea. Out here in the desert, he'll shoot that crossbow at anything that moves, I swear. I asked him, what good did it do to plug that old mule—except to get the old man riled up for no reason? Goldie says—and he was stone sober at the time—he likes to make a hit on a wild target so he can watch the animal threshin' around in a break-dance until it bleeds to death. That's how PCP addicts get their jollies. Killing things, sometimes killing themselves."

Tommy said, "Well, old Sam has sworn to get revenge for that senseless cruelty. You probably knew he was born here—in that hotel down the street. Sam could have made a tourist attraction out of this ghost town and gotten rich off it, but instead he chose to keep it a secret from the world. I can see where Borrowed Time made an ideal hideout for the likes of you and Goldie, all right."

"Except for one big drawback," the red-bearded ruffian admitted. "This cul de sac is a trap. Number one, we couldn't park our machines up here, no way we could hoist 'em up to the tunnel and be ready for a quick getaway if we got cornered. Number two, with only one entrance and exit, the fuzz could lay siege to us and starve us out, if they knew we were in here. That's always bugged me and Goldie. And now if what you're saying is true, and I got no reason to doubt your word, the cops are sure to find our wrecked choppers and start exploring. If you found us, they can find us. But there's one way out for us. All three of us."

"Three of us?"

"You're trapped in here the same as we are, ain't you? The point I'm trying to make, sonny, is that you managed to get into Borrowed Time even with that rock ladder gone. How? I'm making you a proposition. Show us how you did it, and I unload this crossbow and give you a couple hours' head start for home. Is it a deal?"

Tommy appeared to hesitate, but his eyes had narrowed in cold calculation of the surprise life-or-death move he had to make.

"Okay, it's a deal! Come here—I'll show you." Tommy took a couple of steps away from the jail and raised his left arm to point at the gable of the Gunsight Lode Hotel. "Look closely at the top of the hotel chimney. See where it touches the overhang of the cliff?"

Hilton turned to squint curiously in the direction Tommy was pointing. That was when K6ATX's fist clubbed a sledging blow to the corner of the criminal's jaw and knocked him to his knees, triggering the crossbow as he fell.

CHAPTER THIRTEEN

GHOST TOWN HOSTAGE

Surprise was the only advantage Tommy Rockford had going for him, and he had expended that. It was an added bonus that in falling, Rusty Hilton's crossbow had been accidentally triggered, the deadly steel-tipped arrow zipping off into space to shatter itself against the cliff wall facing the jail.

But Hilton was built like a professional wrestler, his thick-boned body slabbed with gristle and muscle, probably scaling two hundred and forty pounds to Tommy's rawhide-lean hundred and eighty. During the moment he had Hilton flat on his back on the ground, Tommy danced around behind him. When the red-whiskered tough came to his hands and knees, Tommy landed a left-handed karate chop to the back of Hilton's neck which would have knocked out an ordinary man.

Hilton, bawling deep in his throat like a wounded bull, let his eyes glaze over but wasn't even slowed in getting back to his feet. Tommy danced back out of reach of the criminal's lethal fists, confident that he could out-box his dazed opponent but equally aware that if Hilton ever got him in a bear hug he would have the life crushed out of him.

Gorilla-long arms dangling at his sides, Rusty Hilton dropped into a half-squat, bouncing on his heels, a maneuver which Tommy mistook for a boxing-ring maneuver to get his balance on the balls of his feet. Instead, it was a ploy used by barroom brawlers or back-alley muggers—a means of getting his hands to the ground and scooping up a double fistful of dirt and pebbles. Even as K6ATX lanced out a right jab which connected solidly with Hilton's left cheekbone, his opponent whipped up both hands and sent a stinging shower of sand squarely into Rockford's eyes.

Momentarily blinded, Tommy staggered back, forced on the defensive now against a foe he could hardly see. Something exploded behind his right ear and spun him around. His knee joints went rubbery and he dropped like a garment falling off a hook, landing on his back.

Struggling to keep his own senses from skidding over the edge into a black void, knowing Hilton could kill him with a single kick or blow, Tommy's eyes cleared enough for him to see Rusty Hilton, sucking air into his lungs with a noise like a steam locomotive laboring up a grade, surrender the advantage a follow-up charge would give him. Instead, the ruffian lurched over to pick up his crossbow, at the same time plucking another arrow from the plastic quiver on his back.

The fight was over almost before it had started. The sand and gravel thrown point-blank into his eyes had done Tommy in; he had made the fatal error of assuming his adversary would fight by the rules.

Above the ringing in his skull Tommy heard the ratchet of Hilton's crossbow make its clattering sound as the bowstring was notched back to maximum tension and a new arrow was slid into its groove. The knuckle on Hilton's trigger finger whitened toward attaining a pressure which could drive the steel barb completely through Tommy's body.

"A nice try, big feller, but no cigar," Hilton panted huskily, still weak-kneed from the two blows the nineteen-year-old had managed to land. "All it got you is the same thing Goldie give to old Sam Sutkliffe's mule last winter. A chance to be buzzard bait!"

Tommy fished a bandanna from his jeans pocket and swabbed at his stinging eyes. "Killing me won't accomplish anything, Hilton. In this climate, dead bodies can be mighty uncomfortable to have around—and graves are hard to dig in this rocky soil. Besides, Hilton, I'm a darn sight worth more to you alive than dead. Have you given that any thought?"

With his free hand Hilton reached up to tenderly rub the growing welt where the heel of Tommy's palm had pounded his neck, sending a numb sensation all the way down to his heels.

"What use are you to me, dead or alive, big feller?"

"Well, there's something you don't know, Hilton. Before I came up here I was in touch with the outside world by radio. By now the CHP knows where to look for you two."

Something akin to fear flickered in Hilton's eyes for a moment. Then he scoffed, "Don't hand me that kind of bull, kid. I saw that walkie-talkie you were carrying when we first ran across you in the lower Gulch. You weren't talkin' on it before Goldie's handlebar clipped you on the gourd, and my Harley ran over it a couple of ticks later and smashed it flat."

Tommy thought, *I've got to keep him talking, keep his mind off killing me.* Aloud, he said "You made a bad mistake leaving me for dead, Hilton. After I came to I went back to my car and got some messages on the air. Friends know where I am. It's only a question of time before the cops show up in Avalanche Gulch, if they haven't already. No matter whether I'm dead or alive—you and Goldie are finished."

Hilton tugged at his lower lip, brow knotted in thought. "Just before you clobbered me," he said, "you were showin' me how you got into Borrowed Time. Somethin' about the hotel chimney?"

Rockford laughed sardonically. "When I said just now I was worth more to you alive than dead, I wasn't referring to our getting out of this ghost town. The hotel chimney bit was just a trick to shift your attention away from me. I was going to tell you there was a vertical shaft in the cliff, opening above the hotel roof, so that I could crawl down like Santa Claus and drop into the chimney. So far as I know, Hilton, the only way in or out of here is through that escape tunnel you already know about. The one that has a thirty-foot drop now that the flood has swept away the piled-up tailings."

Rusty Hilton continued to rub his bruised neck. He knew he had been within a hair's breadth of being knocked out by Tommy's karate chop, which had happened too fast to defend against.

"All right, young feller. You say you're worth something to me. Mind explainin' that?"

"You've put me in the same status as those American hostages were in Lebanon and Iran, remember? You can use me as a bargaining lever when the law enforcement officers show up in Avalanche Gulch and block off your only escape route. You can tell 'em, 'Either give Goldie Lesher an' me a good head start, or Tommy Rockford dies.' As long as I'm alive, you've got a bargaining chip. Without me, you two are dead ducks, and you know it."

Hilton suddenly seemed to come to a decision. "You stand here in front of the doorway," Hilton ordered, "and don't budge. I'm goin' inside for my equalizer. These crossbows are too clumsy."

The outlaw disappeared inside the jail. Tommy was trying to make up his mind whether to risk running for it when Hilton emerged, minus his crossbow and quiver. He had strapped a gun harness around his middle, from the belt holster of which he removed a pistol which Tommy recognized as a deadly Magnum .357.

"I'm wastin' no more time with rappin'," Hilton said. "You're takin' me over to that tunnel and showing me how Goldie and me can get out of this mantrap—tonight. I know it's only a question of time before the fuzz closes the net around us."

Tommy felt despair run through him like a cold wind. Even if he was free to use the two-meter rig he had left in the knapsack over at the hotel porch, a radio signal could not get out except from the open field near the cemetery, with its line-of-sight exposure to the crest of Telescope Peak. Carrying his radio to that open field would be impossible as long as he was a prisoner.

Worst of all, no one really knew of his predicament or his whereabouts, despite what he had told Hilton. He had not been able to contact Uncle JC up on Telescope Peak because of the electrical storm; nor had he gotten through to the hams who were gathering at Badwater and Furnace Creek, and his buddies at Stovepipe Wells.

Tommy knew that eventually search parties would stumble onto the Santa Bonita ham club's VW van parked in the shed at Seldom Seen Sam's cabin. Uncle JC had already reported that Tommy had left the air to respond to an emergency radio message of some sort from Chub Downey, who was using a Citizens' Band rig. That might send trackers reconnoitering down into Avalanche Gulch, but considering the destruction done by the recent flash flood, they would find no clues except Tommy's footprints in the mud going up the Gulch, then turning around and coming back to the cabin.

Police investigators, trying to locate the killers of the casino guard in Las Vegas last night, would sooner or later discover and identify the wreckage of the two getaway motorcycles. They would probably assume, as Tommy had, that Hilton and Lesher had perished in the flash flood.

More than likely his ham friends would also take for granted that the bodies of Tommy and Chub lay buried somewhere under the steaming silt that floored Avalanche Gulch. And K6ATX would wind up as another listing in *QST* magazine's "Silent Keys" column...

Holding his revolver on Tommy, Hilton opened the jailhouse door and shouted, "Goldie—Goldie! You awake?"

A muffled reply came from inside the jail.

"I've hooked me a prize fish, Goldie!" Hilton shouted gleefully. "Bring me one of those wrist irons and a flashlight. We're going into that tunnel and it'll be as dark in there as a gorilla's armpit, the way daylight's failin'."

Unidentifiable noises issued from inside the jail. A few moments later Goldie Lesher lurched across the threshold, his face looking as bleached and rubbery as a corpse's under the shaggy cap of golden curls. His red-rimmed, slitted eyes widened in surprise as he caught sight of Tommy Rockford being held under the threat of his partner's Magnum .357.

Dangling from Lesher's right hand was a pair of Nineteenth Century handcuffs, red with rust, which had no doubt been hanging in the jailer's office for decades. In the other hand Lesher carried a six-cell flashlight.

"All right, kid, arms behind you," Hilton ordered Tommy. "I been watching your eyes while we been talking. Still schemin' on gettin' the jump on me, ain't you? Don't mind admitting you pack quite a wallop for such a young buck. Neck feels like you like to taken my head off, I could sue you for whiplash. So you're goin' under these irons while we're checkin' out that tunnel."

Because the Magnum was aimed straight at his chest, Tommy complied with the order to put his arms behind his back. He heard Goldie Lesher sidle around behind him, the iron manacles clanking ominously. An instant later Tommy felt the yellow-bearded outlaw snap the heavy fetters around his wrists, notching them until they threatened to cut the circulation from his hands.

Now, for the first time, Tommy felt there was no possible hope of maneuvering out of this desperate situation.

"I hope you've got the key to these bracelets," Tommy panted. "They're cutting into my skin worse than a tourniquet."

Goldie Lesher shuffled back into Tommy's range of vision, saliva sliding from his red mouth as he gave a sarcastic giggle. "I got the key, right enough, but what if I didn't? Before your hands swell up on you, the coyotes will be gnawin' at your carcass anyway. You won't feel nothin' a-tall."

Tommy fell in step between the two burly fugitives as they came even with the Gunsight Lode Hotel, then turned at right angles and approached the mouth of the exit tunnel. Lesher went ahead, switching on the flashlight. Tommy followed, with Hilton bringing up the rear with his Magnum still out of holster.

The three exchanged no talk as, bent almost double, they worked their way a hundred feet to the open end of the passage. The rays of Goldie's flashlight revealed the two shiny copper filaments dangling in front of the opening—the antenna wires which Tommy had anchored to the horn-shaped yellow boulder on the rimrock forty-odd feet directly overhead.

Hilton, obviously the more intelligent of the two junkies, got a grip on one of the shoring timbers and leaned out, peering upward toward the pearl-gray, sunset-tinted sky as he traced the parallel hanging wires up the face of the cliff and out of sight over the rim.

"You tellin' me you slid down those wires?" Hilton gasped.

"It's the only way I had to reach this tunnel," Tommy said. "I'd never want to do it again. Even with heavy gloves on, the wires felt like they were cutting my hands to the bone."

Hilton had a look downward toward the floor of the canyon, and shuddered. The porcelain insulators marking both ends of the wire ended barely ten feet below the floor of the escape tunnel, leaving a long and certainly fatal drop to the rocks below.

"Just how," Hilton demanded suspiciously, "were you aiming to get back out of here? You're young and stout with arms like a bull ape, but you couldn't hope to climb back up them wires."

Hilton obviously believed the wires were solidly anchored to something over the rimrock, and Tommy saw no reason to tell him of his original plan to retrieve the loop of wire so as to provide a means of descending to the safety of the canyon floor below the tunnel. An opportunity to use those wires might come up later. After all, miracles do happen. It was best he held his secret.

Tommy said dolefully, "I assumed there had to be some other way to get out of Borrowed Time than this tunnel. You tell me I'm wrong. Which means we're all trapped in this mess together."

Hilton muttered, "So far as Goldie and me been able to figger it out, the avalanche sealed off the ghost town to begin with, but the miners who were caught in Borrowed Time were able to dig this escape tunnel while their grub held out. The job shouldn't have taken long for hard-rock miners. You notice the rock is fairly soft, easy to dig in, otherwise they wouldn't have had to brace the tunnel with timbers to keep it from cavin' in. We figger nobody came back to the camp except Seldom Seen Sam and his folks. When the old couple cashed in their chips, Sam was the only one left alive who knew about the tunnel, or even that a part of Borrowed Time escaped bein' smashed under all that loose rock."

"Which is why," Goldie Lesher added, "me an' Rusty figgered this was the world's best hide-out for a couple of fellers wanted by the FBI and every pig in California and Nevada. Especially the boys in the federal narc squads who knew we used to smuggle hard stuff across the border from Old Mexico, when we were runnin' with the Satan's Angels bikers. That's why, after we pulled off the caper in Las Vegas last night, we came back here to hide out until things cooled off."

Hilton laughed sardonically. "We hauled in fifty thou, yet here we can't spend it to buy ourselves a fix, even at the prices the pushers sell it for on the street—and it won't be too long before we're out of the makings, both of us. That makes us pretty desperate hombres, kid."

Goldie Lesher switched off the flashlight to conserve the batteries. He said, "Well, what are we goin' to do with this punk? I'm dead for sleep and so are you. If he don't know a way to get out of this tunnel without splashin' our guts on the rocks down there, then why are we hangin' around yakking with him?"

Hilton turned to Tommy in the semi-gloom. "Look, kid—what's your name? Tommy? My head ain't functionin' too clear right now... But I ain't so beat I haven't been givin' some thought to what you said about you bein' valuable to us as a hostage."

For the first time since he had failed to knock out Hilton by force, Tommy felt a glimmer of hope.

"So," Hilton resumed, "I'm postponin' your execution until tomorrow. I need time to sleep, and then think things out. Like you said, maybe you're worth more to us alive than dead."

Nothing more was said until they had groped their way back to the ghost town. The inner canyon was pooling with blue-black color now. The sun set early in this, the deepest place in North or South America.

"Naturally," Rusty Hilton went on, "you'll be awake all night trying to figure out some way to kill us and escape. You couldn't do

Goldie or me any harm while we were sleepin' off our fixes, because we bunk in the jailhouse and we have booby-trapped the doorway with a crossbow. Just the same, we'll take extra precautions. You won't sleep in the jail with us. We ain't pikers. We'll fix you up with the best accommodations in this camp's deluxe hotel. Won't we, Goldie?"

Hilton led the way up the rickety porch steps into the Gunsight Lode Hotel. The lobby held the rancid stored-up heat of a long summer day. Behind the reception clerk's dusty counter stood an antique iron safe, three feet square and four feet high. How on earth, Tommy wondered, had the pioneers of Borrowed Time been able to transport such a heavy piece of freight to this secret place?

The six-inch-thick laminated steel door was ajar; the beam of Hilton's flashlight, playing over the vault's interior, showed that it had been emptied of whatever treasure it might have held in the far-off days when Borrowed Time was booming.

"We'll use the safe for an anchor to keep you from driftin' downstream durin' the night, Tommy," Hilton said. "Goldie, unlock one of his bracelets and snap it over the handle of that safe."

The handle, Tommy noted with despair, was in the form of a six-inch iron ring. Goldie Lesher reached in a pocket of his jeans and took out a heavy iron key, which he used to open the fetter from Tommy Rockford's left wrist. Giving his prisoner's arm a brutal jerk, Lesher pulled the open handcuff over to the safe door and snapped it in place through the iron handle ring.

Hilton took the key from his blond partner and, walking over to the hotel's room-key rack a dozen feet away, played the beam of his flashlight on the board so that Tommy could see him hang the handcuff key to one of the cuphooks.

"There you are, Tommy!" the red-bearded sadist chuckled. "All you have to do to set yourself free tonight is drag that safe over to this rack and pick up the key to those wrist irons."

As Lesher followed his partner over to the doorway, he turned to fling a final jibe at their prisoner: "Gettin' that key should be easy for a husky critter like you, kid. I don't think that safe weighs more'n a couple ton."

With that Tommy's captors were gone, heading back toward the jailhouse they had preempted for their home in exile from the law. Tommy Rockford, left alone with a belly aching from hunger, knew the key to his freedom, only a dozen feet beyond his reach, was as inaccessible as if it had been hidden in a crater on the moon.

And not much farther away from where he stood helplessly shackled to the heavy safe, was his backpack, on the rocking chair out on the porch where he had tossed it—was it only this afternoon? A backpack that held not only life-saving food, but a two-meter radio that could give him a link to the outside world—providing he could get down the canyon to that open field beyond the jailhouse, the only place where a radio signal could get out. That open field, too, might as well have been on the moon.

Tommy saw a bat flutter on silhouetted wings from the ceiling to the doorway of this haunted hotel, heading out on its nocturnal forage for insects. He envied the bat. It was free... something he doubted he would ever be again.

CHAPTER FOURTEEN

MORSE CODE MESSAGE

As an eerie nightfall pooled in the rock-walled chasm outside the Gunsight Lode Hotel, Tommy Rockford felt an overwhelming claustrophobia smothering him. Weighing like a tangible pressure in the air about him was the ever-present realization that millions of tons of loose rock were poised and waiting to slide over the south rim, needing only a mild seismic jolt to dislodge them. When that happened, the surviving remnants of Borrowed Time, including this haunted hotel, would disappear forever. If some future archealogist should ever excavate his remains, how would he account for the fact that Tommy's skeleton was handcuffed to the ring handle of a safe?

Tommy knew his sanity depended on shaking off such morbid thoughts. For the first time since this nightmare began K6ATX had time to think about the fate that had overtaken the innocent Chub Downey, replacing the anxiety over his own safety with a deep sense of melancholy he could not shake off.

Chub, for all his ghetto background of street-smart toughness and swagger, was at heart just an innocent kid putting a brave front to a world that had already dealt him more than his share of hard knocks. That he had to die at the hands of a pair of case-hardened dope addicts carried an irony which added to Tommy's depression. He tried to take comfort from the probability that Chub had been shot without warning, and had died in the midst of a euphoria only a dedicated rock hound could know on his first visit to Death Valley.

Tommy experimented with pulling the safe door wide open, which put him three feet closer to the rack where Goldie Lesher had hung his key to escape. Three feet, twenty feet, what was the difference? His doom was just as certain. Tugging the thousand-pound vault across the uneven floor to get within reaching distance of the key rack was of course impossible.

Would Lesher and Hilton return in the morning? There was no guarantee that their drug-rotted memory cells could even sustain any record of what they had done to their prisoner. Even if they did return—would they feed him?

The mere thought of food intensified the pangs which tormented his innards. How large was the stock of food which the two fugitives had stashed away in this ghost town where they felt they would be safe indefinitely? There was no way to rationalize things when you were dealing with mentalities that had been warped and crippled by the abuse of illegal substances.

Tommy dug into his jeans with his free hand and brought out his disposable cigarette lighter, wondering if it had survived the flash flood. It lighted on the third flick, thanks to the low humidity level of the desert. He peered around by its feeble glow to confirm a memory left in his subconscious—that he had seen a lamp somewhere nearby, along with a five-gallon can of kerosene.

The lamp and the fuel can were there, sitting on top of the clerk's counter, both within his reach. One-handed, it took some maneuvering to raise the soot-blackened glass chimney from its brackets, flick the lighter and touch the flame to the oil-soaked wick. The glass bowl of the lamp, he noted, was half full of fuel.

Replacing the lamp chimney, Tommy let his pupils contract to accommodate the illumination, feeble though it was. He visualized how somebody, perhaps many years ago before the avalanche had buried most of the camp, had filled that lamp bowl with kerosene from the five-gallon can. Seldom Seen Sam, who said he had been born in this hotel, may have glimpsed the guttering flame of this very lamp at his moment of birth.

Tommy remembered how the old prospector had said he made his home in the Gunsight Lode Hotel. There were clues pointing to Seldom Seen Sam's presence in this place in the recent past. Besides the week-old newspapers on the counter, there were several calendars pinned to the wall behind the safe, ranging in age from this year's to more than fifty years back. Sam had probably put them there. He noticed a scribbled inscription on the square for December 15 last year—"*Hekter shot with arrer. Berried him.*"

To keep his mind off his own miseries, K6ATX picked up the

lamp by its ring-shaped handle and had a look inside the open safe. At first glance the vault appeared empty. Then, in a back corner, Tommy found a canvas-bound ledger marked HOTEL REGISTER, and a small, mouse-nibbled book which Tommy mistook for a New Testament.

He retrieved the latter from the safe, hoping in his hour of distress to derive some comfort from the sacred writings which he knew had sustained his father and mother in times of difficulty.

But the dust-powdered, leather-bound volume proved to be a personal diary. Stamped on the front cover, in imitation gilt that had tarnished green with age, was the book's title: DAILY JOURNAL, followed by a line in indelible pencil, *Roxanna & Rudy Sutkliffe.*

They were the parents of Seldom Seen Sam, now resting under the weathered wooden headboards out in Borrowed Time's boothill cemetery. This diary might well contain the history of the doomed camp, before and after the catastrophic avalanche!

In spite of his hunger pangs and the numbing constriction of the iron manacle which was clamping off the circulation in his right hand, Tommy Rockford found himself absorbed in scanning the yellowed pages of the Sutkliffes' personal record.

The earliest entries, dated in the 1870s, were written in a spidery Spencerian script common to the Victorian age, penned by old Sam's mother, recounting her marriage to Rudy Sutkliffe and her coming to Borrowed Time. Then, in the middle of the book, was an entry that caused Tommy Rockford's heart to start pounding:

> *Well what everone knowed would happen some day happent today. The Avalanche let go. Borrowed Time is on borrowed time no longer. Whole east end of the canyon including wagon road an more than half the camp is now buried under tuns of bolders. Must of been 40 souls lost mashed to a pulp. The Lord's vengunce on Madame Zedra and her dance hall girls, say I! Rudy says God spared us an maybe 25 other miners. The thing to worry about now is how are we going to get out before the rest of the camp is squashed flat by another slide? Or we starve to death? May God help us is my fervunt prayer.*

Apparently the survivors of Borrowed Time believed in the adage that "God helps them that help themselves," for on the evening of the day the rockslide had sealed off the camp from the world, Tommy found an entry penciled in a labored backhand, probably by Rudy Sutkliffe, then proprietor of the Gunsight Lode Hotel:

> *Roger Levenson an Bill Horton called a mass meeting in our Hotel of all survivors in camp this P.M. They say if doled out careful we have enough grub to last maybe a couple weeks. Supplies in the general store are buried under the slide. Thank God our hotel water well, the only one left in camp, is not damaged, so we will not perish of thirst, the most awful death of all. Roger says by working nite & day the men can dig a tunnel through north cliff an reach daylight in Avalanche Gulch before grub runs out. Have to dig by hand can't risk using dinamite or black powdder for fear blasting would jolt loose rest of avalanche. Meeting ended with prayer. God's will be done. We are in thy merciful hands, Amen.*

Fascinated, Tommy Rockford leafed through the brittle yellow pages, finding the story they told more absorbing than a fiction thriller. This was a true story, a human drama with the rawest kind of suspense, as described in the simple words of a semi-literate man and woman who had experienced the drama they were describing and had survived to tell the story.

Most of the entries were in Mrs. Sutkliffe's trembly hand—presumably her husband was busy helping dig the escape tunnel. She outlined the day-by-day progress of the work, as the miners whose lives had been spared in the lottery of fate toiled around the clock with pick and shovel, rationing their dwindling food supplies in a desperate race against time to chisel an escape hatch through the rocks into Avalanche Canyon, only one hundred feet away.

Exactly twenty days from the date of the disaster, Roxanna Sutkliff penned a climactic entry, the ink blurred by what may well have been the woman's tears of thanksgiving:

> *Allmighty God be praised for His boundless mercy! Just after midnight Levenson's pickax holed through into Avalanche Gulch! All that remains now is enlarge the tunnel enough to crawl out and to put the tailings into wheel barrers and dump the rock down into the Gulch so as to form a ramp to take us to solid ground and everyone in Borrowed Time will be spared a slow death by starvation. It was clost*

to only two days' grub left. Rudy an me hate to leave the camp. We may return later. Rudy is already talking about staking out a claim on the abandoned Gunsight Lode. Praise God from whom all blessings flow.

Frustration needled K6ATX as the radio ham found the next dozen pages had been ripped out of the diary. Apparently the Sutlkiffes had indeed returned to what was left of Borrowed Time by way of the escape tunnel, for the next entry bore a date nine years later and picked up a narrative which had been inspired by Roxanna Sutkliffe's becoming pregnant:

Rudy an me decided to remain here at Borrowed Time until the baby comes. Our merciful Father has kept us safe an comfortable here for nigh onto 10 years now. If He sees fit to bless us with a son we will stay while Rudy keeps digging for the Lode. If it is a girl though Rudy promises we will move out. Borrowed Time ain't no fitten place to raise a girl-child, whereas a son could help Rudy dig back to the Gunsight Lode an be happy doing it. We know this camp has a great future ahead of it. . . I feel so poorly! But nearest doctor is at Independence nearly 200 mile away. God help me.

Mrs. Sutkliffe's delicate script appeared in the journal three days later, for the last time. She heralded a joyous event:

Was delivered of a boy child 3:30 a.m. We name him Samuel Uriah after his two grandfathers. Weighed 7 lb 4 oz by our gold scales. GOD BE PRAISED! I feel very poorly. Dear Lord, if in your infinite wisdom you must call one of us home, let it be me an bless and watch over our man child who brightens our lives after all these hopeless barren years. Thy will be done.

Baby Sam was only one day old when his father Rudy Sutkliffe added a poignant terminal entry in his painful printed scrawl:

Berried my woman this morning. God bless an keep Roxie she was a good wife. I will fotch in a Piute squaw to raise little Sam until I can manage alone. Can trust Injun woman not to give away secret of how to reach Borrowed Time. The buried lode is the only thing I can leave our son. When Sam is old enough I will tell him silver lode that is still there waiting to make him rich. Know I won't live long enough to dig to it through that loose rock slide. Nobody else on earth knows it is there except me.

By the flickering light of the oil lamp, K6ATX determined that there was only one more entry in the journal. It bore a date eighteen years later than Rudy Sutkliffe's announcement of his mate's death following childbirth. Its message was equally tragic:

BERRIED DAD BESIDE MA TODAY. HE WAS 92.—SAM

It was Seldom Seen Sam's one and only entry in the book which had been archived all these years in his parents' safe; the remaining pages were blank. With a feeling of deep reverence Tommy stowed the book away in his hip pocket for safekeeping.

Tommy's absorption in the human drama he had found on the pages of the ancient diary was interrupted by an alien, persistent tapping noise from somewhere inside the building. He realized it had been going on for several minutes now. He would have thought it was the secretive sound a packrat might make scurrying about in the upstairs rooms and hallways of the hotel, or perhaps it was a loose shingle chattering in a vagrant wind gust. Except that the taps had a repeating pattern: four taps, then a pause, then two more taps. Four taps, pause, two taps...

Tommy's pulses began pounding. What had he told Chub this morning on the way to Death Valley? "Four dots in Morse code is the letter H. Two dots is the letter I. Put them together and you get HI, the universal greeting of hams using CW!"

The only two letters of Morse code which Chub had learned during their lesson this morning, using the van's horn for a key.

Tap-tap-tap-tap!...... Tap.... tap!

Tommy's heart did a flip-flop. With that extra space in the final two-tap sequence, the two-dot letter "I" became two separate letter "E"s, changing HI to HEE. Chub Downey had made that error several times this morning, before he caught on to the proper rhythm, a common mistake for beginners.

For a wild instant Tommy wondered if Chub's ghost had returned to haunt him—until he remembered that his scientific bent precluded his believing in the supernatural.

"Hey!" K6ATX called out excitedly. "QRZ? Who's calling? Can it be possible that's you, Chub Downey?"

CHAPTER FIFTEEN

BAIT FOR A TRAP

The tapping ceased. A faint rustle of sound directed Tommy's attention overhead, to the railed balcony overhanging the lobby on three sides. A cascade of talcum-fine dust floated down like smoke into the cone of yellow light cast by the flickering lamp.

Not knowing what to expect, Tommy cupped a hand behind the lamp chimney and blew out the light, somehow feeling safer in darkness which closed in like black paint.

Tommy could hear floor boards creaking as something moved stealthily toward the stairs leading down to the ground floor. In the Stygian shadows Tommy sensed, rather than saw, a bulky figure moving down the stairs, each tread protesting under the weight.

Then a cautious whisper cut through the darkness from the stairway: "You sure them two Satan's Angels aren't around, Tommy?"

There was no mistaking that voice. Chub Downey had returned from the dead!

"They're staying down at the jailhouse, Chub," Tommy answered, straining forward as far as his fettered right arm would allow, his free hand flailing the air waiting for his fat buddy to cross the lobby floor. "Kid, they told me you had been killed! What on earth happened to you? Where have you been all afternoon?"

Chub's familiar chuckle sounded just across the counter from Tommy's outstretched fingers. A moment later their hands clasped in the darkness and for Tommy Rockford it was almost as if he had reached out and touched the Hand of God Himself.

"I sure ain't dead, Tommy! By the way, how did you like the Morse code I laid on you, eh?... I been hiding upstairs since the middle of the afternoon. I was busy exploring this hotel, right after I checked in with you on my CB radio, hunting for Seldom Seen Sam's room where he told me he kept his uranium ore specimens. Then I heard voices outside! I went to the front window just in time to see those two dirtbags coming out of the tunnel I had just discovered. Knew from their leather jackets and one being redheaded, the other a straw blond, that they had to be the Crossbow Killers from 'Vegas. It like to scared me to death, Tommy."

"You were lucky you were indoors when they arrived, Chub. If they had spotted you—"

"You're tellin' *me*? I watched 'em trotting off down the street. I saw them turn into that stone-walled building, and decided the best thing for me to do was hustle back out through that tunnel and give you a call—"

"Chub," Tommy said, "I'm dying to hear your story, believe me, but if you don't get this handcuff off my wrist, gangrene is going to rot it off. The key is over there on a rack—"

"I know," Chub said, moving off along the counter toward the rack of keys. "I was watchin' when those roughnecks brought you in here and locked you to the safe. When I saw the blond feller hang the key to a hook I said to myself, 'Come dark, I'll sneak downstairs and turn Tommy loose!' "

Tommy heard Chub groping his way around the end of the counter and over to the key rack. Metal jingled as the rock hound found the handcuff key and removed it from its hook. A moment later, after fumbling to find the keyhole in the iron bracelet, Chub inserted the key and Tommy felt the notched jaws of the handcuff open and restore the surge of circulation through his wrist, which at the moment had no feeling left in it.

While Tommy was trying to massage some life back into his hand, Chub rattled on: "Like I was saying, I decided I'd better get over to the tunnel and call you on the CB rig. But just when I got to the open end of the tunnel, the biggest mess of water I ever saw came tumblin' down Avalanche Gulch. It wiped away that heap of mine tailings which was my only way to get back down into the Gulch! I had left my specimen bag out in the bushes and I saw it get swept away. Right then I realized I was trapped, maybe for keeps. I was scared, man! I just couldn't believe there would be that much water in the month of June in what is supposed to be the driest spot in the US!"

Tommy said, "It was a flash flood, Chub. A fairly common phenomenon where you've got mountains high enough to reach passing storm fronts... In fact, millions of flash floods helped make the topography of Death Valley what it is today."

"Well," sighed Chub Downey, "I can't say that I like learning my geography lessons first-hand. It was a scary sight, man."

"Uncle JC warned me on two meters that a cloudburst had hit Telescope Peak while I was hiking up the Gulch hunting for you, but his warning came too late for me to reach safety ahead of the water. But why didn't you give me a call, Chub? I was monitoring the band. You knew that. I died a thousand deaths wondering if that flood had caught you down in the Gulch, Chub. Especially after I dug your rock hound bag out of the mud and debris."

Chub said contritely, "I was too scared to talk into the radio, Tommy, for fear those two hoodlums might hear me. I just sat there at the mouth of the tunnel shivering in my boots for I don't know how long. Then I decided it wasn't a very safe place to be, that I'd better hustle back and hide in the hotel. I had hardly started back when I heard you yelling, wanting to know if I was still in the tunnel—"

"So you answered 'Ten thirty-four.' *Trouble at this station, help urgently needed*. That was pretty cool thinking, Chub. You got your message across with a minimum of yelling."

"I was sure those Crossbow Killer guys must have heard me yell at you. I got back here to the hotel and scuttled upstairs, and that's where I've been ever since. But how come you wound up in here locked to the door of the safe, Tommy?"

Still working on his benumbed hand, which was beginning to throb with pain now that the circulation was coming back, Tommy briefed his redheaded buddy on his afternoon's adventures, winding up with his narrow escape from being impaled by a crossbow arrow while visiting the Borrowed Time cemetery.

"Well, I'm ready to go now," Tommy panted. "I've got chow for us out in my backpack, on the porch. We've got to get out of here."

Chub resisted the pull of Tommy's hand on his wrist. "Before we leave, Tommy, you've *got* to come up to Seldom's room and see what I found! My pocket violet ray lamp makes his rock samples glow in the dark with more colors than a rainbow. And my mineral detector chatters like firecrackers going off when I put it near Sam's uranium ore. You won't believe it unless you—"

"Chub, you darn fool rock hound, we're heading for that escape tunnel *now,* understand? I'm famished, but I can wait to eat until we're back at Sam's cabin. Until then, every second we spend in here is at the risk of our lives."

Protesting vigorously, Chub Downey was powerless to prevent Tommy Rockford from shoving him bodily across the lobby and out onto the porch. There K6ATX retrieved his backpack off one of the rocking chairs, pulled Chub down the steps and across the street toward the mouth of the escape tunnel, dimly visible in the wash of starshine which penetrated the Borrowed Time defile.

Then the two boys were stopped dead in their tracks by a voice that issued from the black throat of the tunnel, as menacing as the hiss of a cobra: "How about coolin' it, fellers? You ain't goin' nowhere. This is dead end."

Starlight glinted off the polished steel tip of an arrow resting in the hardwood cradle of a crossbow, as Rusty Hilton emerged from the tunnel's black maw, teeth glinting like a reptile's fangs under his bushy red mustache.

"For a college kid, you're pretty dumb, Tommy," the bald-headed outlaw jeered. "Goldie and me knew *somebody* was hiding in this camp today, so when you asked us what happened to the fat kid here, we told you he was dead, and you swallowed the story. That was dumb mistake Numero Uno."

"Thank you," K6ATX responded. "You're inferring I made mistake Numero Duo?"

"*Si si,* amigo! We used that handcuff key to bait a trap to draw your pal out of hiding. You were pretty stupid not to wonder why we would leave the key hanging on a nail in plain sight. Well, the bait worked. Your buddy showed up from wherever he was hiding and unlocked your cuff. I knew this tunnel would be the first place the two of you would head for, so I decided to camp out here even if it took all night. Which means we've got *two* hostages to bargain with in case the fuzz show up tomorrow. I figure Goldie an' me are going to be able to buy our way out of this mess without skinning our noses."

Hilton leaned the crossbow against the tunnel wall without uncocking it and then drew the .357 Magnum from its holster.

"I prefer using the bow and arrow because of the silence factor," Hilton explained, "but without Goldie here to help me, a gun's handier. Now you two young fellers turn around and head back to the hotel.

We've got special accommodations reserved for you—the royal suite, you might say. The room where old Seldom Seen Sam lived when he wasn't out roaming the hills with his mule hunting for gold, the daffy old coot."

Hilton produced a flashlight from a pocket of his jeans and directed its funneling beam toward the porch steps leading into the Gunsight Lode Hotel. The two boys, knowing sure death from a point-blank bullet would be their reward if they attempted to break away, plodded disconsolately back to the lobby they had left a few moments ago with such high hopes of escape.

"Up the stairs," Hilton ordered, indicating the way with his flashlight beam. "Just don't make any false moves, okay?"

Chub Downey, apparently unaware of the gravity of their situation, spoke up with juvenile excitement in his voice, "I know where Mr. Seldom's room is! That's where I hid out all afternoon. I was watching you two guys from the window. But I knew sooner or later Tommy would show up to rescue me."

"Rescue is hardly the right word to use in this situation, Chub," Tommy said dolefully. "Hilton has out-smarted us."

Climbing the rickety stairs, each tread still covered with moth eaten carpet runner worn threadbare by the hobbed bootsoles of miners who had built this lost camp a century ago, Chub and Tommy reached the balcony with Hilton dogging their heels, pistol in one hand, flashlight in the other.

Without being directed, Chub went down a hallway to his left and opened the first door he came to.

"If you've been here already," Hilton said, "You know where Sam's coal oil lamp is. Light it. I want to give you two hostages a little briefing before I rejoin Goldie over at the jailhouse."

The hotel room which Seldom Seen Sam had used for his home when he was not out prospecting was barely ten by twelve feet in size. There was a mouldy cot covered with an army blanket in one corner. The one window was barred with a basket-woven lattice of heavy strap iron, the work of some long-ago camp blacksmith. The inside walls appeared to be of two-by-twelve pine planks laid flat, rather than flimsy clapboards. This indicated that Seldom Seen Sam's parents, when they built the hotel, had intended this room as a safety vault for the storage of customers' valuables, which probably included nuggets and high grade ore samples from the Gunsight Lode bonanza.

Chub crossed the room to a table cluttered with rock specimens, papers, tobacco tins and other bachelor litter. A moment later the young rock hound had lighted a match and touched it to the wick of a coal oil lamp. By its lemon-yellow glare, other details of the room came into view—faded newspapers pasted to the walls and ceiling to keep out drafts, a corner table cluttered with cans of tinned food, unwashed dishes, blue-enameled cooking utensils, and an uncounted number of cardboard boxes filled with ore specimens, probably gathered by Seldom Seen Sam over a period of decades, each sample representing the promise of a fabulous lode. A small, rust-encrusted cookstove squatted in one corner, its stove pipe askew like a top hat on a drunk man.

"All right," Hilton said briskly. "As you will find out, this strongroom is escape-proof. Goldie and I would have put you in here this afternoon, Tommy, if it hadn't been that we needed to lure your fat buddy out of hiding first."

Tommy said dully, "I'm surprised you and Lesher didn't select the hotel instead of the jail to live in."

"Goldie," Hilton said, "is hooked on PCP—angel dust. When he gets a high on, he seems to want to climb up on a high place and jump off into space, thinking he can fly. So I make sure he's as close to the ground as he can get."

"Unless he's your brother, I don't see why you put up with having to nursemaid Lesher," Tommy said.

Hilton's bottle-green eyes turned bleak. "It goes back to when we were both grunts in Vietnam. Goldie was in the same artillery outfit I was. One night in the Mekong Delta we were ambushed by the Viet Cong. I got fragged pretty bad with a grenade. Goldie Lesher risked his neck to carry me to an aid station. The medics saved me. I'll be in Goldie's debt as long as we live. And that's closer than being blood brothers, son."

Hilton walked over to the door they had just entered and lifted a huge laminated padlock hanging from a nail. The outside of the door was fitted with a massive iron hasp to accommodate the lock.

"This is where you guys will spend what's left of the night," the outlaw said. "If the fuzz closes in on us anytime tomorrow, we'll be using you two hostages to buy our way out."

Chub said anxiously, "And if they don't show up—what then?"

"In that case," Hilton said, "Goldie and I will rig up some kind of a rope ladder and slide down out of that tunnel tomorrow night. Once outside, we've got fifty thousand in greenbacks from the Pharaoh's Palace heist to buy our way out of any jam."

Chub, asked in a frightened voice, "If you two escape... what's going to happen to us?"

Hilton said wearily, "Right now I'm too tired to worry myself with that problem."

Tommy Rockford slumped down on the cot. The room stank with the compounded odors of stale tobacco smoke, rancid bacon in a skillet on the cookstove, food scraps, unwashed blankets and clothing, and scorched coffee grounds.

"I know the two of you will spend the night trying to claw your way out of this room," Hilton predicted, "but if I were you I would save your fingernails. Believe me, I have done durance vile in slammers a lot worse than this."

Tommy had buried his face in his hands, fighting off a despair as deep as he had ever known. Now he glanced up and said curiously, "Your vocabulary intrigues me, Hilton. 'Durance vile' comes from Shakespeare, doesn't it? Behind that dirtbag hair and beard and the Satan's Angels get-up must be a man with considerable education, maybe even a refined upbringing."

Standing in the doorway, Hilton mused, "You're very perceptive, kid. I went to UCLA on a football scholarship, earned a degree, then I got patriotic and volunteered for the military. They sent me to Vietnam. Who would believe it now? But my folks up in Turlock keep my diploma framed on the wall to prove I'm not the dropout I appear to be... Dropout? Maybe I am. The war sort of screwed me up. I came back from 'Nam a disillusioned man. Maybe it was the shabby way the public treated us returning vets, like we were criminals instead of heroes."

K6ATX went on, "I don't understand it. With your background, with a college degree, how come you have to skulk around on back roads on choppers, shooting people with crossbows, snorting coke or whatever kind of drug you're hooked on—"

Hilton mused as if to himself, "I started out smoking pot when I was in high school, about your fat buddy's age. Kept on through college. Then I went into the army. Over in 'Nam I started soaking my joints in LSD. A gook in DaNang got me started on harder stuff, heroin, cocaine. That's why a man with a chemical dependence has to hustle to make enough to support his habit. I don't recommend my way of life, Tommy, but I'm in too deep to ever make it back out."

Hilton stepped out into the corridor and swung the heavy door shut. The two prisoners heard the big padlock snap shut through the hasp like a shark snapping its jaws together. Both remained staring at the locked door as their captor's boots thudded along the balcony, down the stairs, across the lobby and outdoors, heading for the stone jailhouse down the street to rejoin his partner.

CHAPTER SIXTEEN

NEWSCAST FROM NEVADA

When the last footfall had faded away in the night's stillness, Chub Downey turned to K6ATX and said excitedly, "Tommy, you remember how Mr. Seldom told us he had uranium ore samples stored in the hotel where he lived? Well, he wasn't lying."

Tommy groaned. At the moment, getting some food in his famished stomach was his first priority. He shrugged the backpack straps off his shoulders, unzipped the canvas bag and took out the canned food, gorp and fruit drinks he had hastily packed this morning, an eternity ago.

"You must be starved," Tommy said to Chub Downey as he stuffed his mouth full of trail mix. "Help yourself."

"Already eaten," Chub answered. "Mr. Seldom has all kinds of food stashed in that cupboard above the stove. Tommy, I've got something to show you that'll knock your eyeballs loose."

Downey hurried across the room and brought back his Little Jim Dandy mineral detector. Tommy was too busy reaming a hole in a can of tomato juice and swigging down the nourishing liquid to object as Chub clamped the Geiger counter headphones over Tommy's ears.

"You never heard anything like this, even at the exhibit at Exposition Park in LA," Chub said. "Now listen."

As he spoke, the young rock hound switched on the Little Jim Dandy. Even before he carried the sensor disc closer to a cardboard box filled with rock samples at the foot of the cot, Tommy Rockford could hear the rapid clicking in the headset, gaining in volume and frequency as Chub swung the Geiger counter back and forth above the box of ore. There was no question about it, Seldom Seen Sam had found an extremely rich sample of radioactive mineral, presumably uranium, on one of his prospecting expeditions around Death Valley.

Tommy stopped chewing and swallowing long enough to comment, "Very exciting, Chub, but we have more important things to think about—such as trying to save our lives. Plus getting some sleep. We can't let our strength get too depleted."

Chub Downey wasn't listening. He hurried back to the kitchen table where he had placed his own backpack earlier in the day and returned with his portable violet ray lamp, a device used for detecting fluorescent minerals in the field.

"I'm going to blow out the lamp," the rock hound said, "and show you what the rocks on the table look like under black light. This afternoon I covered myself with Mr. Seldom's smelly old blanket so as to get some darkness, and even with that set-up it was like finding a box of chunks chipped off a rainbow!"

Tommy reached out to restrain Chub from extinguishing the lamp. "Hold on a second, kid. Before I enjoy your sound and light show there are some things I need to do."

As he spoke, Tommy Rockford was pawing in his own backpack for his two-meter handie-talkie. He snapped the switch to receive—and confirmed what Chub had reported about radio reception inside this rock-walled crack in the mountain. It was asking too much that an electromagnetic wave could enter or leave these hotel walls.

Hefting the compact ICOM in his hand, Tommy said gloomily, "Just think, Chub—this little piece of high-tech gear could rescue us from this mess if I could only use it out in the middle of that open field under the sky near the cemetery, where there's a line-of-sight shot at JC's QTH on Telescope Peak. But how could I ever trick Hilton into letting me carry a radio out there in the open?"

"I heard plenty on Mr. Seldom's radio today," Chub said. "It was tuned to that station in Las Vegas we were listening to driving down the valley this morning, so we know an AM signal can get down into this hole. I heard KNX in Los Angeles too."

Even as Chub was speaking, Tommy caught sight of Seldom Seen Sam's radio receiver, mounted on a shelf under the iron-latticed window. Tommy's grandparents had owned one like it—a 1930s vintage

Philco superheterodyne in a "cathedral" style walnut case. It operated on dry cell A and B batteries, but how had the old prospector managed to pull in a signal, down here in a deep canyon?

Walking over to inspect the venerable Philco, Tommy got his answer. A lead-in wire led from a Fahnestock clip on the chassis, out the window, and straight up into the night. K6ATX guessed that the wire paralleled the face of the cliff to reach an antenna strung in open air above the rimrock. That was the only possible explanation for how Sam could have brought radio reception to Borrowed Time. An insulated ground wire led from a binding post on the radio set, out the window and down—probably to the water well alongside the hotel, which would make the best possible ground.

"It's five after eight," Tommy said. "KVGS is a news-and-music station, so this is probably their news-on-the-hour break. Maybe we can find out if search parties are out looking for us."

He switched the set on. After an interminable delay waiting for the tube filaments to warm up—a delay which modern radio listeners have been spared, thanks to the advent of solid state technology replacing vacuum tubes—the tinny nasal voice of a Las Vegas announcer issued from the old-fashioned speaker, winding up a summary of market news.

A station signature and time signal followed—confirming that Tommy's solar-battery wristwatch was precisely accurate—after which the announcer said, "You have been listening to the national news-on-the-hour from KVGS, the pioneer voice of Las Vegas, fun capital of the West... This is Dan Casmer switching you live to our mobile unit at Furnace Creek Ranch in Death Valley, where our on-the-scene reporter is waiting to bring you the latest developments concerning the interstate manhunt following the Pharaoh's Palace robbery and murder some twenty hours ago. Come in, Barry Clark."

Tommy was only vaguely aware of Chub passing him two opened cans—one of baked beans, the other half peaches in sugar syrup—which Chub had found in Seldom Seen Sam's cache of food. As Tommy bent his ear closer to the loudspeaker grill the Nevada station went into a QSB or fade. Then he heard the beginning of a transmission from KVGS's short-wave mobile unit: "... Barry Clark, reporting live from the California Highway Patrol unit at Furnace Creek Ranch in Death Valley National Monument.

"Due to an unprecedented thunderstorm that produced rains

which erased all tracks in the valley by midday, no trace has yet been found of Rusty Hilton and Goldie Lesher, the two Crossbow Killers who murdered guard Hal Morehouse at Pharaoh's Palace shortly after midnight and escaped with a satchel full of loot.

"For the benefit of late tuners-in, the two killers escaped from Las Vegas on two motorcycles, a red Harley and a yellow Yamaha. It is known that Hilton and Lesher, well-known members of the notorious Satan's Angels motorcycle gang, continued their escape across country, avoiding roads and highways. They escaped with an estimated fifty thousand dollars in gambling receipts, a spokesman for Pharoah's Palace security police reported tonight.

"At daylight, sheriff's deputies conducting a ground and air search traced the fugitives' motorcycle tracks across the sagebush flats, crossing into California at the Pahrump Valley due east of Tecopah. A US Mail truck driver reported seeing the two cyclists entering Death Valley by way of Jubilee Pass at ten AM. The CHP has roadblocks sealing off all roads leaving Death Valley.

"That brings you up to date on the Crossbow Killer case," Clark went on. "And now for another breaking story of major interest in this area, the mystery of two missing radio hams from Santa Bonita. I have here in our broadcasting van Mr. J. C. Ellison of Seattle, who with a group of Amateur Radio operators had come to Death Valley earlier today from Santa Barbara County to participate in their annual emergency radio competition with fellow radio hams around the world. Mr. Ellison, I understand that two of your group from Santa Bonita are missing and are feared to be victims of flash floods which struck on the west side of Death Valley today. Could you share with our KVGS listeners what you know about this?"

Tommy and Chub stared at each other, holding their breaths as Uncle JC's familiar voice issued from the speaker, a voice raspy with fatigue and anxiety:

"Certainly, Mr. Clark. My nephew, Tommy Rockford, a Cal Tech student who is a well-known radio ham from Santa Bonita, aged nineteen, and a friend of his from Los Angeles, Chub Downey, seventeen, locally famous as a champion Little League baseball pitcher, have been unaccounted for since noon, somewhere in Death Valley. They were carrying a van loaded with radio club equipment to an undisclosed destination below sea-level in Death Valley. We have had no radio contact with them since shortly before noon, at which time my nephew had just received some kind of alarming emergency radio message from the younger boy, who was out collecting rocks in an unidentified canyon."

The announcer asked in his professionally funereal tones, "Where were your nephew and the other boy at the time you last heard from them?"

"We don't know," Uncle JC said, his voice husky with emotion. "It was somewhere at a sub-sea-level site—but Death Valley's sea-level perimeter covers hundreds of miles, as you know. As soon as it gets daylight tomorrow the National Park Service plans to use a helicopter to patrol the sea-level contour line in a effort to locate Tommy's VW van and his camp, and we can organize our ground search from there. It's our only hope. If they were on the west side of the valley they might well have been in the path of this morning's flash floods. In which case..."

Uncle JC choked back a sob and left his tragic thought unspoken.

Barry Clark went on, "We fervently hope that such a mishap did not befall Tommy Rockford and Chub Downey, Mr. Ellison. And now, we return you to our Las Vegas studios to resume our regular programming—*wait!* Wait—I have just been handed a bulletin which may give us the answer to where the missing radio hams are! Stand by, folks—the CHP officers are bringing in a Death Valley celebrity for us to interview—the famous prospector and recluse known as Seldom Seen Sam, who I understand has news for us!"

Tommy grabbed Chub and went into an ecstatic victory dance.

"What's with you, man?" Chub asked confusedly. "I don't see—"

"Don't you understand, Chub? Seldom Seen Sam has arrived at Furnace Creek! He'll be able to tell the officers that he saw us and talked to us this morning at his cabin near the mouth of Avalanche Gulch! That's all they'll need to have rescue parties zeroing in on us tomorrow!"

Tommy broke off as the two of them plastered their ears to the grillwork of the Philco's speaker, as the signal from Las Vegas threatened to fade out. But they distinctly heard the announcer introducing Mr. Samuel Sutkliffe, better known as Seldom Seen Sam the prospector. They heard the eccentric old desert rat clear his throat self-consciously and drawl into the microphone:

"Shore thing, yessiree, I seen them two lost boys yo're describin'.

They passed me an' my jennie mule Hernia this afternoon, out in the middle o' the Devil's Golf Course. They stopped to talk a spell, said they was lost, that they was tryin' to git to a certain place, and could I help 'em."

Tommy's jubilation turned to dismay. "Why, the old duffer is talking crazy—or else he's deliberately lying about us!"

Uncle JC's voice spoke from the background, putting an anxious question to the garrulous old hermit: "Did they tell you what place they were trying to find, Mr. er—Sutkliffe?"

Seldom Seen Sam's answer put a chill in Tommy's heart:

"They shore did! Said they was goin' to set up some kind of wireless station in Ubehebe Crater. That's in the north end of the Valley, a few mile west o' Scotty's Castle. They said—"

Chub Downey cried out in bewilderment, "What's he trying to do to us, Tommy? Even I know that Heebie Jeebie Crater is in the opposite direction from here—"

Uncle JC broke in sharply, echoing the thought in Tommy's mind: "I can't imagine my nephew getting lost in Death Valley! He knows this area like the back of his hand. Mr. Sam, are you sure—"

Ignoring Uncle JC's question, Seldom Seen Sam, obviously basking in his new-found attention, continued reminiscently, "Back in the Twenties, I knowed ol' Death Valley Scotty as well as I did my own Daddy, yessir. My Daddy was the one who discovered the Gunsight Lode, you know... Did I ever tell you about the time Death Valley Scotty woke up an' found this baby rattlesnake had crawled into his boot durin' the night? He wasn't fully awake at the time and mistook this little rattler for a loose shoe lace. Well, he—"

The announcer cut in, "Thank you, Mr. Sutkliffe. And next—"

Chub gave an outraged yelp. "Hey, don't stop him before he tells us what Scotty did with that baby rattlesnake!"

Tommy waggled his head in hopeless anger. "The old man is deliberately trying to keep search parties away from his beloved ghost town, Chub. Ubehebe Crater is a good seventy-five miles north of here. I don't think Sam wants to injure us deliberately. He's trying to keep a vow to his dead father—to preserve the secret of Borrowed Time. And he'll cook our goose doing it."

The volume swelled on the antique radio as Uncle JC introduced several radio hams gathered inside KVGS's mobile van—W6AMD Roy, WA6IBR Spud, K6CRJ Doc, and Uncle JC's newly-adopted son

Noisy Noyce, KA7XNN. They were eagerly making plans to drive up the valley to Ubehebe Crater tonight, hoping to find K6ATX's radio camp.

Because this ancient AM receiver of Seldom Seen Sam's was now their only link with the outside world, and to conserve what power was left in the precious batteries, Tommy turned off the set. That was Chub's signal to blow out the lamp.

"All ready for my violet ray show?" the rock hound asked eagerly, snapping on his "black light" lamp and aiming it toward the ordinary-looking rocks arranged on the table. Under the invisible rays the rocks now gleamed in fluorescent colors—reds, yellows, greens. Under any other circumstances Tommy would have been as thrilled as young Chub. But not tonight.

"The old man pasted labels on the rocks," Chub explained. "That is how I knew which ones to get together for my violet ray lamp. That pink one is calcite, and those speckled green ones have got uranium in 'em. That lighter green one is a fossil of some kind, I think maybe a chip from a mastodon tooth. Did they have mastodons in old-time Death Valley, Tommy? You told me this valley used to be a fresh-water lake—"

K6ATX slumped onto the cot in the darkness and threw himself face-down on the musty blankets, the rusty iron springs protesting under his weight. Holding a tight check on his temper, doing his best to control nerves that were rubbed raw, Tommy replied, "Look, Chub. That's a whale of a rock show you've got there. But I'm bushed. I almost got my brains knocked out this morning. I'm played out. I've got to get some sleep, okay?"

Chub, his teeth glowing with a weird greenish light under the violet ray lamp, said in an abashed voice, "Sure, good buddy. I guess I let my rockhounding get the better of me. But ever since I walked into this hotel with my Geiger counter I couldn't wait to find old Sam's room and the rock collection he told me about this morning."

"I know," Tommy sighed. "You're in rock-hound heaven. But now let me get some sleep, huh? You can play with your rocks all night if you want, but just let me hit the sack, okay?"

He heard Chub mumbling a chastened apology and felt a pang of guilt that he had hurt the kid's feelings. He also knew he would not be doing Chub's morale a favor by explaining to him that all the time they could count on would be the daylight hours tomorrow.

If the police dragnet hadn't closed in on the two Crossbow Killers by sundown—a very doubtful eventuality, what with Seldom Seen Sam shifting the search to the Ubehebe Crater area—then Tommy knew that his and Chub's value as hostages would sink to zero. For their own protection, Hilton or Lesher would murder them before attempting their own escape from Borrowed Time under cover of darkness tomorrow.

CHAPTER SEVENTEEN

DYNAMITE FOR THE LAW

A gray wash of daylight streaming in through the iron-barred window overlooking the single street of Borrowed Time brought Rockford awake next morning.

For a long, disoriented moment he lay on the sagging iron cot, one cheek cradled in the mildewed army blanket, his eyes ranging about the shadowy room without comprehension as to his whereabouts. Then he saw Chub Downey lying on the floor beside the cot, body curled up in a fetal position with knees to chest, his violet ray lamp still clutched in his hands. Tommy would hate to awaken the youth, who would find his worst nightmares could not equal reality.

Tommy swung his legs stiffly off the cot and stood up, aching in every muscle due to the long hours he had turned and tossed on the swaybacked cot springs. The skin of his cheeks and jaw itched from the stubble of beard which hadn't known a razor in going on two days now. Thirst burned his throat and stomach.

"What a bummer of a way to start another Field Day!" K6ATX groaned aloud. He stifled another thought that had followed in his mind: after manning a key or mike in eight annual Field Days since the FCC had issued him his ham ticket and call sign at age ten, this weekend might mark the last Field Day he would ever have...

His throat was parched, reminding him of the deep, cool, fresh-water well located between the hotel and the assay office next door. That well was the only reason why Seldom Seen Sam—and now the two Satan's Angels—had a chance of surviving in the ghost town. But that water was of no use to anyone locked in this room.

Thump-thump-thump-thump!

The unmistakable sound of a helicopter's rotors biting the heated desert air startled Tommy. The sound swelled and died away in a quick Doppler effect as the chopper passed southbound over the narrow slot separating the steep-slanted cliffs which concealed Borrowed Time's buildings from the view of any pilot flying over.

At least an aerial search was under way for him and Chub Downey, as had been announced over the air last night. The 'copter could belong to the Inyo County Sheriff's Aerial Squadron, the National Park Service, or the CHP. He wondered if the sound had reached Goldie Lesher and Rusty Hilton, asleep in the jailhouse.

It dismayed Tommy to realize that the helicopter search party would primarily be looking for the ham club's VW van. They wouldn't see it, parked as it was under the roof of the stable shed next to Seldom Seen Sam's shanty. It had been a familiar landmark long before the first aircraft flew over Death Valley in 1912, so would not provide sufficient reason for a chopper to investigate.

An acute thirst told Rockford how much his system had dehydrated during the hot night. His canteen was emptied yesterday. Tiptoeing so as not to awaken Chub Downey, Tommy located old Sam's tin-lined, rat-proof grub box and checked out the canned goods it contained. There were no fruit juices. The only canned liquid was tomato juice, but so heavily salted that Tommy knew it would only aggravate his thirst. All the canned soups and meats were also too salty to consume without a supplement of water. A cool drink was the only cure for what ailed him. Lack of water for the hot day ahead would be unendurable; they would begin hallucinating.

He made a circuit of the four walls of their prison, and checked the floor for trapdoors and the ceiling for any opening into the attic. Hilton was right. This room was escape-proof.

His thoughts turned to Uncle JC and his ham radio friends. By now, they would have had time to explore the deep, rocky funnel of Ubehebe Crater—half a mile wide, five hundred feet deep—where Seldom Seen Sam had sent them on a wild goose chase with his false story that K6ATX had chosen the volcanic pit as the site of their Field Day QTH. Meanwhile the addled old desert rat was probably preening his tobacco-stained mustache down at Furnace Creek Ranch, posing for the TV and wire service cameras, maybe gabbing over the radio at the Park Ranger's office, enjoying his celebrity status.

"JC won't waste too much time looking for us up at Ubehebe," Tommy rationalized. "He knows the club had given me orders to locate this year's Field Day QTH in Death Valley and below sea-level. Ubehebe Crater is not only outside the valley, but even the bottom must be at least a couple of thousand feet above sea-level."

A prodigious yawn from Chub Downey brought K6ATX back to reality. He turned to see his rotund friend lumbering to his feet, blinking groggily, knuckling his eyes and grinning.

"Hi—must of overslept," Chub apologized. "Don't know when I got to sleep. Not until the batteries petered out on my violet ray lamp, I guess. You'd have to be a rock hound to understand."

Tommy laughed. "You didn't exactly sleep in till noon, pal. It's 5:58. Which means we're only two minutes away from KVGS's six o'clock morning newscast. Suppose we read the mail, shall we?"

A few seconds before six o'clock Tommy switched on Sam's old Philco AM receiver. When the tubes warmed up the voice of Las Vegas announcer Barry Clark—a familiar and welcome voice, now—issued from the cobweb-festooned loudspeaker like a friendly greeting:

"...sums up the latest national headlines. Now for regional news: Nothing new about the two missing radio hams from Santa Bonita, missing since noon yesterday, possibly in the vicinity of Ubehebe Crater. In other news, the California Highway Patrol reports that two motorcyclists answering the description of Rusty Hilton and Goldie Lesher, who committed the crossbow murder and robbery at Pharaoh's Palace casino here yesterday, have been seen traversing a seldom-used desert road south of Highway 60 between Blythe and Yuma, apparently headed for the Mexican border, where US Border Patrol roadblocks are being set up at all ports of entry between Mexicali and Nogales. The latest returns from the municipal sewer bond election at Henderson yesterday indicate—"

Tommy switched off the radio and snorted with disgust. "So much for the accuracy of KVGS radio news," he sniffed. "Lesher and Hilton have been seen heading for the Mexican border...phooie! That means they've called off the Death Valley search, probably."

Chub Downey had finished yawning, stretching and scratching himself and had gone over to the iron-barred front window which gave him a view of the street in front of the Gunsight Lode Hotel and the entrance to the escape tunnel leading to Avalanche Gulch.

"Bad news, Tommy!" Chub exclaimed, beckoning for K6ATX

to join him at the window. "Makes me wish that Lesher and Hilton *were* heading for Mexico this morning. It looks like they're fixing to blow something up!"

Heart pounding with alarm, Tommy Rockford leaped to Chub's side and stared out the window. Not fifty feet below, the two Crossbow Killers were lugging some kind of a wooden box over to the tunnel. They vanished inside, then reappeared without the box.

"Why do you say they're fixing to blow up something, Chub?"

"Because that box is full of dynamite sticks!"

Tommy bent a skeptical stare at his young friend, wondering if Chub's over-active imagination was running away with him again.

"How would a city kid like you know what dynamite looks like?"

"Because I was down in the basement of this hotel yesterday, poking around. Mr. Seldom has boxes and boxes marked 'Dynamite' stored down there, Tommy, along with kegs of black powder like the miners used for blasting tunnels in the old days."

The two bearded fugitives crossed the street and entered the hotel lobby. Both men were barefoot this morning. Tommy said, "They couldn't be planning to dynamite that escape tunnel—the only possible way they have to get out of this trap! It doesn't make sense. Even for junkies with burned-out brains."

Chub said gloomily, "Unless they aim to lower themselves into Avalanche Gulch on a rope or something, and blow up the tunnel behind them, to keep anyone from finding us. Tommy, I—I'm scared!"

Tommy hurried over to the door, with its foot-square, heavily-barred opening. Through it they had an oblique view of the lobby below. He was in time to see Goldie Lesher entering the lobby door. The pungent fumes of the marijuana joint dangling from the corner of his mouth reached the boys' nostrils as they watched Lesher disappear down the steps leading to the hotel's cellar.

Cinnamon-bearded Rusty Hilton appeared in the doorway but remained on the threshold, scratching his broad back against the door frame. He called out to his companion below, "This reminds me of the first time we met, on the north bank of the Mekong after our outfit got fragged by the gooks, remember? You said the only skill you'd learned in the army wouldn't help you with any civilian job except safe-cracking. Well, this booby-trap calls for a demolition expert to install—so you didn't waste your time with the on-the-job training you got in 'Nam, after all."

Goldie Lesher came back upstairs, this time carrying a large spool of copper wire and a small box with a plunger on the top which Tommy recognized as a remote-control detonator, probably one Seldom Seen Sam had used to explode dynamite charges when he was working a quartz mining claim back in the hills.

"It don't take a hitch in the army to learn to crimp a fuse to a dynamite cap," groused the yellow-haired addict.

Tommy Rockford could contain himself no longer. Just as Hilton was stepping out onto the porch to let his partner pass through the hotel doorway, the radio ham shouted "Hey, you guys down there—what are you going to do with that dynamite?"

Goldie wheeled about, his hooded, reptilian eyes narrowing as he squinted up at the balcony trying to locate where Tommy was.

"If the pigs close in on us, it'll be sometime today," Goldie shouted back. "We figure they ain't apt to spot that tunnel mouth half-way up the wall of the canyon outside, but if they do—and come through that tunnel after us—Rusty an' me will be watchin' from our pad at the jailhouse and we'll give 'em a welcome they don't expect." Lesher patted the detonator box under his arm. "One jab of this plunger," he said, "just as the pigs with their law badges are comin' out of that tunnel and—BOOM! Party's over."

Tommy relaxed. It was obvious that Lesher and Hilton were ignorant of the erroneous radio newscast which had reported them fleeing toward Mexico at this moment. Gripping the iron bars of the door opening with both hands, K6ATX shouted to Rusty Hilton, the better-educated of the two criminals: "Rusty—have you considered what would happen if you let your buddy blast a whole box of dynamite sticks? You'd not only make the law officers into hamburger, you'd collapse the wall of that tunnel and seal yourselves off from any chance of escape. That's dumb as heck!"

Hilton shouldered past his partner in the doorway and stepped into the dimly-lighted lobby, staring up at the door of the balcony strongroom they had converted into a prison cell.

"Goldie's blast would be a last resort, our ace in the hole," Hilton called up. "First, we're going to let the fuzz know we're holding you and the fat kid as hostages. If they won't negotiate with us—ka—boom! They're vaporized."

Tommy said fearfully, "And if they do agree to give you a head start in return for sparing our lives—where does the dynamite trap fit in as your 'last resort'?"

Hilton shrugged. "If we can't bargain our way out of here with you two kids as hostages, then the dynamite will make certain the fuzz can't come back with reinforcements to starve us out."

Tommy felt that he was arguing with a mentally-retarded baboon. Hilton's plan carried no reason or logic. It was suicidal.

"And if the dynamite ruins your escape tunnel, where will that leave you? Better think about it, Hilton."

Goldie answered with a snag-toothed grin: "Dynamite won't ruin the tunnel, it'll widen it. That tunnel was dug with pick and shovel. Dynamite will just make the entrance wider. But the law pigs won't be there to see it, or use it."

Before Tommy could speak what was on his mind, the canyon reverberated again to the throbbing rumble of a helicopter, this time on a northbound course. The rotor-thumps grew in volume, thundered briefly overhead, and faded away into silence.

"They're closing in, Goldie!" Hilton cried, a note of desperation in his voice. "If they spot the wrecks of our motorcycles down in the gulch, they'll guess we're using this ghost town for a hideout. But I'll lay you odds that old Seldom Seen Sam is sitting up in that whirlybird, guiding the search. He hasn't forgotten how you put an arrow into his pet mule's belly last winter. This would help him even the score."

Goldie said harshly, "I'll hook up the blasting wire. We'll need that boobytrap sooner than I expected, if we hear that chopper settin' down nearby. But we'll be ready for 'em, Rusty."

Goldie vanished through the doorway. Tommy and Chub, hurrying back to peer out the front window, were in time to see Lesher entering the tunnel mouth, while Hilton waited outside. In a short time Lesher reappeared, unreeling his spool of detonating wire behind him as he headed toward the jailhouse. Tommy knew he had attached one end of the wire to a detonating cap affixed to a stick of dynamite in the case of explosives they had left in the tunnel. The other end of the wire would be connected to the remote-control detonating device at the jailhouse.

Tommy shouted down to Hilton, "Listen to me, will you? Maybe you won't cave in that getaway tunnel, but an explosion could jar loose that avalanche rock up above the rim and send boulders the size of boxcars raining down into this canyon to smash what's left of Borrowed Time—including all four of us!"

Hilton grinned sadistically. "You mean two of the four. If the fuzz hasn't shown up by sundown tonight, Goldie and me are splitting. We've already found enough rope to lower us to the bottom of the canyon from the mouth of the tunnel."

Chub Downey, his voice squeaky with terror, cried out, "You wouldn't leave us behind to die of starvation, would you?"

Hilton started walking in the direction of the jailhouse, following the wire Goldie Lesher had laid on the ground.

"Nothing personal, kid," he called back, "but Goldie and me can't afford to leave any witnesses behind. You both have to die."

Tommy Rockford tried to swallow and found he couldn't, not with a tongue that felt as dry as a wad of cotton.

"Hilton, we're dying of thirst up here. In the name of humanity, can you at least bring us up a bucket of water to drink?"

Hilton walked on, ignoring Tommy's desperate plea.

CHAPTER EIGHTEEN

K6ATX'S SECRET GADGET

For the first time since their Death Valley ordeal had begun, Tommy Rockford saw the beginnings of panic glimmering in Chub Downey's eyes, eyes that windowed a soul in torment.

Up to now, Chub had been too mesmerized by his rockhounding discoveries to think about personal danger. But Hilton's parting ultimatum ended that, bringing him face to face with reality.

From the hip pocket of his jeans Chub drew out the purple glass doorknob which Seldom Seen Sam had given him. He lifted it to his cheek, rubbing it against his skin as if it were a crystal ball with supernatural powers, a talisman to turn to in time of trouble.

"Tommy," Chub husked out as he met Tommy's gaze, "Hilton means they're going to kill us no matter what, doesn't he?"

When Tommy hesitated, groping for words of reassurance, Chub went on shakily, "We've been listening to old Sam's radio. Seems if we can listen, couldn't we *talk* out of here too? I've got my CB transmitter—"

Tommy shook his head despairingly.

"If we coupled the CB to the wire antenna on Sam's old radio, I don't think anyone within earshot would be listening on the CB channels. And as for my two-meter ICOM, I'm afraid it's technically impractical, pal. FM radio has many advantages, like squelching atmospheric noise, but it's basically a line-of-sight thing, and no FM signal could penetrate these cliffs. You've tried it. Sam's radio is AM, and he has a topside antenna. *But we're going to get out of this mess,* and you know why? Because we are *smarter* than Lesher and Hilton!"

Chub's lower lip began to quiver. Tommy saw moisture gathering in the corners of his eyes and in that moment he knew his number one priority had to be to shield this tough-luck Los Angeles ghetto kid from the terror building up in him. He had to divert Chub's attention. For starters, he decided on diversionary conversation. Why not Chub's second most favorite topic—baseball?

"Chub, if you could do a live replay of any baseball moment in your past, what moment would you choose to live over again?"

Chub frowned. "I guess it would be to find myself standing on the pitcher's mound at the All-City championship game, score tied in the top of the ninth, two out, two on, the count three and one on the batter. I'd wind up and fire a fast ball and then a scroogie past him—and then it would be my bloop single in the bottom of the inning that would drive in the game-winning run. . . How's that?"

"If I remember right, that's a rerun of what actually happened a month ago—which is why you're wearing the MVP ring, right?"

Tears slid like quicksilver down Chub's apple-red cheeks.

"Don't treat me like a baby, Tommy. I know we're in this jam together. But I know if anybody can outwit those junkies, you can."

Chub turned away, fighting to keep back unmanly tears.

Tommy's roving eye settled on Chub's Little Jim Dandy Mineral Detector leaning against the table where Chub had been using it last night to listen to the clicks in his Geiger counter headphones when he brought the sensor disk close to Seldom Seen Sam's box of radioactive ore samples.

By some fantastic association of ideas, the seeds of an escape plan took root in Tommy Rockford's brain in that moment.

"Chub," K6ATX said, a new note of excitement in his voice, "do you remember, on the way over to Death Valley yesterday, we were arguing about which of us had the most worthwhile hobby, radio hamming or rockhounding, and we wound up in a barefooted tie?"

Chub nodded glumly, his spirits still mired in depression.

"Yeah, and it looks to me like it was *my* hobby that got us into the jam we're in. But how was I to know that those Crossbow Killers were using this ghost town for a hideaway?"

Tommy got to his feet and reached in his hip pocket for the screwdriver kit he always carried in a flat leather pouch. As he did so, another wallet-shaped object fell to the floor. He recognized it as the mildew-mottled, morocco-bound booklet in which Seldom Seen Sam's parents had kept a diary of their lives in Borrowed Time camp, which he had removed from the downstairs safe last night for examination.

At this moment he had no idea how, but he believed that that century-old journal might also fit into the vague, crazy scheme for survival which had popped into his head at the sight of Chub's mineral-hunting device. A plan which might not save their lives, but which might possibly buy them more time than Lesher and Hilton were planning to grant them if their value as hostages ran out—and if radio reports of the police canceling their Death Valley search were true, their hostage value had already expired.

"Chub, bring me your mineral detector," Tommy ordered briskly, opening the snaps of his pocket tool kit and selecting a tiny Phillips screwdriver. "I am about to build a miracle gadget. I will also need a chunk of Sam's uranium ore to make it work."

Chub Downey brought him the Little Jim Dandy and, fishing in a box of rocks on the table, picked one out of the pile.

"Mr. Seldom has labeled this one carnotite," Chub said, "and according to my *Handbook of Western Minerals*, carnotite contains uranium in minute amounts."

Tommy took the fragment of carnotite, which to his uneducated eye appeared to be an ordinary chunk of sandstone such as he'd pick up in a creek bed in Mission Canyon behind Santa Bonita. The faded label attached to the ore specimen by a fine rusty wire was inscribed in faded ink: *CARNOTITE from Routt County Colo. 1957.*

As Chub looked on with a perplexed scowl, Tommy placed the rock on the floor, donned the headset attached to the Little Jim Dandy mineral detector, and switched on the Geiger counter. The crackling noises in his ears sounded like crumpling cellophane, highly amplified. Carnotite was indeed radioactive.

"Whatcha doing, Tommy?" Chub asked curiously, as he saw his friend studying the metal meter box at the upper end of the handle of the mineral detector. It contained the Geiger counter dial, a jack for the earphone plug, and the battery pack which supplied the power to operate the unit.

"Listen," Tommy said, aware that his pulse had speeded up as the vague plan began to take on sharper focus in his mind. "How much uranium ore does old Seldom have? I'm going to have to borrow more than just that hunk of carnotite. I'll explain why I need it after I finish working on my little mystery gadget here."

Chub's beefy shoulders lifted and fell. "He has maybe a dozen chunks. Some is labeled Uraninite, which my Handbook says is the same as pitchblende. Seldom's label says it was from Gilpin County, Colorado. That doesn't jibe with what he said about all his prospecting being done around the Panamint Mountains and Death Valley. All of his radioactive stuff is labeled as coming from Colorado and Utah."

Tommy was carefully unscrewing the baseplate of the mineral detector's control box and battery case. He said, "I have a hunch Seldom Seen Sam swapped some of his Death Valley minerals to some collector from out of state, in exchange for radioactive material from the Rockies. There's no uranium mining around Death Valley."

K6ATX picked up the two-meter hand-held transceiver he had just taken from his backpack and examined it thoughtfully.

He was thinking, *It all depends on how much those two killers know about electronics, whether I can get away with this crazy idea. They are pretty ignorant, probably. But as long as I have a million-to-one chance of fooling them, it's worth trying...*

The compact little IC-2AT two-meter rig had a metal bracket accessory screwed to its back, enabling the user to hook it over his belt for carrying purposes. With some careful bending of the bracket, the steel clip could be spread enough to enable it to be attached firmly to the underside of the battery case of Chub's Little Jim Dandy mineral detector.

Chub Downey seemed to forget his terror as he became absorbed in trying to figure out what strange thing his friend was up to. Finally he could stand it no longer. "*What* are you doing, Tommy?"

"Making a gadget that may get us out of this mess," Tommy responded enigmatically. "I am going to mount my two-meter radio under the battery case of your Little Jim Dandy mineral detector. Then I'm going to inform our Crossbow Killer friends that there is a treasure cache buried somewhere in this ghost town, and that I can locate it with your Little Jim Dandy. Follow me so far?"

"You don't make sense to me," Chub grumbled. "I must be dumb."

"Not as dumb as Hilton and Lesher. The idea is that they will let us go outside to start hunting for that 'treasure.' They won't suspect that the Geiger counter is also carrying a two-way radio!"

Chub scowled dubiously. "All they have to do is look and they'll see it's a two-meter rig attached to my Little Jim Dandy—"

"You know it's a radio, and I know it's a radio, but will those two dope addicts know that?" Tommy asked. "I'll tell 'em it's the power supply for the mineral detector, if they ask, and I'm gambling our lives, Chub, that they won't even notice. I don't think they'll even be curious enough to ask. The bottom line is, if we *combine* our two hobbies, rockhounding and ham radio, maybe we can turn the tables on that Crossbow Killer pair!"

As he was speaking, K6ATX selected a small screwdriver from the miniature tool kit he always carried with him, and opened the case of the handie-talkie. This exposed a mass of transistors, diodes, resistors, micro circuitry and other miniaturized components. They meant absolutely nothing to Chub, but to an electronics major from Cal Tech, who also had been into Amateur Radio in all its phases since boyhood, exploring the innards of both the radio and the mineral detector control box was elementary.

He quickly located and identified the two wires leading to the radio's external phone jack, snipped them with his pocket wirestripper and diagonal pliers, and, uncoiling the pigtails, led the wires through a ventilator hole in the radio set and attached them to the headphone jack inside the Little Jim Dandy.

"Now I'll explain what I've been doing," Tommy said. "I've rewired this equipment so we can accomplish *two* things with your headphones. First, I can tune in your radioactive ore noises with the Little Jim Dandy. Or by changing some switch wiring, I can pick up radio signals from the two-meter band, muting the radio speaker and shunting the signal to the headset. Savvy so far?"

"Nossir," Chub confessed. "It's still all giblets to me."

Chub Downey, like most Citizens' Band hobbyists, knew next to nothing about the technicalities of electronics, and admitted it. His ignorance came as no surprise to Tommy, nor did it reflect on Chub's mental capacities.

"It wouldn't do for Hilton or his pal to catch me working on this little conversion job," Tommy said. "Suppose you go over to the window and warn me if you should see them coming."

As Chub stationed himself obediently by the iron-latticed front window and began his lookout duty, Tommy Rockford began putting his skill as an electronics technician to its supreme test. Their very survival, he was convinced, depended on how well he could combine the functions of their two hobbies, rockhounding and Amateur Radio—or or put another way, geology and electronics—into this makeshift marriage between a mineral detector and a radio transceiver.

When he had finished the initial phase of his secret gadget, the two-meter handie-talkie appeared to be an integral part of the mineral detector. Any rock hound, ham operator or CBer would know better, of course, but Tommy doubted if Hilton or Lesher would know the difference—especially if they had blown their minds with dope.

Chub whispered anxiously from his guard post at the window, "Hey—they're walking back toward the tunnel again, Tommy. And Hilton is carrying what looks like a stereo boom box—"

Alarm stirred in Tommy Rockford as he leaped to the window in time to see Rusty Hilton and Goldie Lesher heading into the escape tunnel. Chub was right—Hilton was carrying a twin-speakered AM-FM stereo radio and casette recorder, the "ghetto blaster" usually carried around city streets, audio blaring at full amplification, as what had become a social status symbol.

"That's bad news, pal," Tommy whispered. "It means they know they can't bring in any radio signals until after sundown, so they're taking it to the mouth of the tunnel where they can stick the whip antenna out into Avalanche Gulch and pick up a Las Vegas broadcast station and tune in the news."

Tommy checked his watch and saw it was nearing nine o'clock.

He switched on Sam's antique radio, reduced the volume to a whisper, and said "I have a hunch Hilton's trying to tune in on the latest news bulletins about the Crossbow Killers—and the search they know must be on for the two of us. No matter how you slice it, this is a bad development. If they learn the police have called off the search for them and shifted the manhunt to the Mexican border, they'll know they don't need us any longer."

As the ancient Philco warmed up they heard John Lockhart's familiar voice from KVGS signing off his Bandbox of Golden Oldies program to once more introduce the studio newscaster, Dan Casmer.

"First, Las Vegas news," Casmer announced briskly. "The search for the Crossbow Killers responsible for the slaying of a security guard at Pharaoh's Palace some thirty-six hours ago has been shifted from the Death Valley area to the Mexican border near Yuma, a trucker having reported to the Border Patrol and CHP that he had seen two motorcyclists matching the descriptions of Rusty Hilton and Goldie Lesher heading south from the desert town of Blythe. They are believed to be carrying in excess of fifty thousand dollars stolen from the local casino."

Tommy Rockford turned pale under his tan. He was almost positive that at this very moment, this radio newscast was being monitored by the two dope-crazed Crossbow Killers on their boom box, out at the far end of the Avalanche Gulch escape tunnel. If so, that ended any need of a bargaining lever involving hostages.

For Chub's benefit, Tommy speculated with a confidence he was far from feeling, "I think the Highway Patrol is putting out a fake news bulletin to trick the Crossbow Killers into thinking that law enforcement people think they've already made it across the border into Sonora. That would make Lesher and Hilton let down their guard, take unnecessary chances, probably stumble right into a police trap."

The Las Vegas newscast resumed before Chub could answer:

"...once again we switch you to our mobile unit at Furnace Creek ranger station in Death Valley for the latest word on another manhunt going on in that area, a rescue mission. Come in, Gary Clark in Death Valley."

Tommy and Chub stared at each other with mounting concern as the voice of KVGS's roving field reporter issued from Seldom Seen Sam's loudspeaker:

"Thank you, Dan Casmer in Las Vegas...We have here in the KVGS mobile van Mr. J. C. Ellison, uncle of the missing Tommy Rockford of Santa Bonita, and also our old prospector friend Seldom Seen Sam Sutkliffe, the desert celebrity who has become a legend in his own time. Mr. Ellison, what is the latest progress report on your search for the two lost radio hams?"

Uncle JC's voice has a sore-throat raspiness which told Tommy that JC hadn't slept since coming down off Telescope Peak following the cloudburst yesterday: "I'm afraid I have no progress to report, Mr. Clark. Our overnight journey to Ubehebe Crater area where Mr. Sam sent us proved fruitless. We have also searched the area from a CHP helicopter without results. The fact that Mr. Sam saw Tommy and his young friend Chub Downey of Los Angeles, driving their van north across the Death Valley salt flats at about the time the rainstorm broke on the Panamints, relieves our minds that at least the boys weren't victims of the flash floods which tumbled down the mountainside yesterday, as we had first feared."

"Then what do you think may have happened to them?" the radio announcer asked. "This is big sky country, for sure, but two boys in a van shouldn't be able to hide from helicopter surveillance for very long—even if they had any reason to hide. Supposing we ask Mr. Seldom Seen Sam for his opinion?"

The old prospector spoke up eagerly: "I'll tell you what I think happened to them two young wallopers, yessir! I think they stumbled into them two Crossbow Killers on the road, and them toughs murdered 'em and buried 'em in a shaller grave somewhere on the road toward Ubehebe, or maybe in the Sand Dunes where grave diggin' is easy—"

"But why should they want to add two more murders to their list, Mr. Sutkliffe? Do you think they are psychopathic killers who just kill for the fun of it?"

"Why would they kill the two kids?" the old desert rat repeated. "To steal their van, that's why! The police are lookin' for two guys on motorsickles. They could put their sickles in the van and get through roadblocks farther down the road."

Announcer Clark said gravely, "That certainly puts a new and ominous complexion on the case, Mr. Sutkliffe. Thank you for appearing on our show. And Mr. Ellison, we also thank you, and hope on our next broadcast we have happier news about your nephew and his friend. Now we return you to our central studios—"

Tommy Rockford again switched off the antique Philco to conserve the precious batteries. Chub was saying something about Seldom Seen Sam being a wicked man to tell such lies about them and send folks looking for their graves in the sand dunes miles to the north, just because he wanted to keep searchers from snooping around Avalanche Gulch and maybe stumbling onto the secret of Borrowed Time.

Numb with despair, Tommy removed the toe plate from the mineral detector and then, crushing the chunk of uranium-bearing carnotite under his heel, poured the fragments inside the Geiger counter device and replaced the toe plate. This time when he switched on the headphones he was rewarded with a loud clicking sound as the mineral detector picked up the carnotite ore concealed inside its own detector mechanism.

Chub returned to the window to resume his lookout duty. After an interval he said wistfully, "You know, Tommy, if you and I don't get out of this mess alive, there's one thing I'll regret most."

"What's that, Chub?"

"There's a mystery here in Death Valley that I would give an arm and a leg to solve. If those crooks kill us, I'll never know the answer. I don't know if I can stand it."

Tommy, unable to figure out Chub's fatalistic mood, his calm acceptance of death, asked curiously, "What is this big mystery?"

An impish light burned in Chub's eyes as he replied, "You remember when that radio reporter was interviewing Seldom Seen Sam and he was talking about Death Valley Scotty, the guy who built Scotty's Castle?"

"Actually, old Scotty was a stone-broke phoney, Chub. The Castle was built by a millionaire insurance man from Chicago who had hired Scotty as a guide. Anyway, what are you getting at?"

"Remember he was telling about how Scotty found a baby rattlesnake in his boot and mistook it for a loose shoestring? Well, the mystery is, what did Scotty do next? I don't want to die without knowing! In fact I dreamed about that baby snake all night."

Tommy Rockford threw back his head and roared with laughter. He realized that Chub had been pulling his leg all along, in an effort to boost Tommy's morale. He said, "Chub, you are the most! For a moment there I thought you had cracked under the—"

Chub waved him into silence. Peering out the window, he called back over his shoulder, "They're coming back out of the tunnel, grinning like their throats are cut. They heard the same news we did—which means they know they don't need us as hostages—"

CHAPTER NINETEEN

A JUG OF COLD WATER

Tommy strode over to the window to join Chub. He was in time to see Rusty Hilton striding toward the hotel entrance below. Goldie Lesher, carrying the "boom box" portable stereo, was heading back toward their living quarters in the ghost town jail. Both men seemed to be in unusually boisterous spirits.

Hilton entered the hotel lobby and came up the stairs, his motorcycle boots pounding the tin-carpeted treads. Reaching the doorway of their prison, Hilton peered in at the two boys through the barred opening, his lips spread in a jubilant smile.

"I've got some hot news for you, fellers!" the outlaw announced triumphantly. "State police have called off the hunt for me and Goldie. They think we're heading for the Mexican border, probably already crossed over into Sonora. No pun intended, but that means the heat is off here in Death Valley!"

Tommy said hopefully, "Then you can disconnect that dynamite booby-trap before your spaced-out partner accidentally triggers that detonator and blows all of us off the map."

Hilton ran a grubby palm over his sweat-beaded scalp.

"Might be a good idea, at that. Goldie can get uncontrollable when he's high on angel dust. He is capable of doing anything. That's why I always chain him to his bunk at night—for fear he might get the notion I'm a seven-headed rattlesnake and do me in when I might be stoned out of it myself."

Chub, to Tommy Rockford's dismay, chose this moment to bring up a subject which Tommy had wanted to keep furthermost from Hilton's mind: "Now that the cops aren't looking for you, what are you going to do with us, Mister Hilton? Turn us loose? We're getting powerful thirsty."

Hilton peered at his prisoners through the barred opening for a long moment, his brow furrowing thoughtfully.

"I came up here to offer you two guys a proposition—because I admire your guts. Neither one of you have caved in and started blubbering for mercy since we first took you hostage."

Tommy walked over to confront their captor at close range.

"What kind of proposition could you offer us? You hold all the cards in the deck."

Hilton grinned. "What would you give right now for a gallon jug of fresh, cold mountain spring water from Sam's well?"

Tommy felt himself salivating at the very mention of water.

"What do we have to offer that would be worth a gallon of water? Which you know darned well would be worth more than a gallon jug filled with diamonds."

A sly look entered Hilton's squinty eyes.

"I'll fetch you a gallon jug of fresh water, right now, in return for some information."

"What information?" K6ATX countered suspiciously.

"Look, Tommy. I'll level with you. You know that Goldie and me have lost our wheels. And this ain't the time of year or the kind of country to travel on foot. We can't hole up here another day. Not that we don't have plenty of grub, grub enough to last us a month, stashed away in the jailhouse. But—there's another reason why we can't risk staying around any longer. But we have to have transportation. Highjacking a car out on the highway is out of the question—summertime traffic in Death Valley is practically zilch."

"I get it," Tommy said. "Your drug supply's running out."

Hilton nodded bleakly. "Goldie's smoking his last PCP Sherm right now. When that high wears off he'll be in bad shape. Our nearest supplier is in San Bernardino. I have a few lines of coke left, but when that's gone I'll be climbing the wall myself."

"So what is your proposition?"

Hilton gripped the iron bars of the door opening, squeezing the knuckles white, a mounting desperation showing in his eyes.

"Let's reason this out together, Tommy. You and the fat kid here came to Death Valley in a Volkswagen van, according to the radio. We also know your van hasn't been located by the people out searching for you, which means you hid it. I want to know where. There are lots of places, but I can't waste time looking for them. Off-hand, I'd say you parked it in front of Sam's old shack on the north rim of the Gulch, except that's out in the open. So that means you hid it in some nearby gully. But which one?"

Tommy and Chub exchanged glances. Hilton was obviously not familiar enough with Seldom Seen Sam's abandoned shack to remember it had a lean-to stable under the tamarisk tree where Tommy had left the van, making it invisible from the air.

"When are you coming to the point, Hilton?" Tommy wanted to know. "Quit playing cat-and-mouse with us."

"Okay, here's the deal. I'll fetch you a nice jug of cold water if you tell me where you hid the van, and turn over the ignition key. Don't make Goldie and me force you to strip so we can locate the key in your clothes, which we could easily do. The two of us would leave tonight, park the van in Barstow down in the Mojave Desert, and hop a freight train to San Berdoo."

"Why should you need a key to start the VW? I imagine you have hot-wired a few cars you've stolen in your time."

"We wouldn't want to be stopped at a routine road block for questioning and the cops find out we'd jumped the terminals on our ignition. That would land us in the slammer on suspicion of grand theft auto. That's a risk we can't take."

Jabbing Chub with his elbow to emphasize that he wanted his rock hound pal to stay completely out of the conversation, K6ATX said, "I don't have the key on me, Hilton. But I'll accept your deal. Bring us the jug of water. When Chub and I have had a good swig, I'll tell you where the van is parked. You'll find the key in the ignition."

Hilton's mouth lost its stern fixture. He formed a ring with his thumb and forefinger in the A-OK sign and said "One jug of water coming right up. I know you've got too much sense to try and double-cross me, Tommy, or play games with me."

After the Satan's Angel had made his way back downstairs and out of the lobby, Chub said accusatively, "Why did you blow it like that, Tommy? You could have said somebody else drove us in and dropped us off—"

Tommy, for some reason Chub could not fathom, was actually

grinning. He walked over to the table where Chub had been playing with the rock samples last night, cleared off a space, and again took Rudy and Roxanna Sutkliffe's old Borrowed Time diary out of his hip pocket.

"Don't interrupt me now," he admonished Chub. "I've got work to do before Hilton gets back with that jug."

From a tin can nailed to the wall, Tommy took a stub of indelible pencil, deciding against using his own modern ball-point pen for what he planned to write in the old diary.

Wetting the pencil point on his tongue, Tommy began printing something in crude capital letters on a blank blue-ruled page of the diary, his brows drawn together in a knot of concentration.

The creaking noise of an unoiled windlass being cranked, in the area between the hotel and the tumbledown assay office, told both boys that Hilton was hoisting a water bucket out of the well.

Tommy continued his mysterious writing job in the yellowed pages of the Sutkliffes' personal journal. He did not look up as he said, "Chub, you were telling me on the way over from LA what your old grandmother said were the two most powerful forces of mankind, just before she signed you over as a ward of the state. Remember?"

The young baseball prodigy nodded somberly. "I'll never forget! Grammy said the two greatest forces in the universe are love and greed. God is love, but the Devil is greed, and she said too many folks chose to eat out of the Devil's garbage can of greed when they could be feasting with the Lord at his banquet table of love." Chub's lips spread in a grin of recollection. "I remember when I was a kid, dreaming of becoming a big baseball star like Babe Ruth or Steve Garvey or Pete Rose, Grammy used to quiz me about what the two greatest powers on earth were, meaning love and greed. And just to aggravate her, I'd answer, 'A sinking fastball and a change-of-pace pitch.' She would paddle me for being what she said was sacrilegious."

The grin changed to a scowl. "But what has my old Grammy's Sunday School stories got to do with that guy bringing us a jug of cold water, Tommy?"

K6ATX, having apparently finished whatever he was scribbling in the old diary, re-read it carefully and then thrust the book back into his hip pocket as he swung around to face Chub again.

"Greed," he said, "is what motivates the devil's disciples on this earth—and wouldn't you say that Rusty Hilton and Goldie Lesher qualify as devil's disciples?"

Chub shrugged, not quite comprehending. "According to their leather jackets they are Satan's Angels, yes."

"What I am trying to say, Chub, is that both men have to support expensive drug habits—maybe hundreds of dollars a day. That was why they held up the casino in Las Vegas. The fifty thousand they got after killing the guard won't last them very long, assuming they are able to reach a drug pusher. Well, I figure I can make Hilton's greed work against him, and hopefully save our necks at the same time. We sure haven't anything to lose by trying. That's where my little Geiger counter-radio transmitter combo enters the picture. And the thing that will prime the pump is an old diary of Sam's parents that I found last night in the safe."

Totally mystified by Tommy's words, Chub did not have time to frame a question when they heard Hilton's booted feet coming up the stairs and along the balcony to the door of their prison. Tommy whispered sharply, "No matter what you hear me say to Hilton, don't butt in and say anything, understand? Just keep quiet. Your blabbing tongue could ruin everything I've got planned."

Chub was round-eyed with confusion as he whispered back, "Tommy, compared to me a corpse at a wake is a chatterbox."

Hilton's shaggy-bearded face reappeared at the barred opening in the door. They saw him stoop to set down the plastic jug of water he had drawn from the well, and heard his ring of keys jingle as he fitted one into the big padlock outside.

"Both of you go over and sit on the cot," Hilton ordered. "I know you're both desperate enough to jump me and I don't blame you. But I've got to open this door in order to set the water jug inside. I didn't drop any rat poison in it, if you're wondering."

As soon as Tommy and his chubby friend had obeyed orders and withdrawn to old Sam's cot across the room, Hilton unlocked the door and set the water jug on the floor. Raising his left foot, he rested the heel of his boot on the top of the jug.

"One nudge of my foot and the only water you'll get is what you can lick off the floor boards—and get your tongues full of splinters," Hilton said. "You get a drink when I get the van key."

Tommy felt his parched lips and tongue go cotton-dry merely at the sight of cold water less than a dozen feet away.

"Hilton, on my word of honor, I don't have the key here with me. I left it in the ignition in the van."

"So where is the van hidden?"

"It's parked in the shed under the tamarisk tree at Seldom Seen Sam's shack, which is why it wasn't spotted from the air. And we gassed up coming through Furnace Creek Ranch yesterday. You can cover three hundred miles on a full tank, meaning you won't have to risk stopping at any service station between here and Barstow."

Hilton seemed to be pondering the validity of Rockford's answer, his blood-shot eyes smouldering with distrust.

Finally he said, "Okay, I'll believe you—for the time being. When it gets dark Goldie and I will lower ourselves into Avalanche Gulch with some old rope we found in the jail closet. It's only half a mile over to Sam's shack, so if the van isn't there like you say, it won't take me long to get back here and make you sorry you lied to me. If you did, now's your last chance to correct it."

Tommy said desperately, "I promise you, the van will be there at Sam's cabin—unless somebody has discovered it already and driven it off. According to the radio news, that hasn't happened."

Noting the surprise on Hilton's face, Tommy gestured toward the elderly Philco receiver on the wall shelf. "We've been listening to the same news broadcasts from Las Vegas that you have. That's why we know you and Lesher could make your getaway in our van, because the police think you escaped into Mexico on your motorcycles and have called off their surveillance up here. Just the same I would advise you to keep off the main roads, hide by day and travel by night. Because there's still an All Points Bulletin in every CHP car, identifying that van as carrying signs advertising it as Santa Bonita Radio Club property."

Hilton eyed Tommy Rockford with growing uneasiness.

"Why should *you* be giving *us* advice on how to escape? You know Goldie and me don't intend to leave either one of you alive to tell tales out of school later on. We've already got murder raps hung on us, so two more won't make any difference. The only reason we didn't cut you down yesterday was because we thought you might be valuable as hostages. That isn't true now."

Hilton's words brought Chub Downey close to collapsing. But incredibly, Tommy Rockford was facing down the outlaw with a growing smile which seemed to exude supreme confidence.

"What I'm about to say may be hard for you to understand,

Hilton, but you and Goldie aren't going to kill either one of us! And do you know why? *Because I can pay you to not only let us survive, but send us on our way unharmed!*''

Hilton looked startled. After a long moment, he inquired in a skeptical growl, ''Are you crazy with the heat? What's your deal?''

The young radio ham played his trump: ''I can pay you more than half a million dollars in silver bullion, ten times what you got for killing that man in Las Vegas. Right here in this canyon. I can take you to that silver and let you see it with your own eyes!''

CHAPTER TWENTY

$500,000 IN SILVER

Hilton started a sarcastic laugh, then snapped his jaw shut. Greed—one of man's baser instincts—kindled in the beady depths of his eyes. Greed left no room for suspicion or ridicule.

"Who are you trying to kid, Tommy?" Hilton jeered. "According to the radio, your family ain't wealthy. Your old man runs a travel agency in Santa Bonita and he's only offering five thou reward for information leading to your return, dead or alive."

Tommy decided the moment was ripe to bait his trap. He started to reach in his hip pocket to pull out the Sutkliffe diary—the essential central prop in his play-acting plan—but froze when he saw Hilton's right hand blur to his side and whip out the Magnum pistol from its holster. The muzzle swung like a snake's head from left to right, right to left, covering both boys, as K6ATX belatedly explained what he was about to do.

"I wasn't reaching for a weapon, Hilton, I was reaching for a book I found last night in the hotel safe. It contains information that will verify what I said about that $500,000 silver cache."

Hilton holstered his pistol, embarrassed at having betrayed the extent of his own nervous tension.

"Go ahead and drag out your book," he said. "If you'd had a gun you would have used it before now. The skin-tight jeans you young fellers are wearin' now, you couldn't hide a razor blade."

Tommy Rockford drew the morocco-bound volume from his pocket and riffled the brittle leaves with the ball of his thumb, making sure he had gained Rusty Hilton's complete attention.

"This old book was the day-to-day diary that Seldom Seen Sam's dad and mother kept more than a hundred years ago, when this camp was booming, and after. They owned this hotel. On page 23 it tells how an avalanche cut off the road leading into this canyon from Death Valley, and destroyed half the camp under millions of tons of rock. It also tells how the trapped survivors were able to dig that tunnel out to Avalanche Gulch and escape. But the Sutkliffes came back later. In fact, Seldom Seen Sam was born right here in this hotel, maybe in this very room. His mother died of complications of childbirth that same day. This diary also tells how Sam buried his father out there in the Borrowed Time graveyard. This diary has been collecting dust in the hotel safe downstairs ever since. I'd say it has great value to California historians."

"So," Hilton grunted, "what has all this got to do with a half a million bucks worth of silver? And where do I fit in?"

"Have you ever wondered why old Sam was so paranoid about anyone finding out about Borrowed Time's existence?" Tommy asked. "The answer isn't entirely in the fact that Sam's brain has deteriorated to an extent that he could probably be declared legally incompetent. There was a motive behind his secrecy."

Tommy handed the leather-bound diary over to Hilton, who accepted it as gingerly as if it had been a live scorpion.

"Look on page 43, Hilton. Toward the middle of the book. You will find an entry written by Sam's father which tells you why Sam has such a phobia against letting anyone know about this town."

Hilton leafed through the book to page 43. His lips mumbled the words aloud as he worked his way through the scribbling in indelible pencil, so dim as to be almost illegible, in crudely-printed capital letters. The date was a century old:

> THE SILVER INGOTS STORED IN THE WELLS-FARGO OFFICE ARE APPRAISED AT NEAR $500,000 MARKET VALUE. THEY REPRESENT GUNSIGHT LODE PRODUCTION FOR FINAL THREE MONTHS OF THE CAMP'S LIFE. TODAY I MOVED THE SILVER TO WHERE NOBODY CAN FIND IT IN CASE SOME TOUGH HOMBRES COME BACK TO PICK UP THE SILVER THEY KNOW WAS LEFT IN THE EXPRESS OFFICE AT THE TIME OF THE AVALANCHE. I WON'T TELL SAM WHERE I BERRIED IT TILL HE TURNS 21, IT WILL BE THE ONLY LEGACY I'LL LEAVE OUR SON I RECKON BUT IT WILL KEEP HIM IN COMFORT FOR LIFE. HIS MAW

WOULD HAVE LIKED THAT BLESS HER SOUL.

—RUDOLPH M. SUTKLIFFE

Tommy Rockford's voice broke through Rusty Hilton's gathering excitement as the Satan's Angel finished reading the faded entry in the journal and handed the book back:

"Now you can understand why Seldom Seen Sam didn't want anybody snooping around this ghost town of his! He is the only person living who knows that half a million dollars' worth of raw silver lies buried somewhere between these canyon walls. The irony of the whole thing is that Sam himself doesn't have any idea where that silver is. He probably spent years hunting for it before he gave up and turned into a single-blanket jackass prospector."

Hilton growled skeptically, "But the diary said that the old man would tell Sam where the cache was, when he turned twenty-one."

Tommy replied, "Compare the date of that entry in the diary with the date of Rudy Sutkliffe's death on his grave marker. You'll find that Sam was only eighteen when Rudy died, too young to share the secret. His father took his secret with him to the grave."

A vein ticked wildly on Hilton's temple. Then the enthusiasm faded in his eyes. "The silver's probably buried under all that avalanche rock. It might take a thousand years working with a thousand bulldozers to locate it."

"No, Hilton. The diary makes it clear that the avalanche was the cause of the camp being abandoned, leaving the heavy silver bars stored in the Express office. It follows that Rudy Sutkliffe buried the silver later, at some place accessible to us today."

Hilton's expression changed to one of rekindled interest.

"You have stumbled onto the cache, is that it? You said you could lead me to it, in return for us letting you go."

The time had come for Tommy to play his ace. The most skeptical person in the room at the moment was Chub Downey, who knew his pal was playing a dangerous game of make-believe.

"I didn't say I knew exactly where the silver is buried," K6ATX said, "but I do have a scientific instrument that can locate that cache for you, Hilton. If you have any loose change in your pocket, put it on the floor and I'll give you a demonstration."

The outlaw's hand shook as he pawed in a pocket of his Levis and drew out a handful of loose change, which he spilled on the floor at Tommy's feet. "Okay, hot shot—show me."

While Chub Downey looked on with total skepticism, Tommy Rockford carried the Little Jim Dandy mineral detector over to where Hilton stood staring down at the scattered pile of dimes and quarters. He allowed K6ATX to clamp the Geiger counter headphones over his ears. Tommy said, "I am assuming that you know how these machines work—"

Hilton shook his head. "I've seen foot patrols in Vietnam hunting for frag mines with one of these gadgets, but I don't have the foggiest notion how they work. Except they start buzzing when they get near buried iron. Could be a land mine—or a bottle cap."

"Okay," Tommy said, "instead of anti-personnel mines, we're looking for silver, a large mass of it. Just listen to what happens when I pass the detector over even a small pile of silver coins—"

Chub stared with mouth agape as he saw Tommy Rockford wave the pie-plate-shaped detector unit over the wooden floor. Chub was only vaguely aware that Tommy had "salted" the detector with crushed radioactive carnotite, and that he had wired a control switch so the crackling noise of the Geiger counter reacting to the carnotite could be fed into Hilton's earphones or shut off at will.

Using the Little Jim Dandy as he might a vacuum cleaner, Tommy kept the headphones switched off as the detector moved along above the warped floor boards. But when the metal detector neared the scattered silver coins, the pressure of his thumb on a toggle switch made the headphones come alive with a crackling noise that deafened Hilton's ears. Then, moving the detector's sensor disk away from the coins, Tommy switched the headset into silence.

"Now you see how it works," Tommy said. "This super-sensitive machine could locate that $500,000 cache if it came within a hundred feet of the spot where Rudy Sutkliffe buried it. If Seldom Seen Sam had had the advantage of such a simple high-tech machine as this he could have located his father's buried silver long ago."

Rusty Hilton removed the headphones from his ears.

"So far, you've sold me," he conceded. "What's your angle?"

Eyes flashing with triumph, K6ATX said, "Give me the freedom to explore this canyon with this metal detector, and I'll have pinpointed the location of Sutkliffe's buried silver by sundown. It will probably be buried a few feet under the surface, of course, but there are plenty of tools around to dig it up with. In case I haven't located the spot today, I guarantee the job will be done by tomorrow. Since the police have called off their Death Valley search, your staying here another day or two presents no problem. Especially where a fortune in pure silver ingots is involved."

"I suppose you'd want a fifty-fifty split of the silver?"

Tommy could see the guile flickering in the depths of Hilton's reptilian eyes. He could almost hear what Hilton was saying to himself: Once the silver is in my hands, there's no reason why I would have to pay Tommy a red nickel. Just finish him and the fat kid off with a couple of crossbow arrows, and be on our way...

"You keep one hundred percent of the silver, you and Goldie," Tommy answered. "Plus my VW van to make your getaway in. All I ask in return is a chance for Chub and me to be free to walk over to Furnace Creek Ranch and start forgetting this whole nightmare."

Rusty Hilton appeared to be picking Tommy's proposition apart in his mind, searching for hidden traps. Finally he reached a decision.

"Okay, you've got a deal. What could I lose? You and the kid can ride out with Goldie and me in your van tonight. We'll let you out somewhere along the highway to Shoshone where you can hitch a ride back to Furnace Creek Ranch before the heat sets in. Of course, that's if and providing we make actual eyeball contact with your buried silver bricks. I want proof that somebody else hasn't stumbled across it in all these years since the stuff was buried. Fair enough?"

Tommy frowned dubiously. "You said we would leave tonight? I might need to hunt an extra day—"

Hilton shook his head. "It's Goldie I'm worried about. If he doesn't get a fix soon he'll turn into a raving maniac. And the nearest pusher, like I told you, is in San Bernardino. Goldie's supply of PCP comes first. I can give you till sundown to locate that buried silver, but no longer. That's my final offer."

Tommy pretended reluctant acceptance of Hilton's deadline.

"You've made yourself a beautiful deal, Hilton. Silver bars are easier to fence than, say, silver coins. Your fence won't ask any questions. The cache will be like owning your own bank. Anytime you need money, you can come back here and dig up another silver bar."

Hilton handed the headphones back to Tommy and moved over to the doorway.

"I'll go brief Goldie on the deal," he said, backing out the doorway and closing it. "It'll take something pretty powerful to persuade him not to get started for San Berdoo in daylight. Then I'll be back and you can start work with your gadget."

The two boys heard the metallic snap of the huge padlock being closed over its hasp, followed by the clumping of Hilton's boots heading down the lobby stairs and out the front door. Then, breaking what had amounted to some kind of paralysis, both pounced on the gallon jug of water at the same moment.

They took turns gulping the life-restoring liquid down parched gullets. In the end, Tommy had to forcibly restrain Chub from over-drinking, a mistake which could have caused serious results in his dehydrated condition.

"Tommy," Chub panted when their drinking orgy was over, "I can understand that you bought us the rest of this day of life. But what's with all this buried silver business? You know my Little Jim Dandy won't pick up non-ferrous metals like silver. Maybe you're an expert radio ham, but you don't know from nothin' what my little dime-store Geiger counter can do."

"Chub, I assumed you'd caught on by now that there *isn't* any silver cache! I made that up, as a way to fool Hilton."

"But the Sutkliffe diary—the words Hilton read—"

"That's what I was writing in the diary just before Hilton came up here. I had a pretty good idea that greed would make him believe my far-fetched story about buried silver ingots. He did!"

"Well," Chub protested, "I still don't get the drift of it."

Tommy felt his tension unwinding for the first time in hours.

"You haven't caught on to my scheme yet, Chub? That makes you almost as dumb as Hilton. I wired my two-meter transceiver into the circuitry of your metal detector, right? Well, all I was trying to get Hilton to do was let me out of this hotel so that I can use that radio to send out an SOS and bring someone to rescue us!"

Chub Downey shook his head dolefully. "Stop fooling yourself, Tommy. You know that radio waves can't get out of this rocky hole."

K6ATX's voice held a note of triumph as he said, "You're mistaken, Chub. There is one place in Borrowed Time canyon where a radio signal can reach the outside! That's the open field between the jailhouse and the cemetery, which is wide open to the sky. If I can reach that open area with my two-meter rig, I will have a line-of-sight shot at Uncle JC's base camp on Telescope Peak!"

Chub Downey scratched his scalp confusedly. "But what good—"

Tommy smiled patiently. "Don't you understand, Chub? JC left Noisy Noyce and some other radio operators up there to man our Field Day two-meter communications. If I can put out a distress call they should be able to copy it—and send a Sheriff's helicopter to rescue us! My job would be to stall for time—'treasure-hunting' with my secret gadget until the chopper got here! I could do it!"

CHAPTER TWENTY ONE

A SMELL OF SMOKE

Before Chub could react to Tommy's sensational words a sound of voices raised in bitter argument and a thud of boots entering the lobby warned them that their captors, one of them dope-crazed, were on their way upstairs.

Tommy and Chub were seated on Sam's cot when Rusty Hilton unlocked the door of their prison room and stepped inside, followed by Goldie Lesher. The latter was obviously in wretched physical shape, both hands wracked by uncontrollable tremors, his face ashen, his bloodshot eyes peering like a rabid animal's from behind a screen of tousled hair. Goldie staggered when he walked and would have fallen had not Hilton seized an elbow to steady him.

"Goldie is facing a withdrawal problem," Hilton explained, "so he wants us to get out of here right now, take your van, and be on our way to find his PCP supplier in San Berdoo. I've convinced him that the fifty thou we got in the Las Vegas caper won't last us very long and that we should gamble on you finding where the old man stashed those silver bars."

"A chance to make a half-million-dollar haul, free and clear of any objections from the law, at no risk to your own necks, is what I would call an opportunity that won't come again," Tommy said. "You wouldn't be hitting the road until after dark anyway."

Goldie struck a match to light a brown Sherman cigarette which Tommy knew was laced with angel dust. Inhaling deeply, he snarled "How long's thish shilver hunt goin' take? Thish ish the lasht fix I got. After thish blitz wearsh off I might blow a fuse."

Tommy said, "I'll work as fast as I can, but remember, I may have to cover every square foot of the canyon floor with my detector before I locate the cache. That'll take time."

Lesher wiped his mouth with the back of his hand, malignant pungent-smelling smoke forking from his nostrils.

"Aw' right. Le'sh get at it. But I'm shtayin' here at the hotel while you two do the huntin'. It's hot as the hinges of Hades out there, enough to fry your brainsh, an' it ain't even noon yet."

Heart pounding with excitement, Tommy picked up Chub Downey's Little Jim Dandy mineral detector, with its two-meter radio riding piggy-back disguised as a battery container. As Chub started to follow the two Crossbow Killers out into the hall, Goldie seized the teenager by the shoulder and shoved him backward with such force that Chub sprawled on his back alongside the cot.

"You're shtayin' here, Lard Tub!" Lesher snarled.

Seeing the fear and despair in his companion's eyes as Chub struggled to his feet, Tommy said reassuringly, "Wait here where it's relatively cool, Chub. As soon as they have their hands on the silver cache they'll turn us both loose. I trust Rusty here to keep his side of the bargain."

Rusty Hilton closed and locked the heavy door on Chub's prison. Then he gestured for Tommy to lead the way downstairs while he dropped behind to lend a supporting arm to Lesher.

Walking through the lobby door onto the porch was like opening a hot oven. The pent-up heat of dozens of yesterdays had no chance to escape the rock-ribbed canyon, and today's sun was punishing Death Valley as if trying to uphold this desert area's reputation for being the hottest spot in the fifty states.

Rusty assisted Goldie Lesher into one of the porch rocking chairs and then walked down the steps to where Tommy Rockford had begun his treasure-hunting charade by putting on the headphones. At the moment Tommy was conserving battery power; he would get no radio reception until he reached the vacant field under open sky.

Pretending that his mineral locator was turned on, Tommy began sweeping the pan-shaped sensor back and forth, right and left, while he moved slowly in the direction of the cemetery. Rusty Hilton, bald head shining under the sunlight reflected off the north cliff, shuffled along beside K6ATX, sweat beads beginning to run down the red creases on his hairy neck.

"First off, we'll see if Sutkliffe dumped the silver bars into the town well," Tommy suggested. "Ideal hiding place, with the standing water adding protection against discovery by outsiders."

"Sounds logical," Hilton agreed, mopping his flushed face with a grimy bandanna handkerchief. "I hope we locate it quick, though. I don't handle this kind of heat too well."

From his rocker on the porch, Goldie Lesher watched Hilton and their prisoner vanish around the corner of the hotel, heading for the cemented rock coaming of the Borrowed Time well, the only source of water for drinking and cooking the camp afforded.

Peering down into the well, Tommy could see his silhouetted reflection on the water some twenty-odd feet below. He had invented such a logical story of Rudy Sutkliffe hiding the silver bars left behind in the Express office that he almost believed it himself.

"Hear anything?" Hilton asked expectantly, as he saw Tommy waving the metal detector over the open well.

Tommy shook his head. "Just some static caused by the iron in the windlass," he reported. "This locator is directional, sensitive in a cone-shaped beam something like a flashlight would cast down into that well. If the silver was under that water, you could hear these headphones whistling clear over there."

Clearly disappointed, Hilton gave a final glance down into the well, its walls hewn out of native bedrock. "This was probably a mine shaft," the outlaw speculated, "only they hit a vein of water and had no choice but turn it into a well."

Tommy agreed. "Finding water was actually better than striking an ore body of high-grade silver. I imagine when they first located the Gunsight Lode they were probably having to haul their drinking and cooking water by muleback from Bennett's Wells or maybe even Furnace Creek."

Carrying on the treasure-hunting masquerade, Tommy worked his way past the well coaming, waving the Little Jim Dandy back and forth as if it were a broom, a few inches above the flinty earth.

He could hear the ragged sound of Rusty Hilton's labored breathing, sucking air in and out of his lungs as if it was being filtered through a wet towel. With any luck at all, the intolerable heat would make Hilton stop bird-dogging his heels after awhile. Tommy's whole scheme depended on at least getting out of earshot of his captor, long enough to put his two-meter rig into operation.

With deliberate slowness, K6ATX worked his way past the

weathered false front of Honest Jas. Garrett's Assay Office & Miner's Tool & Supply Depot. Next to it was the tarpaper-roofed shack identified as Dell's Tonsorial Parlor. Beyond that was the Wells-Fargo Express agent's office, the next to the last building which was shielded from the direct sunlight by the overhanging cliffs which hid the ghost town from being spotted by the pilots of aircraft overflying the area, even at treetop altitude.

Fifty feet beyond the express office, past the horse troughs and hitching rails, stood the stone jailhouse which the two Crossbow Killers had appropriated for their hideaway. There the shade ended and the open sky began, and through that opening in the foot of Telescope Peak the sun's heat poured with all the fury of a devil's cauldron, making the entire scene shimmer in the reflected heat waves as if viewed through a sheet of rippled window glass.

"My second guess as a spot where Sutkliffe might have buried his cache would be the stock corral on the far side of the jail," Tommy commented, mopping his own flushed cheeks with the long sleeve of his baseball jersey. He dared not remove the garment, knowing the sun's rays would soon blister his flesh. Meanwhile the heat was sucking the juices from his body at a rate which would soon leave him as dehydrated as a corn husk. But he would have to endure that punishment long enough to outlast his captor...

Hilton, already gasping like a fish out of water, said "I'd lay odds you'll find it in the cemetery. Maybe buried in Sutkliffe's own grave, which he probably hacked out of the bedrock years before old Seldom Seen Sam had to bury his carcass."

Tommy replied, "Well, I will have worked my way down to the graveyard within a couple of hours, and we'll find out."

The prospect of stepping out of the shade of the canyon wall beyond the jail was more than Hilton could contemplate.

"Look, Tommy," he said hoarsely. "It's fairly cool inside the slammer there, thanks to the thick stone walls. You don't need my help to work that gadget, do you?"

Tommy Rockford's heart leaped with anticipation. Another fifty yards and he would be out in the center of the open area at the western end of Borrowed Time's canyon, with a view of the blue dome of the sky and, a life-or-death matter to him now, an unobstructed view up the canyon-gashed flank of Telescope Peak itself.

"Go ahead and enjoy whatever comfort the jail offers you,

Hilton,'' Tommy said magnanimously. ''You know darn well I'm not going anywhere, but if you think I've got any tricks up my sleeve, you can always watch me through the jail windows. . . and reach me with your crossbow.''

Hilton lurched ahead and turned in at the jail doorway from which yesterday he had watched a crossbow arrow streaking through space toward the cemetery where Rockford had paused to study the epitaphs on the headboards of the graves of Roxanna and Rudy Sutkliffe. Turning to stare at K6ATX from the shade of the doorway Hilton said in a not-unkindly voice, ''Sorry you have to walk out into that furnace, Tommy. Hurry it along as fast as you can. If you feel like you're about to keel over, stop work and come in here and pour a couple of buckets of water over your head.''

''Thanks, Hilton, but this job can't be speeded up. What if old Sutkliffe poured those silver bars down a post hole? This locator has a narrow beam. I don't want to overlook one square foot of this canyon floor. Don't forget, my life is riding on this.''

Hilton waved his understanding and disappeared into the shelter of the stone jailhouse. A few minutes later, when Tommy Rockford was passing the doorway with his metal detector, his captor came out with a dripping gunny sack which he had soaked in a bucket of water.

''Hang this over your head,'' he invited Tommy. ''It won't short-circuit your headphones or anything, will it?''

For a moment they met each other's eyes, captive and captor, and something almost like rapport passed between them. Then Tommy reminded himself, ''If this silver hunt was for real, the minute Hilton found out where the cache was, he'd put me out of my misery with that pistol of his. The only reason he's being thoughtful is because he thinks I hold the key to a buried fortune. . .''

''Thanks, Hilton. This sack will dry out pretty fast, so I may be back from time to time for a refill.''

''Okay. You'll get it. Good luck.''

Adjusting the sopping-wet burlap over his head and shoulders, Tommy took his first step out into the blazing sunshine. He picked up the pace, not wanting to delay his own moment of crisis a moment longer than he had to. The killing temperatures, perhaps registering two hundred degrees on the ground, had nothing to do with his growing sense of urgency.

He did not know whether Hilton was watching from a jail window or not, but on the assumption he was, he kept up the pretense of sweeping the mineral detector from side to side, covering a four-foot wide swath of ground as he headed out into the open field under the rimrocks. Slowly, carefully, patiently covering ground.

Above him, the crown of Telescope Peak shimmered in the heat waves reflecting off the salt flats of Death Valley, the sky more brass-colored than blue, and so bright it hurt the eyes. Up there on the peak—the loftiest point on the Panamint Range at 11,049 feet—Uncle JC had set up the ARRL Field Day base camp day before yesterday, and on that fact Tommy was staking his future.

Pulses playing tom-tom solos on his eardrums, Tommy turned on the radio clamped under the battery case of the Little Jim Dandy.

K6ATX was confident his one-and-a-half-watt ICOM hand-held model packed more than enough wallop, even in midday, to punch a signal to the top of Telescope Peak where his cousin Noisy Noyce and other hams would be standing by.

The headset responded with an RF carrier and a human voice—the sweetest sound Tommy had ever heard in his life—reached his ears with the receiver at low volume:

"W7OE, Over-Eater at Furnace Creek, this is the intercom station on Telescope Peak with Fred, KB6JIP, Jump in Price, at the mike. . . Answer on both is affirmative, sir. The Lompoc station at Dante's View will be operational when Field Day begins. Ditto with the Vandenberg guys over at Badwater. I can see their QTH with the binocs, solar cells all set up for business. Back to you."

Tommy Rockford pressed his talk button and signed K6ATX, hoping to break the frequency in the heart-beat of time between KB6JIP's sign-off and Uncle JC's transmission. With his radio in receiving mode, he strained his ears to pick up an answer, but heard nothing. Obviously KB6JIP was listening to JC's reply.

The sun had already steamed the water out of the gunnysack Tommy was using for a head cover. He had to keep swinging the mineral detector right and left over the ground, as if searching for signals which would indicate the presence of a large mass of bar silver buried nearby, to keep from rousing Hilton's suspicions.

The carrier from Fred's radio returned, indicating that Uncle JC had finished his transmission. KB6JIP, whose KB6 prefix branded him as a recently-licensed amateur, came on with a clipped "Roger-dodger W7OE, this is KB6JIP off and clear."

The critical moment had come.

Tommy Rockford knelt down, assuming Hilton was watching him from the jail, ostensibly to rest a moment while he mopped his face and neck with the gunny sacking, but in reality to get his lips close to the microphone contained in the hand-held radio.

His voice, pitched low enough so it would not carry to the jailhouse where Rusty Hilton might be watching and listening, was fraught with a desperate urgency as he started what was probably the most important radio transmission of his life: "KB6JIP, Telescope Peak, this is K6ATX, King Six Alpha Tango X-Ray, calling May Day and standing by. Emergency! May Day! Do you read me?"

Tommy switched from send to receive. An interminable interval of silence, which was probably measured in seconds, ended when KB6JIP's startled voice sounded in the headphones:

"Ro*ger*, K6ATX! You're blasting in here on the peak! Yours is the call we've been listening for around the clock! Where in heck are you, old man? Are you okay? Everybody will want to know. Over."

Tommy sucked in a deep, deep breath, the intolerable strain of feeling cut off from the world at last lifted from his spirit. He was sure that radio hams all around Death Valley, busy setting up for Field Day operations which were due to begin a short time from now, had listened in on the control station making contact with K6ATX, and would recognize it as the call sign of the missing radio ham they had all been waiting for.

Without formal preamble or call signs, Tommy Rockford spoke again into his handie-talkie mike, "Fred, can you tape this QSO and play it back to my Uncle JC? I'm sure he can't copy me."

"Can do, Tommy. Just turned the recorder on. Will play it back to W7OE/6 as soon as I can rewind. Go ahead, K6ATX!"

Hardly able to control the hammering of his heart, K6ATX forced himself to keep his voice low as he spoke clearly and distinctly into the mike, "This is K6ATX. Chub Downey and I are being held prisoner by the two Crossbow Killers who pulled off the casino robbery in Las Vegas night before last. Now get this. Our QTH is not on the topo maps—it is a narrow gulch with overhanging rimrocks, invisible from the air, located immediately south of Avalanche Gulch, which is directly east of Telescope Peak. This QTH contains the buildings of a mining camp known as Borrowed Time, with a jailhouse which the two Crossbow Killers have been using as their hideout. If Uncle JC has access to Seldom Seen Sam, have him use Sam as a guide to this place.

"The only possible access would be by helicopter. Inform pilot there is a small, perhaps two-acre level field which is visible from the air at the west or upper end of Borrowed Time Canyon. Sam knows about it—his parents are buried in the graveyard there. This is the only possible place a chopper could enter the canyon. Time is urgent as Chub and I have been threatened with death before the day is over. Warn chopper pilot that Crossbow Killers are armed and dangerous, repeat, armed and dangerous.

"They plan to make getaway tonight in the club's VW van which is parked in a shed beside a miner's abandoned cabin on the north rim of Avalanche Gulch near the bench mark indicating sea level.

"If you wait to capture the two killers when they come for the van it will be too late for Chub and me. This is K6ATX standing by—how copy?"

The instant Tommy Rockford signed off, the two-meter control station atop Telescope Peak came back: "Roger one hundred percent, K6ATX! Stand by while I call your Uncle JC and put your message on the air. I'm sure he'll have some questions. They have a Sheriff's helicopter standing by at Furnace Creek, ready to take to the air at a moment's notice."

Tommy, continuing the charade of scouring the surface of the open field with his mineral detector for the benefit of Rusty Hilton whom he was sure was watching from the shelter of the jailhouse, heard KB6JIP calling W7OE, followed by a pause during which he assumed Uncle JC was answering. Then K6TZ's powerful carrier came on again and JIP was saying, "That's roger, I have been in QSO with Tommy! He sent a May Day call and says he and Chub are in terrible danger. Stand by while I play back the tape..."

A few seconds of silence, then Tommy heard his own recorded voice advertising his and Chub's desperate plight to the world:

"This is K6ATX. Chub Downey and I are being held prisoner by the two Crossbow Killers who pulled off the casino robbery at Las Vegas night before last...Our QTH is not on the topo maps..."

As he listened to the replay of his transmission, Tommy Rockford's nostrils suddenly picked up an ominous, alien odor. A smell of smoke, heavy and acrid in the heated canyon air, as if the incredible heat of the sun had started the ground to smouldering.

Spinning around to face back down the canyon, K6ATX was

aghast to see a malignant red ribbon of flame flick like a serpent's tongue through a broken window in the lobby of the Gunsight Lode Hotel. Already, ugly billows of smoke were vomiting from the lobby doorway, past the empty porch rocking chair which Goldie Lesher had been occupying, filling the air with a swirling, opaque haze that held the creosote stench of burning tarpaper.

Ripping the headphones off his head and dropping the Little Jim Dandy to the ground, Tommy Rockford started toward the jailhouse, screaming at the top of his lungs: *"Help! Help! The hotel's on fire! The hotel's on fire!"*

All K6ATX could think about in that terrible moment was that upstairs over the inferno that was gutting the hotel lobby, Chub Downey was a doomed soul, trapped, helpless, facing cremation in a locked room...

CHAPTER TWENTY TWO

THE DIVE OF DEATH

Rusty Hilton, a beer can clutched in one hand, his red beard and mustache dripping beer foam, stepped outside the jailhouse just as Tommy Rockford reached the door. The outlaw swore an angry oath as he caught sight of the burning hotel.

"That darn fool Goldie! Every time he gets high on angel dust he either tries to fly off a roof or he rips off his clothes or he sets fire to something. I should never have left him alone—"

Tommy Rockford seized Hilton's shoulders in both hands and shouted frantically, "Give me the hotel key! Chub's up there—"

Hilton stared incredulously at the radio ham who seemed bent on shaking his head off.

"Hey, cool it, son! Are you crazy? You'd burn to a crisp before you got halfway up the stairs, from the looks of that fire—"

Tommy was a husky athlete and he was in the pink of condition. Hilton had already sampled the power of Tommy's fists. He now felt that strength at work again, as Tommy shook Hilton back and forth as if intending to break his neck. "Hand over that key or I'll take it away from you—"

Shocked into submission by the berserk fury of his attacker, Hilton made no effort to draw his holstered gun. He tossed the beer can aside to paw into a pocket of his Levis and draw out an old-fashioned brass key to which was attached a metal tag branded ROOM 3 GUNSIGHT LODE HOTEL, BORROWED TIME, CALIF.

Letting go his death-grip on Hilton's shoulders, Tommy snatched the key and sprinted off in the direction of the Gunsight Lode Hotel.

The highly-inflammable tarpaper which lined the ceiling and walls of the lobby accounted for the thick black smoke and the appalling headway the fire had made, but an odor of raw kerosene was very strong in Tommy's nostrils. Kerosene?

Halting alongside the porch to assess his best chance of getting inside and surviving to reach the second floor where Chub Downey was trapped, K6ATX heard someone shouting above the crackle of the flames. He looked up to see Goldie Lesher, stripped to his boxer shorts, leaning over the balcony railing above the porch, waving a five-gallon coal oil can and screaming words which Tommy could not distinguish. Here was the most shocking display of what narcotics could do to crucify a human that Tommy had ever seen.

Screaming incoherently, Lesher hurled the oil can in the air and turned to disappear through an open second-story window.

Seconds were precious now. Entering the hotel through the front door was impossible; no one could get past the threshold alive. Tommy ran to his left, rounding the east corner of the ghost town hotel in hopes of finding a rear entrance—and sobbed a broken cry of thanksgiving as he caught sight of a flight of rickety stairs leading to an upper doorway in the east end of the building. If it had been intended for use as a fire escape, its time had come.

Rockford vaulted up the stairs three steps at a time. The protective railing fell away into pieces under his grasp, and he felt the time-rotted treads split under his weight. Reaching the second story platform, Tommy found himself confronted by a closed and locked door leading to the hall in front of Chub's prison.

He stepped back and, lowering his head and bunching his shoulders into a battering ram, lunged at the door as if he was a football player diving at a tackling dummy. He felt wood break under the impact of his hundred and eighty pounds of bone and muscle, panels splintering and caving in, the iron lock holding.

Recoiling, Tommy kicked savagely at the broken panels, causing the door to tear loose from its hinges. The momentum of his charge carried the radio ham staggering into the upstairs hallway where cinder-laden smoke eddied as thick as paint, stinging his lungs.

Remembering emergency training he had picked up as a Boy Scout in his youth, Tommy flung himself to the floor, knowing that hot air rises and his chances of breathing were better the lower he got. Through the whorling smoke he could see that the lobby was a mass of flames, and a shock went through him as he realized that the cellar below that inferno was filled with dynamite and blasting powder. If the fire reached those explosives, the hotel would disintegrate into a spray of debris from one second to the next.

Wriggling his way along the hall until he came to Chub's door, Tommy sucked his lungs full of air at the floor level and then rose to his feet, the choking smoke swirling about him. He wondered where Goldie Lesher was, somewhere behind that churning smoke...

K6ATX groped blindly for the padlock, found it, fumbled the key in his wild haste, fell to his knees and slapped his hands around until he recovered it. It seemed to take superhuman concentration to fit the key into the padlock, making him wonder if Rusty Hilton had betrayed him and given him the wrong key.

Then he heard the padlock snap open and he was yanking it loose from the hasp. He twisted the doorknob and half fell, half dove into the room which had been Seldom Seen Sam's quarters.

He bellowed Chub's name, seeing no sign of his friend. The room was relatively free of smoke, although fumes were filtering in through cracks in the floor boards and he could feel the heat of the downstairs holocaust against the soles of his Nikes.

Then he spotted Chub Downey, kneeling behind the table, stuffing old Sam's rock specimens into a canvas bag. Even with his life at stake, his rock hound instincts made it imperative that he rescue what he could of the old prospector's geological collection.

Knowing it was useless to make himself heard above the furnace roar of the burning lobby, Tommy Rockford staggered across the room, tore the sack of rock specimens out of Chub's grasp, seized the young rock hound by the armpits and bodily dragged him toward the doorway. Chub did not resist, his eyes as dull as a zombie's.

Out in the hall, Tommy pulled the overweight kid to his knees, gesturing toward the fire escape door and motioning for Chub to keep as close to the floor as possible, under the deck of smoke. The air was beginning to fill with live cinders now, pelting down like red snowflakes, stinging when they landed on bare flesh.

Both boys were choking violently as they finally reached the broken doorway leading to the outer stairs. As they came to their knees and crawled out onto the narrow railed platform, Tommy knew the ancient steps would never hold up under their combined weight.

He was right. They were halfway down the fire escape when dry-rotted bracing timbers buckled under them, and the entire stairway collapsed, plunging them a dozen feet to wind up in a jumble of splintered two by fours and pine planking.

Scratched and bleeding, Tommy grabbed Chub by a wrist and led the way toward the street, fighting to get away from the zone of superheated air next to the burning building. By common consent they headed toward the mouth of the nearby escape tunnel, where the fire was sucking a brisk intake of hot air from Avalanche Canyon.

Instead of cooling them off, the artificially-induced breeze was only serving to feed more oxygen to the conflagration which was now licking like an inverted waterfall to devour the whole front of the hotel, curtaining the iron-latticed window of Chub's erstwhile prison room, up and over the eaves to greedily attack the dry oily fuel provided by the asphalt roofing shingles. It had been close.

Through the smoke, Tommy caught sight of the ghostly figure of Rusty Hilton, bald head and face shielded from the heat by a bandanna. Tommy thought, "If he thinks he can save Goldie, he's too late. His buddy has been fried to a crisp by now."

Leaving Chub Downey sprawled prostrate in the mouth of the escape tunnel, Tommy bucked his way through the smoke and heat to reach Hilton's side, out in front of the assay office. This far away from the doomed hotel the heat was tolerable and they could hear each other above the roar of the holocaust.

Meeting Tommy's stare, Hilton shouted hoarsely, "Kid's dead?"

Tommy pointed toward the mouth of the tunnel where he had left Chub, no longer visible behind the roiling black smoke.

"He got out okay. I'm sorry, Hilton, but I'm afraid your pal is trapped up there on the second floor. When I got here he was up on the balcony above the porch, waving an oil can. He must have sloshed lamp oil over everything and touched a match to it. Why?"

Hilton raised an arm, pointing to the western end of the hotel where fire was now fluttering like red pennants from the upper windows. Then he spotted Goldie Lesher, pacing along the second story balcony high above the well and the assay office roof. The yellow-haired ruffian seemed to be going through the contortions of some kind of primitive Indian dance, hopping up and down on bare feet, waving his arms, his mouth a red hole behind screening mustache as he howled incantations into the teeth of an artificial gale created by the blaze.

"PCP jag," Hilton shouted, his lips close to Tommy's ear. "For some reason God only knows he set that fire. It isn't the first time. Angel dust does that to people. I was a fool leaving him alone in his condition. This time I can't do anything to save him."

Goldie Lesher had caught sight of Tommy and Hilton. He waved at them, then dropped to the floor of the balcony and seemed to be writhing in some kind of weird break dance. Suddenly, as if propelled by springs, he bounded to the railing of the balcony, braced there on wide-spread legs, and then froze with arms above his head, palms together, eyeing the ground fifteen feet below.

"Oh *no!*" Tommy groaned. "Is he going to dive? All he has to do is climb over the rail and slide down one of the balcony pillars to the ground! Tell him that, Hilton—he'll listen to you!"

Rusty Hilton shook his head. "When Goldie is on a PCP high, he actually thinks he can fly like a bird. I've saved his life before. But this time I can't get to him on account of the fire."

Watching as if caught in the paralyzing throes of a nightmare, Tommy Rockford saw the blond outlaw flex his knees to give extra spring to his diving leap, seemingly unaware that attempting to broad-jump to the roof of the next building would be suicidal.

Flapping his arms like a bird, Goldie Lesher launched himself into space in a macabre version of a swan dive. Instinctively Tommy shut his eyes and turned away, unable to bear the sight of a human being self-destructing on the rock-hard earth below.

But the expected crunch of sound did not come. Almost afraid to open his eyes, sure he would see a bloody sprawl of splintered bone and shattered flesh smeared on the ground beside the hotel, Tommy turned around for a look—but saw no trace of a broken corpse. The optical illusion was that by jumping into space, Goldie Lesher had taken wing and actually flown off into the smoke.

"My god, my god," Hilton was sobbing. "He was like one of those circus high-divers on a tower, hitting the bullseye of a tiny tank of water below. *Goldie dove straight down into that well!...*"

Tommy Rockford felt a tug of compassion for the grief and suffering he saw written on Hilton's evil features. Tears leaked from the red-shot eyes into the cinnamon beard. A whimpering, keening sound as of a woman weeping issued from Hilton's cavernous chest. Tommy was looking at a totally broken man.

Of one accord, the two headed toward the circular masonry coaming of the Borrowed Time water well. The heat of the fire was almost more than they could bear, but shielding their faces with their arms, they leaned over the rim of the ledge and peered down into the shuddery depths of the mine shaft that was now a well.

Again Tommy saw his silhouette reflected on the foamy surface twenty feet below. But this time, the semi-nude figure of Goldie Lesher floated on the ripples down there, arms and legs extended like some kind of dead water bug, face buried under water.

Feeling that he was about to be sick, Tommy Rockford turned and left Rusty Hilton alone with his grief. Skirting the zone of superheated air as widely as he could, Tommy made his way back to where Chub Downey hunkered in stunned paralysis. He was clutching Seldom Seen Sam's purple glass doorknob in both hands as if it were some kind of magic talisman. The young rock hound stared back at Tommy as if they were strangers, causing Tommy to wonder if the horrors Chub had experienced had destroyed the boy's reason.

Chub let Tommy help him to his feet. He was moaning, "Only thing I saved was Sam's amethystine doorknob, had it in my pocket. Everything else...Mohs kit...my specimens...all lost, all gone."

Like a solicitous nurse helping a post-operative patient walk along a hospital corridor, Tommy assisted his dazed friend down the ghost town street, past the assay office and barber shop, out of the intolerable heat radiating from the Gunsight Lode Hotel. They stumbled over to the porch of the Wells-Fargo Express office and sat down, just in time to see the entire front of the hotel collapse in a mass of flaming ruin and crash to the street where it lay flaming and smoking, subsiding into a devil's garden of pink coals, while the roof, still supported by charred studding timbers, blazed with new fury until it, too, collapsed.

Rusty Hilton was kneeling at the well's concrete and fieldstone curb like a worshipper at an altar railing, his elbows resting on the circular stone coaming of the shaft which would be Goldie Lesher's tomb throughout eternity.

Tommy knelt down beside Chub Downey, both of them needing time to get their own nerves functioning again. Then Tommy realized that his young friend was still suffering under the burden of believing that their own dooms were hopelessly sealed.

"Chub, I've got the best possible good news to share!" Tommy shouted in Chub's ear. "Our gadget worked! I got an SOS through to our hams up on Telescope Peak! Loud and clear, no sweat!"

Dull horror was replaced slowly by a surging new hope in Chub Downey's expression as he stared back into his rescuer's eyes.

"You mean—they'll send someone to get us out of here?"

Tommy nodded, his own ecstasy matching Chub's. "Yes, yes! The cops have a helicopter at Furnace Creek air strip, gassed up and ready to go, they said. It's probably airborne right now. A chopper could make it here from Furnace Creek inside of ten minutes!"

Tommy broke off, catching a look of pure terror transforming Chub's face into a mask as he stared up and behind K6ATX. Sensing danger, Tommy came to his feet and wheeled around—to find himself staring into the round black hole in the barrel of Rusty Hilton's .357 Magnum, the gun aimed straight between his eyes.

"So you managed to sneak an SOS out of here, did you?" Hilton sneered. "So the fuzz is on the way in a helicopter, are they? With a SWAT team loaded with automatic weapons and tear-gas cannisters, all primed to wipe out the bad guys and take you and the fat kid back to strut before the TV cameras, eh? Well, Tommy, when they get here, *they won't find any one of us alive—including me!*"

CHAPTER TWENTY THREE

JAILHOUSE BOOBY-TRAP

The eyes that stared into Tommy's were those of a madman, the eyes of a man who had finally been driven to the ragged edge of mental collapse and was ready to take his own life as well as commit two more murders inside the next few minutes.

Hilton gestured with his gun barrel in the direction of the burning hotel. His voice was harsh: "We're walking back to the well, Tommy. When the cops get here we can't make it too easy for them, eh? They'll start searching for us, never sure if they're walking into an ambush trap or not. Even cops armed with machine guns are scared of crossbows which can kill without sound. We'll make 'em sweat before they finally look down into the well—"

The red-bearded ruffian swung his attention to Chub Downey.

"You stay put, kid. I'll be back for you later. I might even talk myself into letting you live, who knows? You aren't the one who got me into this jam."

Tommy Rockford made eye contact with Chub, hoping against hope that the rock hound would get his message—as soon as he was alone, run for the open field near the cemetery where the chopper will land. You can't trust this fiend to spare your life—

Numbly, Rockford started walking back into the heated zone, heading for the well Hilton intended to become his watery grave, knowing that as Hilton followed him, he was giving Chub Downey his chance for survival.

The assay office and barber shop were totally enveloped in flames as they neared the well. Unknown to either Hilton or his intended murder victim, Chub Downey was following them, a dimly-seen figure behind the smothering screen of ground-hugging smoke.

Like something in a nightmare, Chub saw Tommy Rockford step up on the stone ramp of the well, his back to Hilton. The latter lifted his pistol to take aim at the back of Tommy Rockford's head, steadying his gun arm with his left hand.

It came to Chub in a flash of realization that he was Tommy's only hope. And in that moment of truth the young rock hound believed he could overcome the handicap of not being armed. He still had his own greatest God-given talent. Hadn't a scout for the Los Angeles Dodgers told Chub's coach that he was the greatest control pitcher for his age that California high schools had ever produced?

Chub Downey reached in his hip pocket and drew out what he now considered his most precious possession—the purple glass doorknob Seldom Seen Sam had given him. He palmed the shiny sphere and went into the motions of a baseball pitcher on the mound, preparing to serve up his best pitch to a waiting batter. Except that now, his target would not be home plate and a catcher's mitt. It would be the .357 Magnum clutched in Rusty Hilton's two hands, drawing a bead on the back of Tommy Rockford's head...

There was no time for a wind-up. Chub Downey, pitching from a stretch position he had copied from the likes of Fernando Valenzuela, reared back and let the purple doorknob go with every last ounce of power his arm and back could generate.

As unerringly as a laser beam, Chub's overhand "fast ball" sped through thirty feet of space to strike the knuckles of Hilton's right hand a micro-second before the gun spat flame and exploded with a crack of sound that cut through the rumble of the conflagration.

The ear-numbing crack of the shot brought Tommy Rockford spinning around, trying to figure out why a bullet hadn't drilled into his skull, why instead the slug had sprayed rock dust as it ricocheted off the well coaming, somehow deflected from its target.

He saw the Magnum fly from Hilton's fist. He heard the felon's cry of pain and surprise. Then, from the corner of his peripheral vision, he saw an object he recognized as Chub Downey's amethystine glass doorknob go rolling along the ground as if chasing the gun.

K6ATX moved fast then. He charged past the stunned figure of Rusty Hilton to scoop up the smoking Magnum .347, his thumb earing the weapon to full cock. Beyond Hilton he saw Chub Downey walking toward them, a wraith emerging from the smoke. He wore the broad grin of a jack-o'-lantern—or a pitcher strutting from mound to dugout after hurling a no-hitter.

"Chub—you saved my life!" Tommy shouted incredulously. "Hilton was about to gun me down when you knocked that pistol out of his hand! And I didn't even know you had followed us—"

Chub walked over and stooped to pick up his precious doorknob, which had landed unbroken in a patch of soft sand. He lifted it to his lips and kissed it.

"No big deal, Tommy," he said modestly. "Only half the distance I would pitch a baseball from the rubber to home plate. At thirty foot range, how could I miss? With you as umpire, yet?"

Tommy turned his attention to Rusty Hilton now. The outlaw, still stunned by the sudden reversal of their situation, was sucking a bloody welt on his right knuckles, trying to muster up a defiant sneer as he kept his eyes glued to the gun in Tommy's hand.

"That rod doesn't freak me out! You won't shoot me! You're too square, too uptight with your codes of honor and fair play."

The excruciating heat made it necessary to get away from the burning buildings as soon as possible. Tommy waved up-canyon and shouted, "We'll wait in the jailhouse till the chopper lands."

With Hilton stumbling along in the lead, the three hurried past the now-burning Wells-Fargo office to an area where the heat was not so intense and the air did not sear the lungs.

"Well, Tommy," Chub commented, "I guess I lose the argument about who has the most valuable hobby, ham radio or rockhounding. My hobby would never have brought the cops to rescue us."

Tommy, hugging his right arm to his ribs to keep the heavy pistol aimed steadily at their prisoner, gave Chub a slap on the back with his free hand.

"Right now," he laughed, "I am inclined to say that your baseball hobby is the most important of the three. Without that last pitch of yours I would be floating down in that well with Goldie right now. The rest of my days I'll know I owe my life to you—"

Downey stuffed the purple doorknob back into his pocket. "I think the score is tied, Tommy. You got me out of that burning hotel. You took a lot more risk than I did throwing a doorknob."

When they reached the jail Rusty Hilton headed through the doorway with Tommy close at his heels, jabbing his gun muzzle into the small of Hilton's back to guard against any false move.

It was twenty degrees cooler in the cell block and jailer's office than it was outside. The roaring sound of the fire diminished sharply when Chub closed the iron door behind them.

Glancing around the jail, Tommy saw a number of 1880-style ankle irons and handcuffs dangling from wall pegs just inside the door. Tommy said crisply, "Hilton, wrists together at your belt buckle, please. Chub, fetch one of those sets of bracelets and shackle our friend. We can let somebody else figure out how to release him without a key. A hacksaw or a locksmith, maybe."

Hilton made no move to resist as Chub Downey brought over a pair of rusty iron fetters and secured them to his wrists. As his eyes accustomed themselves to the gloom inside the jail, Tommy Rockford saw that the right-hand wall was provided with two sets of double-deck bunks, each with leg irons dangling from ringbolts cemented into the stone walls. Mining camp justice might have been crude but it was effective in keeping jailed prisoners in line.

Hilton walked over to one of the upper bunks and reached up with his manacled arms to roll back a straw tick mattress. From the bull hide straps which served as bedsprings he drew a shiny black leather satchel bearing a gold-colored logo that resembled the head of King Tut and the words PHARAOH'S PALACE, LAS VEGAS, NEVADA.

Hilton tossed the satchel at Rockford's feet. "The haul we made in Vegas the other night," he said. "Fifty thou, the radio said. The casino's insurance company will pay a good reward to whoever recovers it, five thou at least. You earned it. Or if you want, keep the whole shebang and split it with your tubby friend."

Tommy picked up the cashier's satchel, apparently stuffed with paper money and traveler's cheques to judge by the weight, and tossed it into Chub's arms.

"Chub, the helicopter should be showing up any minute now. Go over to the center of that open field—you'll see your Little Jim Dandy mineral detector where I dropped it. Stand by to help the chopper pilot make a landing. We're in no hurry now."

After Chub had left, Hilton seated himself on a lower bunk, shackled forearms resting on his thighs, and regarded K6ATX with a sardonic grin.

"No hurry, you say? If your helicopter doesn't get here soon it'll be too late for you two. Apparently you don't know that Seldom Seen

Sam loaded the hotel cellar with blasting powder and dynamite to use in his prospecting. When the fire eats through the floor, there'll be a blast they'll hear all the way to 'Vegas."

Tommy said bleakly, "I know about the dynamite in the cellar. The explosion doesn't worry me. But it would rattle the cliffs and bring that suspended avalanche down into the canyon and fill it to the brim with loose rock. That's why the old-timers named their camp Borrowed Time in the first place, knowing all that suspended slide rock would spill sooner or later. I think I'd rather be blown to bits than be squashed like a bug under all that rock."

Uncocking the pistol, Tommy started for the door with the intention of going out to join Chub in the open field, when he caught sight of some strange object resting on the jailer's table in the center of the room. He recoiled as if it had been a coiled snake when he recognized what it was.

A crossbow—perhaps the very weapon which had murdered the security guard of the casino in Las Vegas. The spring metal bow had been cranked back to full-cock position. A lethal steel-tipped arrow lay cradled in the hardwood groove which corresponded to the bore of a rifle barrel. The arrow was pointing at the jail doorway.

Leading from the trigger of the crossbow was an almost invisible nylon fishline. There was barely enough light inside the jail for Tommy Rockford to trace that fishline diagonally across the room to where it was secured to a screwhook in the right-hand door post. Several feet of extra fishline hung from the screwhook.

A booby-trap! A loaded crossbow waiting for anyone coming through the door—

Seated on a lower bunk at the far side of the room Rusty Hilton said resignedly, "Goldie invented that contraption. At night we strung the fishline across the doorway. You couldn't see it. Anyone shoving against it would get an arrow in the guts. Goldie didn't want anyone coming into the jailhouse when we were asleep. Sooner or later old Seldom Seen Sam would have found us."

Before Tommy could reply, their ears were filled with a familiar *thump-thump-thump-thump!* which both recognized instantly and understood its significance.

The throbbing rotor-blade roar of a hovering helicopter!

CHAPTER TWENTY FOUR

PASSING INTO LEGEND

Tommy felt a shiver ripple down his spine as he realized how many times he had walked across the line of fire of that deadly, anachronistic booby-trap. But Hilton had said that only at night was the trigger line stretched across the doorway to trap intruders. . .

Excitement mounted in the young radio ham as he went to a front window, the sound of a helicopter—could it be more than one?—growing in volume overhead. The canyon was obscured with milky layers of smoke, a factor which would make a helicopter's descent into the narrow opening between Borrowed Time Canyon's cliffs extremely hazardous, if not impossible.

"I'll be back for you, Hilton," K6ATX told the outlaw seated on the bunk. "From the noise it's making, that's a troop-carrying chopper, not a two-passenger reconnaissance job."

He left the red-bearded fugitive despondent, face buried in his hands. Closing the jail door, Tommy noted the massive iron key in the lock and twisted it to secure the bolt, just in case Hilton got ideas of returning to the suicide well to join Goldie. Loyalty, at least, was one of Hilton's strong virtues.

Outside, K6ATX broke into a run, out into the open field where Chub Downey, coughing from the smoke, stood waiting at the spot where Tommy had discarded the Little Jim Dandy mineral finder. He was peering skyward, waving his arms excitedly.

His eyes stinging with smoke, Tommy looked up to see not one, but two choppers hovering a hundred feet above the rimrocks. One he recognized as a big ten-passenger Bell Model 204, equipped with a cable hoist and halogen quartz searchlight for night rescue work.

Along the fuselage was a seven-pointed gold star and the words INYO COUNTY SHERIFF AERO SQUADRON 2. Tommy's friend Sheriff Ross Jackson flew the same model chopper back in Santa Barbara County.

The smaller "Huey" helicopter was a Plexiglas bubble that resembled a dragonfly hovering above and to one side of the bigger machine. Tommy recognized it as the camera crew's chopper from KCBS, Channel Two Television in Los Angeles. A video photographer sat in the open doorway, taping the action for tonight's TV news.

The Sheriff's Bell 204 also had its fuselage door open, and Tommy Rockford believed one of the three men strapped in the doorway was his Uncle JC. A uniformed law enforcement officer put an electric bullhorn to his mouth and his words reverberated from the sky like the voice of the Norse god Thor himself:

"Two questions. What is the situation regarding any threat from the two Crossbow Killers? Can I assume you have them under control? Wave for affirmative, don't wave for negative."

The boys waved.

"That's a relief! Question two: how many will we have to air lift? Do you have prisoners? Our basket has a capacity of two only. You have four arms between you—raise one arm for each passenger we have to hoist out of there."

Chub raised both arms. Tommy, casting a vote for Rusty Hilton waiting in the jailhouse, lifted one arm.

"Okay, that's three. We'll have to make two descents with the basket. The air is too turbulent and visibility too obscured by smoke for us to attempt landing in such restricted space. But we can hover and manage an air lift with no problem. Do you still read me? If affirmative, wave."

Tommy and Chub waved frantically.

"Okay, stay where you are. First basket coming down."

Tommy saw the sheriff's officer hand the bullhorn to the civilian beside him. A moment later the familiar voice of Uncle JC boomed down from the skies: "From up here you two guys are a sight for sore eyes. Smile pretty for the TV cameras on the way up!"

Tommy said briskly to Chub, "You stand by and steady the basket when it reaches the ground. I'm going back for Rusty."

"Will do," Chub said excitedly. "Hey, this is fun, man! And I think I see Seldom Seen Sam up in the big chopper!"

"They probably brought him along to serve as a guide. Easier than poring over topo maps trying to locate Avalanche Gulch."

"I hope Sam's aboard," Chub said. "I've got a question I've been dying to ask that old coot. About shoelaces and baby snakes."

Tommy Rockford was already on his way back to the jailhouse. Belatedly it occurred to him that in his absence Hilton might have gotten hold of a gun, or was waiting to open fire with the wicked crossbow. Cocking the Magnum .357 for action if necessary, Tommy arrived at the jail door and squinted through an open rivet hole. He had a clear view of the outlaw still seated on the lower bunk, face in hands, a picture of total despair.

Unlocking the door, K6ATX stepped inside. Peering back through the smoke toward the open field, he could see sunlight glinting on a steel wire cable and a wire mesh body basket being lowered from the hovering chopper toward the waiting Chub.

"Hilton, they're evacuating us by cable hoist—too risky to attempt a landing inside the canyon, too much air turbulence due to the fire, and the smoke cuts their visibility to the ground."

Hilton came to his feet, staring down at his manacled hands.

"Yeah, I heard the pilot talking..." Hilton grinned bleakly. "Tommy, I hate to sound like a curious old woman, but how in thunder did you manage to call in that chopper? I know radio can't get out—not from down in this hole in the mountain."

Tommy watched Hilton crossing the room toward the door. He held the pistol at full cock, alert for any treacherous attack.

"A radio signal *can* get out, from that open field—and I had radio ham friends up on Telescope Peak to copy my signal. That gadget you thought was a Geiger counter, a mineral detector—I had attached my two-way radio under the control box. When I got out there under the open sky, it was easy to get out with an SOS."

Hilton's eyes held a grudging admiration for the clever way the radio ham had outwitted him. "You know, Tommy, sitting here thinking, I realized those old-time miners didn't have a stamp mill and a smelter up here where they could manufacture silver ingots. You weren't really searching for a $500,000 cache, were you?"

"No, Hilton, I wasn't. I forged that entry in Sam's diary to trick you into letting me take my radio outside the hotel. But I got so caught up in the excitement of the treasure hunt, I almost believed Sam's silver was for real!... But we can't waste time yakking, Hilton. We've got to clear out of this canyon before that dynamite blows and the avalanche starts. Let's go—move it!"

Hilton came to a halt some six feet away. He shook his bald head. "No, young feller. I won't be coming with you. If I did, the State of Nevada would only execute me for Murder One."

"B-But I can't just let you stay here and get buried alive, Hilton! Besides, you might draw a life sentence. Serve some time, rehabilitate yourself. Kick your drug habit, get out on parole, make a new life for yourself, It's never too late! You can do it!"

A sad smile twisted Rusty Hilton's lips. "No. I belong here with my buddy Lesher. But you tell the fat kid, if his rock had missed my gun hand, you two wouldn't be taking that whirlybird ride now." The iron manacles jingled as Hilton raised his arms in an awkward salute. "Better get movin', son. You're on borrowed time every extra second you stay down here. Good luck—and—adios."

Before Tommy could interpret the fatalistic implication in Hilton's last words, he saw the outlaw step sideways to put his body into the path of the booby-trap arrow, then reach out to grip the nylon line stretched tautly from trigger to door frame.

"No, Hilton—don't—you can't—"

Hilton jerked the trigger line. Simultaneously the burly Satan's Angel staggered under the impact of a steel-tipped shaft impaling his back between the shoulder blades. Even as Hilton's knees buckled and he slumped dead at Tommy's feet, K6ATX saw the reddened tip of the arrow projecting through Hilton's breastbone..

Fighting off a great soul-sickness, knowing the time for his own escape might well be measured in clock-ticks now, Tommy Rockford turned and sprinted back to where Chub Downey was now squatting in the sheriff's air-rescue basket awaiting the radio ham's arrival. Chub had stowed the Pharaoh's Palace satchel and his Little Jim Dandy between his knees in the basket, while he clutched the steel wire cable securely with both fists. Then Chub saw Hilton's pistol in Tommy's hand and his face went chalk-white.

"You're leaving Hilton behind?" Chub called out as Tommy jumped into the basket, secured a grip on the hoisting cable, and waved a lift-off signal to the pilot in the helicopter a hundred and fifty feet overhead. Receiving no answer, Chub's lips framed three words: "Is he—dead?"

Tommy nodded, too choked with emotion to reply. Suddenly the ground seemed to drop away from beneath them, the basket assuming a slight pendulum motion as the chopper's hoisting drum began reeling in the wire cable. The boys' stomachs held the same queazy sensation they had each experienced many times riding the loop-the-loop roller coaster at Magic Mountain amusement park.

The cliffs seemed to slide downwards on either side of the rising basket, like the walls of an elevator shaft. The helicopter engine and rotor noise swelled in deafening crescendo as the cable hoisted them swiftly out of the superheated air caused by the fire raging in the canyon below them, the wash of the helicopter blades thinning out the smoke.

The basket came up under the belly of the Bell 204 to a smooth, swaying halt. K6ATX was vaguely aware that it was his Uncle JC's strong hands which reached down to seize his wrists and hoist him into the cabin where a squad of heavily-armed deputies had been waiting in case they were needed. Chub Downey, grinning with the thrill of it all, was hauled aboard after him, and immediately scuttled on hands and knees over to where shaggy-bearded old Seldom Seen Sam was seated, a living relic out of the pioneer days of Death Valley, a man more at home leading a packmule across a desert than riding in a helicopter. The old man's eyes were streaming tears as he watched a raging inferno where his parents' hotel, his birthplace, had existed for more than a century, unknown to the outside world.

"Mr. Seldom," Chub was shouting, "I've been dying to ask you—after Death Valley Scotty mistook that baby rattlesnake for a loose bootlace, what did he do?"

"Why," the old prospector's words were barely audible in the cabin, "ol' Scotty tied that sarpint into a bow knot, what else?"

A sheriff's deputy leaned down to retrieve the black satchel from the basket, recognizing it instantly as the bag containing the loot which had cost a Las Vegas casino's security guard his life.

"Pharaoh's Palace is offering a ten thousand dollar reward for the recovery of this money," the deputy shouted in Tommy's ear. "I guess it will be payable to you. I'm sure you deserve it."

Tommy pointed toward his rock hound friend. "I'll assign any reward to Mr. Downey there. He has ambitions to get a college degree in geology. Funding was his big stumbling block toward an education. The Las Vegas reward should help ease that problem."

The deputy asked, "What happened to the Crossbow Killers?"

Tommy pointed toward the smoke-boiling canyon. "Both dead.

It's a long story, sir. I'll be glad to fill you in later."

The officer gestured to the .357 Magnum pistol which Tommy still clutched in an iron grip. With a sheepish grin, Tommy handed the weapon over. "Rusty Hilton's. No, I didn't have to use it."

The deputy grinned, then reached down into the basket to lift out what appeared to be a mineral finder with a two-meter hand-held radio attached to its handle. Tommy Rockford would be explaining the workings of that life-saving device for the TV cameras later.

The helicopter door slid shut and the big bird went into a vertical climb, out of the tumbling smoke clouds into warm, breathable air heated only by a friendly California sun.

Tommy Rockford was staring out the Plexiglas window at the raging inferno that was leveling the remnants of Borrowed Time when the long-awaited explosion came, in a blinding flash of light and a spreading mushroom of smoke and dust. A series of following explosions created shock waves of sound which made the helicopter stagger. The ear-riving boom reminded K6ATX of another blast, the one which had involved a sand-buried sailing ship last summer when he was vacationing on the beach up in Washington State.*

Close on the heels of the blast from the powder magazine in the hotel cellar came a swelling kettledrum-roll of sound, louder, more ominous, as the suspended slope of centuried avalanche rock started its long-destined skid off the tilted flank of Telescope Peak. In slow motion at first, the slide rapidly gathered momentum as it began to spill like a black Niagara over the edge to fill Borrowed Time's lost canyon, snuffing out the holocaust burning in the chasm below and concealing the ghost camp's existence for all time to come. A cataclysm which meant that Borrowed Time was at long last passing into legend, even as it buried Goldie Lesher and Rusty Hilton in the deepest grave in the California wilderness.

To Tommy Rockford, it was like emerging from some kind of nightmare. If in some future era archaeologists ever excavated the site of Borrowed Time, how would they account for human bones at the bottom of a rock-filled well shaft? Or another human skeleton in the ruins of a stone jail, its rib cage skewered by an arrow from a weapon out of the Middle Ages, a crossbow?

---

*See CQ GHOST SHIP! published 1985 by ARRL

Tommy was aware that his Uncle JC was shouting in his ear, "Your Dad and Mother are flying in this afternoon. They'll book into Furnace Creek Inn. Before they get here we'll have a doctor stitch a few tucks in that scalp wound."

Worry and suffering had left their deep furrows on W7OE/6's gaunt, unshaven face.

The helicopter gained altitude and banked around in a steep turn to avoid the malignant cloud of dust and smoke which was now erupting volcano-like from the rock-filled canyon they had just escaped. Tommy consulted his watch and somehow found it inconceivable that the time was still a quarter-hour short of high noon. Field Day had just barely started!

Far below, the shadows of the two helicopters flickered across the swaybacked roof of Seldom Seen Sam's cabin, the Death Valley QTH where their mad adventure had begun.

Seldom Seen Sam, a grizzled relic of another era who still seemed perfectly at ease in a helicopter, rose from his bucket seat and groped out a hand to touch Tommy Rockford's. In a voice freighted with all the grief and disappointment and loneliness that had been crowded into his eighty-odd years, the old man husked out poignantly, "It was my dynamite that teched off the slide, the big one. It lost me everything? Nawthin' is left down there?"

In a voice trembling with infinite compassion, K6ATX replied, "The two hoodlums who shot old Hector are under all that rock, Mr. Sam. And you didn't lose everything. Your parents' graves—the avalanche didn't reach them. And here is something else I saved that I know is precious to you."

So saying, Tommy Rockford removed the musty Sutkliffe diary from his pocket and placed it tenderly in Seldom Seen Sam's gnarled hands, the book which related in their own handwriting the love Sam's parents had lavished on their newborn son so long ago.

Turning to Chub Downey, Tommy suggested, "Why don't you tell Mr. Sam how the purple diamond he gave you saved both our lives, huh? Tell him we owe our escape to his generosity. And your pitching arm—it gets credit for another win."

The little CBS Television chopper veered off to record on color video tape the awesome eruption of smoke which spelled the end of an incredible footnote to California frontier history.

Shimmering through the pure crystalline air as far as the eye could reach, converging magenta mountains enfolded the brooding, sunbaked mystery and beauty of the desert Tommy had always loved.

By air, the helipad at National Monument headquarters at Furnace Creek Ranch was only minutes away. Waiting there for Tommy Rockford would be a reunion with his anxious parents, a square meal. And then the excitement of the most challenging Field Day of his life as a radio ham!

The Inyo County Sheriff's helicopter zoomed up and away like a bird against the storm-washed blue dome. To K6ATX, the sensation was akin to the euphoria an eagle must feel as it soars free, spread-winged on the surging up-draft of a thermal column...

THE END

AUTHOR'S NOTE

Death Valley QTH is the fourth ham radio adventure novel starring Tommy Rockford, K6ATX (the first three were *SOS at Midnight*, *CQ Ghost Ship!* and *DX Brings Danger*), and if the readers of this book are anything like the readers of the first three, you may find yourself with a hankering to become a radio ham yourself.

Well, you'll never regret it! There are about a half million hams in the United States alone, and a new ham puts his station on the air about once every ten minutes.

How do you go about it? It's easy. If you're ten or twelve years old, a good way to start is to become an SWL, or short-wave listener. Be sure the receiver you buy has a BFO or beat-frequency oscillator in the circuit, however; otherwise you can't listen to Morse code, which is the most fun of all—and you have to know the code before you can get a ham license.

After a few weeks of listening to radio amateurs all around the world ragchewing via short waves, you'll get an urge to join the fun. At this point, contact your local radio club for information—they may conduct classes in code and radio theory. If not, or if you live on a farm or other isolated spot, drop a postcard to the American Radio Relay League, Newington, Connecticut 06111, requesting their free package of beginner information.

Your parents may ask, "How expensive is Amateur Radio?"

The answer to that is, "As expensive as you want to make it."

You can build your own eighty-meter CW (code) transmitter, good for a one-thousand-mile range, out of junk parts. It is best to spend the bulk of your radio budget for a good communications receiver, for later, if you find that hamming isn't your cup of tea, you can always use that piece of gear.

You can buy ham gear in kit form and save a lot of money—besides having the fun of putting together a piece of electronic equipment that works.

By shopping for second-hand gear, you should be able to get on the air with a Novice Class station for under $200. From then on the sky is the limit.

Good luck and vy 73,
WALKER A. TOMPKINS, K6ATX

ABOUT THE AUTHOR

If you have seen the credit line, "story by Walker A. Tompkins," flash on your TV screen following some episode of *Death Valley Days*, *Lone Ranger*, *Cheyenne* or *Cisco Kid*, you may wonder if he is the same author who wrote *Death Valley QTH* and its predecessors starring radio ham Tommy Rockford (*SOS At Midnight, CQ Ghost Ship!* and *DX Brings Danger).* He is.

Death Valley, where much of the action of *DEATH Valley QTH* takes place, is a familiar spot to Mr. Tompkins. During the past eight years he has served as historian and guide for twenty-five bus tours lasting four days each, so he knows Death Valley like the back of his hand.

In his home town, Mr. Tompkins is best known for his twice-daily history talks on Radio Station KBLS and his numerous books on regional history and biography. He has been a licensed radio ham since 1952, when he first heard of the Novice Class license, passed the examination and was assigned K6ATX as a station call. He is a former president of the Santa Barbara Amateur Radio Club and has written articles about the hobby for the American Radio Relay League, *National Geographic Magazine*, *CQ*, *Parents' Magazine* and *Popular Electronics*.

During his writing career Mr. Tompkins has traveled all over the world, Egypt and Japan being his favorite spots, with the South Seas and Italy as runners-up. During World War II he served for three years as a war correspondent in Europe.

DEATH VALLEY
QTH
PROOF OF
PURCHASE